FIRST COMES BLOOD

LILITH VINCENT

Copyright © 2021 Lilith Vincent

| All Rights Reserved |

No part of this book may be used or reproduced in any manner whatsoever without written permission from the publisher, except brief quotations for reviews. Thank you for respecting the author's work.

This book is a work of fiction. All characters, places, incidents and dialogue are drawn from the author's imagination and are not to be construed as real. Any similarities between persons living or dead are purely coincidental.

ABOUT THE BOOK

Four ruthless men. A virgin mafia princess to unite them. But first, there will be blood.

On my seventeenth birthday, I learn a terrible secret about my family. My future is in the hands of four brutal men, and what awaits me at their hands is too terrible to imagine.

Four men who desire me. Four men who vow to possess me. Four men who think they can destroy me.

As the only daughter of Coldlake's mayor, I should be kept far, far out of their reach. Instead, I'm being thrown to them as a sacrifice. My father insists only one of them can marry me, but all of them vow to secure my promise.

A promise in blood.

They take. I bleed. Happy birthday to me.

Author's note: First Comes Blood is the first book in the Promised in Blood series and ends on a cliffhanger. These books contain dark themes, violence, and a Why Choose romance with ruthlessly possessive men. The story is dark, dirty, and delicious, so please read at your discretion.

PLAYLIST

Your Guilty Pleasure – Henry Verus
Miss YOU! – CORPSE
Where Are You – Otnicka
BALENCIAGA – FILV
Such a Whore (Baddest Remix) – JVLA
Roses (Imanbek Remix) – SAINt JHN
Drüg – Lucky Luke, Emie
Clandestina – FILV, edmofo, Emma Peters
Promiscuous Motive – Nelly Furtado VS Ariana Grande
Cause I'm Crazy – DJ Goja
Devil I Know – Allie X
Demons – Hayley Kiyoko

Search "First Comes Blood by Lilith Vincent" on Spotify

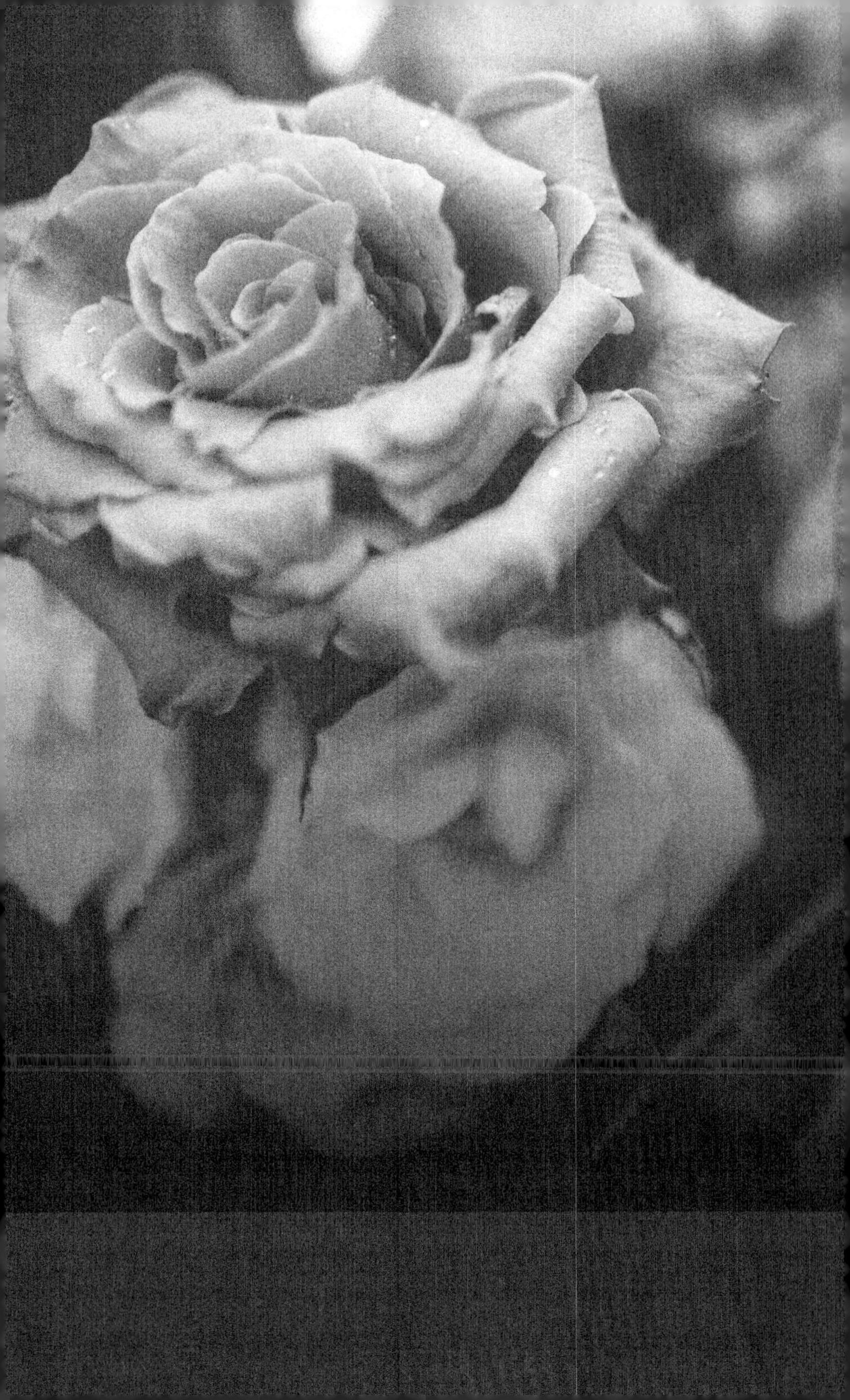

CHAPTER ONE

CHIARA

In one moment, your entire world can shatter.

Irreparable.

Absolute.

Final.

I'm living in a perverse, inverted Cinderella tale of wealth, privilege, and protection. At the stroke of midnight, it's ripped away until I have nothing left. Not even a fairy godmother to pat my cheek and tell me it will be all right.

Nothing will be all right ever again. I belong to them now. My devil princes. Rulers of this city. Harbingers of disaster. Four men who are as dangerous as they are handsome and as brutal as sin.

They hold my life in their hands, and I'm their plaything. A pawn to increase their power in this corrupt city.

They'll take what I love and make it bleed.

But none of this has happened yet. It's not quite midnight on my birthday, and my virginal white dress is clean without even a spot of blood.

My life and heart are in one piece, for a few more hours at least.

Tick tock.

Candles light the dining room, and there are fresh flowers along every wall. The table has an elegant centerpiece in black and gold—Dad's signature colors—and gleams with crystal glasses, silver cutlery, and white bone china. The napkins resemble lotus flowers that are spreading their petals on each dinner plate.

Hanging from the ceiling is a baby blue banner that reads, *Seventeen today!*

It's affectionate and kitschy. That will be my mother's touch, and my heart lifts at the sight. Maybe this will be a happy night, after all, and over dinner I can ask my father about going to college, and this time he won't walk away or change the subject.

There's no time for my mind to run away with this daydream because the moment I enter the room, I'm called to heel.

"Chiara, come here."

Obediently, I go and stand before my father. He's dressed in a tuxedo, spotlessly neat and groomed. His thick black hair is swept back, and a few silver threads glisten among the strands. He's a powerful man, in all senses. Big and imposing with flashing eyes and broad shoulders, but a powerful man politically, too. He's the Mayor of Coldlake. We're wealthy. Influential. Untouchable. People like to tell lies about my family, but the rumors never stick. Bad things seem to happen to our enemies, and they just melt away.

Over his shoulder, Mom's hovering, her hands tightly clasping her elbows, her too thin face even more gaunt than usual. She's wearing a long black evening gown, her blonde hair is coiffed, and she's sparkling with jewels, but her dark eyeshadow makes her face look like a skull.

A specter at the feast.

We studied *Macbeth* in school a few months ago, and the idea that a mournful spirit has come to my birthday party flits across my mind.

I flash Mom a reassuring smile while Dad inspects me from head to toe, from the tiara tucked into my blonde hair to the white chiffon gown that skims my body and pools at my feet. I don't know why he's looking at me like he's never seen this dress before. He chose it for me. I look like a sacrificial virgin on my seventeenth birthday.

I fiddle nervously with the diamond earrings hanging from my earlobes, and he slaps my hand away.

"Stop that. It makes you look nervous, and nerves are for the weak. Do you want to look weak?"

"In front of who?" I peer past him to the table, wondering who's coming to dinner. Dad's been dropping cryptic remarks about an honored guest for weeks but won't tell me anything else. I count the place settings on the oval mahogany table.

Me.

Mom.

Dad.

And…four more places?

Four? "Who's coming to dinner?"

Mom turns even paler, and her throat convulses as if she's going to be sick.

Dad's smile widens. Always that air of mystery. *Father knows best* and *don't ask questions.* Dad's the smartest man I know and there's nothing he won't do for us or the city of Coldlake. When there's a problem or a scandal, he tells us that everything will be fixed, and then it is. According to him, we don't need to know how the problems go away. We're too important for that sort of worry. We're his beautiful girls.

But this isn't politics. This is my birthday party.

"You'll find out." He glances at the clock on the wall. It's two minutes to eight. Two minutes until the mystery guests arrive. The ticking suddenly becomes menacing.

Tick tock.

"Chiara." Mom's voice is shaking. She comes forward to take my hands in hers, and they're cold and bony—like death.

"Please try to eat a little more, Mom," I whisper, gazing into her huge eyes. Lately, she seems to be fading away in front of me. "I worry that you're getting sick."

She squeezes my fingers. "Don't worry about me. You're seventeen today. It's time you learned the truth about—"

The doorbell rings, interrupting her. Dad gives Mom a warning look, and she backs off.

"The truth about what?" I look between my parents, but Dad won't answer, and Mom can't. She's always been in awe of Dad, but lately, she's been downright afraid.

Dad inspects the table, and his face transforms in disgust. He strides over and, with one sharp tug, rips the baby blue birthday banner down and crumples it in his fists.

Mom whimpers, and tears fill her eyes. I grab her hand and hold it tightly, glaring at Dad's back as he throws the banner into a side room. Now nothing in the dining room is ours. It's all Dad's.

I've seen him like this on the eve of an election or a big rally, feverish with the ambition to win at all costs. His charisma means that everyone around him is swept up in his determination. Mom and I become the perfect, smiling wife and daughter. Mom will give speeches and I'll hold Dad's hand and wave to the crowds. As the longest-serving mayor of Coldlake, Dad knows just what to say, just how to smile to convince the people that he's who they want. He's who they *need*.

And he is good for Coldlake. The city is thriving and the people are prospering. You only have to attend the parades or stand on Main Street on a Saturday and see all the happy people shopping and eating to know that this city is something special. Dad's something special.

But tonight, Dad's brought his ambition to my birthday party. As he gazes at me, I feel the full weight of his expectation.

All the hairs stand up on the back of my neck as I hear footsteps coming down the hall toward us, heavy and masculine. Not one set of feet. Many feet.

Before I can take another breath, four men enter the room—big, dangerous-looking men with forceful gazes and intent focus. They line up in a silent row, their expressions hostile. And yet, their faces are familiar. I realize with shock that I know them. They're famous.

Or rather, infamous.

Standing on the left in a tuxedo like Dad's is Salvatore Fiore, chin lifted with arrogance as he straightens his cuffs, diamond cufflinks gleaming. His rich brown hair is swept back, and his strong jaw is clean-shaven. He owns half a dozen casinos in the city. Those are the legit ones, anyway. I hear that there are a dozen more where bets are placed on more than just blackjack.

Next to him is Vinicius Angeli, hands casually in his pants pockets, but his clever eyes alight with interest. Angeli, like *angel*. He's got a face like an angel, terrible in its golden beauty. He's how I imagine the Archangel Gabriel would look if he appeared before me. Rumors of dirty money swirl around him in the news. *Lots* of dirty money.

The third man is all in black, his shirt tight across his prodigious chest. He wears his black beard short and painstakingly neat. He's got better brows than I do. Black curls just touch the back of his collar, and his eyes are narrowed. Judgmental. His name comes to me after a moment. Cassius Ferragamo, nightclub owner. Strip club owner, too, it's rumored, ones that are filled with the most corrupt people in the city, night after night.

Finally, standing a little apart from the others is a pale-eyed, blond man in a suit with a skinny black tie. He has the tousled hair and muscular body of an Australian surfer, but his gaze is so, so cold that I feel the blood in my veins turning to ice. I'd know him anywhere. Lorenzo Scava. No one knows what the hell he does, but it's rumored to be brutal, dangerous, and highly illegal.

Everyone in Coldlake would recognize these men. Their pictures have all been in the news. They're criminals. Extortionists. Mobsters.

Killers.

And they've all come to my birthday party.

Vinicius' mouth quirks in a smile. "Hey, birthday girl," he purrs in a voice like black velvet. Then he winks.

My face reacts on its own, heat stealing over my cheeks. I attend Coldlake Girl's Catholic High School. The only males I come into contact with are family and the old priests. Now, four seethingly good-looking men are all eyeing me like they're wondering how I taste. I feel like I'm completely naked in front of them.

Salvatore finishes straightening his cuffs and steps confidently forward. "Happy birthday, Miss Romano."

As he places his hands on my shoulders, a hot spark that Vinicius kindled bursts into flames within my chest. Salvatore dips his head to kiss my cheeks, brisk at first, but after the first kiss, he slows right down. I'm out of my father's view, thanks to Salvatore's massive back, and his fingers trail across my jaw as a devilish smile spreads over his face. My lips part in surprise, and his hand on my wrist suddenly tightens as his mouth descends on mine.

The seconds his lips are pressed against mine are eons long. Heat flows from him into me. Fire licks up my body. I shouldn't allow this to happen. Before I can put my hand against his chest and push him away, he breaks the kiss. His mouth leaves mine, but I can still feel it.

His eyebrows rise, teasing me. "Pretty girls need a birthday kiss."

"Fiore!" Dad barks.

But Salvatore doesn't move. He stays right where he is, his face inches from mine, his goading expression daring me to call for help. I close my lips and turn my face away, my insides churning.

What the hell is going on?

Salvatore stays where he is a few seconds longer, proving to Dad that he follows no one's orders, I suppose, and then steps aside.

I stay where I am as Dad greets the men, standing between them and me. For a moment, I wonder if he's outraged on my behalf that one of his guests kissed me within seconds of meeting me. He only looks mollified when they all greet him respectfully as Mayor Romano and shake his hand.

It's his reputation he's worried about, not mine.

The men are formally introduced to Mom and me in turn. Only Vinicius smiles at me. Salvatore looks amused, but not in a friendly way. Cassius and Lorenzo both regard me with glacial silence, the former as if I'm massively disappointing him and he's itching to correct me, and the latter like he's wondering whether to sever my limbs above the joint or below. Instead of dousing the heat inside me, their attention makes it burn harder. Every sensibility is telling me to fear these men, and on many levels, I do. Something deeper inside me, something more primal, wants to draw closer.

Dad calls them all businessmen. Important friends and colleagues. I might not know much about people and the world, but I can read. I hear what people say. "I think there's been some mistake."

Dad slips his hands into his trouser pockets, and his hooded gaze flashes with warning. "There's no mistake. They're your dinner guests. Be nice to your guests, Chiara."

"But they're all criminals!" I burst out.

Dad's jaw tightens. He exchanges glances with each of the four men, and then he smiles.

He *smiles*.

They smile too. Four treacherous smiles, all teeth and threat.

"And so?" Dad asks.

"And…we're not." My voice goes up at the end. We're not? Are we? People whisper about the Romano family, that Dad's got irons in many fires and fingers in many pies. Vague things. Nothing that makes the news. Not like these men who seem to be evading a new accusation every week.

There's a dark chuckle from Salvatore. "She's more innocent than I thought." His eyes travel over my lips, my breasts, my hips, as if he's dismantling my chiffon dress with his gaze. My lips are still burning from that kiss.

"Chiara, these are my dearest friends. Show some respect."

Dearest friends? These men? I've heard the accusations about my father, that he's got links to the underworld and friends in low places. Of course, I've had my suspicions…but Dad's always denied the rumors and called them ridiculous. He's my father, and I believe him. He's not the loving, affectionate man that some fathers are, and he expects a lot from Mom and me, but I've always believed he's an honest person. If you can't trust your own father, who can you trust?

Across the room, four men in suits watch me like hungry wolves.

"Sit." It's an order for Mom and me. Mom has her eyes on the floor as she walks quickly toward her chair. I know what she'd tell me if she could find her voice.

Just obey, Chiara. You know it's easier to do what he wants. It will all be over soon.

But I don't dare take my seat. If I sit down, then I'm going to hear terrible things. I know I am. There can be no innocent reason that these four men—these four notorious, dangerous men—are in our house tonight. I look desperately at my father. Dad, what have you done?

What did you promise them?

What do these men *want*?

Mom and Dad are at either end of the oval dining table. The four men stand along one side, and my solitary setting is opposite. They wait behind their chairs for the birthday girl to take her seat.

"Eleonora," Dad says lazily, not even looking at his wife. Mom hurries over to me and tries to push me into my chair, but I resist.

"Sit," she breathes in my ear. "Please, darling. Just get through this night. You're not of age, and nothing can happen to you." Her final unspoken word hangs between us as our terrified gazes meet.

Yet.

But something *will* happen to me. Something to do with me and these men. Not tonight, but soon.

"You don't need to be afraid. I'll find a way to help you before it's time, I promise," she whispers.

My knees weaken, and Mom steers me into my seat before going back to hers. In front of me, the men all sit down. Salvatore.

Vinicius. Cassius. Lorenzo. They stare back at me. I feel like I'm being interviewed for a dangerous job I don't want.

Dad rings a bell, signaling the staff to come in with wine and starters. I sip from my sparkling water, trying to make sense of Mom's cryptic words. *I'll find a way to help you before it's time.* Time for what?

Dad and the men talk as Mom and I pick at our smoked salmon slices. Real estate prices. The industrial developments down at the docks. The new nightclub that Cassius has opened. Dad congratulates them about their latest business ventures, and they smirk as they thank him for deals that have gone through. It sends a shiver down my spine to listen to them.

"Speaking of deals…" He glances at the four guests. "Which of you thinks you should be the one? We can discuss the details in private, but a lady likes to be courted." Dad indicates me with his wine glass and takes a large mouthful.

"Of course she does," Salvatore says, leaning back in his chair and regarding me. His arrogant smile snares my attention. "It should be me, obviously. I'm the richest—and the strongest."

It should be him who gets what? And why does money and strength matter? Salvatore has an aura of impeccable grooming and wealth about him, but I don't know if he means physically strongest or something else. Cassius, who looks like he could bench press a whole lot more, glances at Salvatore and makes a dismissive, "*Tch*," sound.

"Obviously you? Obviously nothing," cuts in Vinicius, and as he glances at me, I'm dazzled again by his good looks. "It will be me because I'm the handsomest and the cleverest."

At the far end of the table, Lorenzo has produced a knife from somewhere and is twirling it in his fingers. The point is wickedly sharp. Mom, who's closest to him, shrinks back in her seat, her shaking hand covering her throat.

I wish they'd all leave, but most of all, I wish Lorenzo Scava would disappear. His face doesn't betray anything, but I have the impression he's enjoying her fear.

"I'm the toughest. I'm unswerving in my duty to others, and the duty they have to me." This is Cassius. His voice is accented as if he's spent several years or more in Italy. He addresses Dad, but then his attention turns to me as he lets his final words hang ominously in the air. A shiver goes through me. I hope he never has any expectations of me.

Salvatore looks down the table. "And you, Lorenzo?"

Lorenzo Scava acts as if he hasn't heard a word of what's been going on. He's still twisting that knife and flipping it across his knuckles while Mom looks more and more afraid.

My hands grip the napkin in my lap until I can't take it anymore. "Stop that!"

Lorenzo snatches the knife out of the air and pins me with a predatory look. I'm trapped in that pale gaze, and I can't move a muscle, even though every nerve is screaming at me, *run*. "It's simple. If I'm not the one, then you'll all regret it."

"*Cane pazzo*," Cassius mutters. *Mad dog.*

"The one what? What is going on?" I look desperately at Dad. If this is a business deal, then it's the strangest one I've ever heard.

At the head of the table, Dad rests his fists on the wood and smiles broadly at me. Anyone would think it's his birthday he's beaming so much. "Chiara. Tonight, you'll be promised to one of these men. On your eighteenth birthday, you'll become engaged, and when you're eighteen and one week, you'll marry, and the Romanos will be joined with one of the most important families in Coldlake."

Around the table, no one moves. Not even Mom. The room is so silent that I can hear the ticking of the clock. I'm the only one with her mouth open and her eyes wide. Everyone knew about this except me.

My four potential fiancés are drinking in my shock like it's the finest wine. Dad's put me on display before them and they're delighted with the goods.

My palms turn clammy and my breathing quickens. This is the future Dad planned for me all along. He's never been interested in discussing with me what I want because he's been envisioning me as the bride of one of these vicious men. He's always liked to brag that he makes the best business deals. Finds the best leverage. Dangles the juiciest incentives. Only this time, the deal isn't for real estate, or a redevelopment, or a trade deal.

The deal is me.

Tick tock.

CHAPTER TWO

SALVATORE

"You want me to marry one of *these* men?"

Chiara Romano's beautiful face drains of color. I'm glad we're here when she first hears what her father wants. You can tell a lot from a person from how they handle a surprise.

Or in her case, a shock.

Her hands are clenched in her lap and her eyes are round. She's petite, almost doll-like with her long lashes and honey-gold hair. The diamonds in her ears and the tiara in her hair set off her fresh-faced beauty. Those lips of hers, though, they're something else. Lush and sweet and receptive to kisses. I wonder what else that mouth can do.

I glance at the others, and realize they're wondering the same thing. How much fun will Miss Romano be on her wedding night? We like a girl who will fight back.

Mayor Romano glowers at his daughter. "Yes, Chiara. Did I not just spell it out for you? One of these men will be your husband. After tonight, you can consider yourself promised. When you marry in a year and a week, you'll leave this house and start a new life with your husband."

I gaze at my future bride over my wine glass, expecting the flood of tears to begin. I can't have a woman who's going to fall apart when she gets a fright. Cassius and Lorenzo enjoy a woman's tears, but if my wife cries, I'll have to beat it out of her.

Chiara's eyes are dry. "But why? This is like something out of the Dark Ages."

I put my wine glass down and lean forward. "It was kind of your parents to spare you from the truth for so long. Kind, but misguided. You were never going to have a choice, Chiara. People like us don't marry for love. We marry for power."

She turns her baby blue eyes on me, and her expression flickers with fear. Chiara Romano needs a better poker face. But that's all right. I'll teach her.

"People like us? But my family isn't like yours. We're not criminals."

On my left, Vinicius pretends to wince at her choice of words. "Please. We prefer the term *entrepreneur*."

"Speak for yourself," Cassius raps out. "I'm a businessman. These are my associates. I don't like your attitude, young lady."

Chiara breathes in sharply, as if Cassius' words have hit her like a whip. If she's already afraid, she won't like what he'll do to her as her husband.

Mayor Romano seems to feel like he's losing control of the conversation and raises his voice. "Where do you think the money comes from to put this roof over your head? Pay for that expensive school of yours? All your pretty clothes?"

"Your job as mayor."

Vinicius laughs. Cassius shakes his head with his brow furrowed. Lorenzo stares at Chiara with cold, hooded eyes. Opposite her husband, Mrs. Romano seems to have fled into the far reaches of her mind. I wonder if Chiara is like that. Weak and fragile.

We'll know by midnight. Each of us has a little present prepared for Miss Romano. If she breaks, then we walk away. Our world isn't for the weak.

"No, sweetheart." Mayor Romano's voice drips with condescension. "It's from the deals I make. The deals that keep this city thriving—with the help of these men, of course."

Lorenzo turns to gaze at the mayor and starts flipping his knife again. No one likes to be talked about like they're an afterthought, especially not us.

"You're going to be an important part of a deal with one of these men."

Vinicius touches the tip of his tongue to one of his pointed canines. "Just one of us? Can't we all have her?"

Cassius' eyes flare with interest. Lorenzo draws his thumbnail over his lower lip and gazes at Chiara like he's imagining something dark and dirty.

My smile widens. "Yes. Why don't we share her?"

Chiara's eyes couldn't hold any more confusion. Poor little lamb. I don't think she's ever been kissed before tonight, let alone imagined what four men at once could do with her. Only one of us can marry her, but we'll all share her, and show her what our world is really about.

The four of us. Brothers, in every way but blood.

The mayor's lip curls. "I only have one daughter. I can only have one son-in-law."

I swirl my wine lazily in my glass and address my future wife. "One thing you should know. You won't ever come between the four of us. Nothing can alter our bond."

The tiniest of smirks flits across Romano's face and is gone. The mayor thinks he can use his daughter to drive a wedge between us. United, the four of us are stronger than he is. Divided, he can play us off against each other.

Chiara noticed her father's smirk. She regards me, and then all four of us, her gaze finally coming to rest on Lorenzo.

Her expression asks, *Your bond? Even with him?*

"Yes. Even this crazy asshole," Cassius growls, jerking his head at the blond man next to him.

Mrs. Romano sits up and clears her throat. "That's all very interesting, gentlemen. But I think you're forgetting one thing. This is Chiara's choice."

The mayor opens his mouth to contradict her, but I'm tired of hearing his voice. I want to speak to my bride. "All right, then. Who among us would you choose, Chiara? Which of us is your future husband?"

Vinicius casts me a smile and smooths his tie. He knows that for any sane girl the choice is between him and me, and he's better-looking.

But looks are the least of what's important. I'm the smart choice. The *only* choice. I'll have her no matter who gets her in the end, but I want my name on that dotted line.

I wait, eyebrows raised.

"What? You want me to choose now?"

I want to hear who she *would* choose. It won't be up to her, but I'd like to hear her say my name before the inevitable happens. It will make the whole business of marrying her less tearful and irritating if she doesn't need to be forced.

The silence around the table stretches. The ticking of the clock on the wall fills the room.

"I won't," Chiara whispers so softly that her lips barely move. She's staring straight ahead at us.

She dares defy *us*.

"Answer the question, Chiara," says Mayor Romano.

My eyes narrow. The only place a woman should put up a fight is in the bedroom. When she's ordered to do something, she needs to obey without question.

Chiara stands up, her chair scraping on the floor. Her face is flickering with powerful emotions. Without another word, she hurries from the room, her head down.

Mayor Romano starts to get to his feet, but I stand up first, buttoning my jacket. "I'll talk to her. She just needs some persuading."

I catch Vinicius' amused expression and Cassius' smirk. What?

I can seem nice. Of the four of us, I'm the most convincing in that department, assuming the charade doesn't get dragged out and my patience worn through. Lorenzo twists his knife over his tattooed knuckles, and his eyes burn in the candlelight. His intent is clear. If I don't bring her to heel, he will.

The house is built around a central courtyard with a huge swimming pool lit up in the darkness. It's a mansion fit for a Hollywood movie star or Wall Street financier. A mayor shouldn't be able to afford this. It's almost as palatial as my own house, which should send alarm bells ringing among Mayor Romano's constituents, considering my fortune has been built on spilled blood.

I find Chiara in a sitting room, the doors pulled back to let in the warm evening air. The room is dark, but she's luminous in her white dress. She has her back to me, head down, small fists clenched.

Silently, I come up behind her and stroke my fingers across her bare shoulders. Her skin is warm and smooth and feels electric against my own. "You ran out on your dinner guests, Chiara."

It takes all my self-control not to slide my hand around her throat and squeeze until she understands never to do such a thing again.

She turns to face me with a gasp, her eyes huge and troubled. "I wish you'd all leave, please. There's been a misunderstanding."

A little child, hiding under her blankets and hoping the monsters will go away. My smile widens. "But I've got a present for you."

Chiara closes her mouth and swallows. "If it's another kiss I don't want it."

No? She might fear me, she might fear us, but she responded the moment I kissed her. Fear and desire twined together. It's an intoxicating blend.

I step toward her, enjoying how she steps back. This girl is going to make me fight for every inch of her body. I can't wait.

I take a flat velvet box out of my pocket and open it, revealing the diamond necklace within. It catches the light and sparkles enticingly.

She turns her face away. "No, thank you."

"It's your birthday present. I bought it especially for you." Bought it. Took it from Vinicius as my cut from his last heist. He posed as the pilot of a billionaire's private plane and held everyone at gunpoint on a remote Venezuelan runway. He needed my international contacts to pay off the airport authorities, and so I got the necklace. I had to wash the blood off, first.

"If I accept your present, I'll be in your debt like my father is. That's it, isn't it? He owes you money and that's why all this is happening."

"If your father owed me money, I'd be coming for his blood, not his daughter, and I'd be brandishing guns, not diamond necklaces."

I move behind Chiara, drape the necklace around her neck and stroke her hair aside. My lips close to her ear, I whisper, "You have a lot to learn about the way the world works. When you marry me, I'll teach you."

I fasten the tiny clasp and admire the way the diamonds sparkle against her skin. Chiara has a beautiful, slender throat, and as I lean over her I want to run my tongue over her delicate skin and feel her pulse beating wildly. I imagine her face down on black sheets, naked except for this diamond necklace and completely at my mercy.

"I don't want anything from you. I don't want to be in your debt.

I feel like you'll ask for things I won't want to give you."

"But I ask for so little." *Just your body and soul. Your cries for mercy. Your total obedience and your life in my hands, forever.*

Her fingers reach up to touch the diamonds around her throat. "What is it you do want?"

I put my hands on her shoulders and turn her to face me. "You."

Confusion flickers in those beautiful eyes, and her lower lip softens. I ache to lean down and nip it with my teeth.

"I've heard so many despicable things about you. Who are you really?"

"I'm a businessman. I own hotels. I run casinos." I stand behind her and point at three gleaming skyscrapers, just visible over the roof of her house. "That one's mine, and the two on either side, among many others."

My lips skim the shell of her ear as I talk, and I feel her shiver beneath my fingers.

"That's only part of the truth, isn't it?" she whispers.

"Clever girl. Shall I tell you the truth?"

She nods, still looking up at the glimmering buildings.

I slide my arm around her waist and pull her back against my chest. She stiffens and clutches my arm. "I win, at any cost. What I set my mind on, I get, including you, Chiara."

"I'm not a skyscraper, or my father. I can't be bought with promises and diamonds."

My composure cracks at her defiance. If she were looking into my eyes, she'd be backing away in fear right now. I stroke the diamonds around her neck and keep my voice soft. "No? And yet here you are, in my arms, wearing my diamonds."

"I'll take them off the second you're gone and throw them away."

Heat ripples through my muscles. She's just crossed the line from naïve to disrespectful. My hand drifts higher, stroking her throat. "You think you're not in danger in this house because your father's close by and it's your birthday. I gave you diamonds. I'm being *nice*. You've forgotten your manners, Chiara."

I grip her throat and squeeze. Her eyes fly open and she grabs my wrist with both hands. Her body flails but I have her clenched tight against me.

Trapped.

Teeth bared, I growl in her ear, "I'll help you remember them. You don't talk back to me. You don't treat what I give you like dirt. I can get to you whenever I want. I can hurt you. I can hurt your mother. I can do whatever the fuck I want in this town, and no one, least of all your father, can stop me."

Chiara gives a strangled whimper, her heels hitting my shins.

"Don't let that pretty mouth of yours put a bullet in your head." I watch her as she struggles, her movements becoming more and more frantic. If she has any sense, she'll only have to hear this once. Finally, I release her and shove her away from me.

Chiara's hand flies to her throat as she doubles over, gasping for breath. I straighten my jacket and smooth my hair. I think she's learned her lesson.

"I can be your friend, or your worst nightmare. Happy birthday, Chiara."

CHAPTER THREE

VINICIUS

I'm standing out by the pool as Salvatore strides past me. "Did you have a nice chat with the birthday—"

He keeps walking with a face like thunder, and growls, "Disrespectful little bitch. I'll enjoy putting her in her place when the time comes."

I grin to myself in the darkness. Salvatore has no subtlety. I suppose when diamonds didn't do the trick, he went straight for threats. Everyone knows you catch more flies with honey.

I saunter around the pool to the sitting room where Chiara is gripping the back of a sofa with a trembling hand and trying to catch her breath. "How was your talk with Salvatore?"

She whirls around, her big eyes opening wide. "What do you mean?"

"You're shaking."

Chiara takes a deep breath, but slowly. "I'm fine, thank you."

She moves past me, but I step in front of her and smile pleasantly. It was clear from her expression over dinner that she doesn't like Cassius or Lorenzo, and Salvatore just scared the shit out of her. All these dragons. I'll be her Prince Charming.

"This must all be so strange for you. You had no idea that your father worked so closely with us before tonight, did you?"

Chiara studies me carefully, searching for the trick.

No trick. I'm just being nice.

For now.

"Sit down with me for a moment. The others have tempers and even I have a hard time making them listen to me." I go to the sofa and make myself comfortable. "I prefer a good conversation, so let's have a talk."

Chiara glances toward the dining room, seeming to wonder if it's safer in there than out here with me.

"I swear I won't make you promise yourself to me in marriage in the next thirty minutes. You must be curious about the four of us. Maybe I can answer your questions." I tilt my head, doing my best to disarm her. "Maybe I can help you."

Slowly, she makes her way over to the sofa and sits down next to me, glancing at me like I'm a bomb that's about to blow up in her face. I relax back with a smile.

"You seem different from the others," she says after a moment.

"What, not completely insane, you mean?" She nods, and I laugh. "That's fair. Salvatore and the others are used to getting their own way. Right now, I imagine they're all furious that you never answered Salvatore's question."

"I'm not going to marry any of you," she says right away.

"Sorry, kitten. Unless something unforeseen happens, then you are going to marry one of us." The one who claims Chiara as his wife will have all sorts of interesting leverage over the mayor. I was arrested last year, and even though the charges didn't stick, the memory still makes me burn with anger. That won't happen again if I have Chiara.

Her face creases in despair. "But this is so archaic. I never imagined that my future was going to turn out like this."

I take a pack of playing cards from my pocket and show them to her. "Maybe I have the solution. How about we play a game?"

"What kind of game?"

"A little bet to settle this once and for all. Salvatore might own the casinos, but I'm the betting man among us. If you ask him, I have a problem, but I can stop any time I like." Another smile, this one self-deprecating.

Chiara glances at the cards. If she were going to walk away, she would have by now. I just have to reel her in.

I split the deck and riffle them together; arch them and stack them back into a neat pile. The familiar hand gestures are slick and pleasing. They never fail to get a betting man's attention.

Or woman's.

Chiara eyes the cards with interest. "What are we betting on?"

I sort through the cards, looking for one in particular. "If you win, then we four disappear from your life forever."

The effect on Chiara is electric. Her spine straightens and her eyes light up. I can feel how much she wants this and I draw out the moment, drinking in every second.

"That's not something you can promise all on your own, is it? The others seem like they do whatever they want."

"Oh, but it is. The others will be angry with me if I lose, but they'll stand by the bet." If I lose.

If.

"Why?"

"Because in our world, a deal is a deal, and the only way out once a promise has been made is in a pine box." We might be a bunch of criminals, but we have a code. We lie, steal, and cheat to get what we want, but our word is sacred.

"And if I lose?"

I find the card I want and flip it around to show her. "Nothing changes. We carry on as before, and one of us will do his best to win your heart."

"I'm not stupid. This isn't about my heart." She glances at the card. "What game are we playing?"

I place the queen of hearts on the table. "Find the Lady." I deal out two more cards, face up, and lay them beside the queen. The ace of spades. The ten of clubs.

Chiara shakes her head. "The game where you show me the queen of hearts and then switch the cards around using sleight of hand and I have zero chance of finding her? No way, that whole game is a con."

I grin at her. "Ah, and I was hoping you wouldn't know the trick."

"There are shills who play this game on the bridge over the river. I walk past them every weekend on my way to church."

"Church? What a little angel you are, inside and out." I pick up the three cards and hold them out to her. "We'll switch places then. You move the cards, and I'll find the queen."

Chiara takes the cards from me, her expression doubtful. "I still don't trust you."

I put my hand over my heart. "Who, me? I'm putting myself in your hands."

She glances at the backs of the cards and her expression becomes totally blank. "All right."

I hesitate, her sudden poker face throwing me off. "Wait, really? Do you know the trick?"

She blinks her long lashes at me. "Who, me?"

I narrow my eyes. Either she's bluffing or she really does know sleight of hand. The others will flay me alive if I mess up this deal for them. They want Chiara, badly. I want her, too. The stakes are high and I could actually lose.

I feel suddenly energized and crack my knuckles. "Interesting. Let's do this."

A smile tilts up the corner of Chiara's mouth. "It's almost as if the idea of losing is exciting to you."

"I've had too many sure bets lately. It's fun living dangerously."

"You really will honor the bet if I win? I don't know if I can trust you."

"You think a man like Cassius would let me go back on my word? Or Salvatore? The man runs a casino."

She flips through the three cards, watching me with her head tilted to one side. "Either I get rid of you all, or everything stays the same. You'll honor that?"

"I swear it."

"I guess I can't say no, then. What have I got to lose?"

More than you realize.

I slide closer to her and murmur in her ear, "You're really beautiful, you know that?"

"Stop trying to distract me. You said you weren't going to use any tricks."

I stroke my hand down her arm. "No tricks. It's not often that a beautiful woman holds my destiny in her hands."

"I'm holding on to these," she says, showing me the backs of the three cards in her hand. "You can flatter me as much as you want but I'm not letting go of them."

I don't give a damn about the cards right now. "The game is all the more interesting when the stakes are high, don't you think?" I slide my hand around her waist. "Think about it, Chiara. You're in control. Doesn't that make you feel powerful?"

She raises her chin to look at me, her eyes as bright as stars. What did it feel like when Salvatore kissed her, I wonder? He likes an ambush. I prefer surrender.

"It's…different."

"Come now," I murmur, dipping my mouth closer to hers. "I've been honest with you. Won't you be honest with me?"

Her gaze flickers to my mouth. "I don't know if I can trust you."

"Why don't we try this and find out?"

I press my mouth to hers. Her lips part and she lets me claim them, one after the other. I feel her inhale as her eyes drift closed. For a sheltered Catholic girl, she has a seductive kiss. Mm, yes, the others will enjoy her, too. Just enough innocence for Cassius. More than enough vulnerability for Lorenzo.

One of her hands is on my chest and the other is clutching those precious cards. She's unguarded, and I reach down to her ankle and slide my fingers up the inside of her leg.

Maybe I like an ambush just a little.

Gasping, Chiara breaks the kiss. We stare into each other's eyes, our breaths mingling. What a bold girl she is. I wonder what it would take to make her go all in.

She pulls away and brandishes the cards. "Let's just get this over with."

I stop her with a hand on her arm. "Wait. Let's make this more interesting. Are you up for that?"

"More interesting how?"

"Don't show me where the lady is. Deal all the cards face down, switch them around, and I'll just pick one."

"But that makes it even less likely that you'll pick the queen. Why would you want that?"

I shrug one shoulder. "I like you, Chiara. After you've won the bet, maybe I'll ask you on a date. You'll never want any of us if we force you."

She looks at the cards in her hand and then back at me. She's still puzzled, but she's going with it. "All right."

Victory races through me, tasting almost as delicious as her lips. A con man knows one thing for sure: you can't con someone who's not greedy. Chiara just got greedy.

She lays the three cards out, face down. Then she starts shuffling them back and forth on the table. "Go on, then. Find the lady."

I tap my heart. "I've already found her."

Chiara glances at my chest. "That's pretty cheesy. Don't try and wriggle out of this. Pick a card."

"I'm not. I've already found my queen."

"Choose anyway."

"Fine, but I have her already so it doesn't count. The middle one."

She reaches for the middle card, and stops. "If I turn this card over and it's the queen of hearts, then either you have the luck of the devil or you've tricked me, and I won't rest until I figure out which it is."

I smile a slow, heated smile. "The devil's definitely on my side, but I don't need his help tonight. This is between just you and me."

Chiara takes a deep breath and flips the card over, revealing the ace of spades. She puts her hands on her cheeks and gasps. "I won! I can't believe I won."

I shake my head. "Sorry, kitten. No, you didn't."

"Don't be a sore loser. I beat you fair and square."

I reach into the front pocket of my jacket, draw out a playing card and show it to her. The queen of hearts. "Told you I already had her."

"What?" Chiara snatches the queen of hearts from me and stares at it. Then she grabs the other two from the table. The ten of clubs and the jack of diamonds. "But…but I had the queen of hearts! I didn't let go of the cards even when you kissed me. How did you get hold of her?"

I smile wider. "First rule of playing with a con man. Suspect everything, especially when things seem to be going in your favor." I may enjoy a risk, but I'm not a fucking idiot. There's no way I'd make a bet like that if I didn't already know I was going to win.

Chiara's shoulders slump as she realizes the trick. "You switched the cards before you even gave them to me. I can't believe I didn't check the cards."

She was too busy enjoying being kissed by me. Now I know she wants me, I'm going to fight twice as hard to make her my wife. I want the security of having Mayor Romano in my pocket wherever I go in this city.

I take the cards from her and throw them aside. "I've got a present for you. A little piece of advice. Trust no one, not even your own family. The only person you can rely on is yourself."

"There's no chance I'll ever trust you again."

I smile, revealing pointed canines. "Especially not me."

My head dips toward hers like I'm going to kiss her. At the last second, I snap my teeth together, and she jumps. "Happy birthday, kitten."

CHAPTER FOUR

CASSIUS

Ten at fucking night, I haven't had the rest of my dinner and I haven't been promised a wife. What the hell am I still doing at the mayor's house?

I take a swig of the whisky I helped myself to after Chiara stormed out of the dining room like a brat. The swimming pool glows blue-white and the garden is studded with lights. I've spotted half a dozen staff. Everything in this house is expensive. It's only acceptable to raise a family like this if they understand that this privilege comes at a cost, and the cost is doing what you're fucking told.

A figure in white walks along the edge of the pool, a sparkling tiara nestled in her golden hair. The chiffon clings to her slender body. I watch her, the taste of the whisky lingering in my mouth. Chiara will look good on my arm as I walk into one of my clubs. She'll be delicious spread out on my bed. I love a small woman that I can completely engulf with my size, and her delicate beauty will look even better when her face is streaked with tears.

But perhaps this would be easier if she were plain. Beautiful women who know they're beautiful are a pain in the fucking ass. As my eyes follow her, though, I can't be sorry that Chiara Romano is utterly delectable. I put my whisky down and straighten my tie. She'll just require more correction.

I stand at the far end of the pool with my hands in my trouser pockets. Chiara's so lost in thought that she almost walks right into my chest. She pulls up short with a gasp.

Recovering herself, she asks, "Have you got something for me, too?"

I don't like her tone. It's bordering on sassy. "Why? Do you suppose you've earned a present from me?"

Chiara shrugs, her face a picture of unhappiness. "It's my birthday. Salvatore gave me this." She touches the necklace at her throat that's heavy with glistening stones.

Of course he gave her diamonds. Lavish gifts and vicious threats, that's his style.

"Vinicius gave me advice."

I laugh softly. "Let me guess. Trust no one? Definitely don't trust him. You can tell he's lying because his lips are moving."

Speaking of lips, Chiara's are swollen. Who's been kissing her, Salvatore again? No, probably Vinicius as part of his games.

"Why do you all want me, anyway?"

She's not my wife yet. I wonder how best to play this. Perhaps after her chat with Vinicius she'd respond best to honesty. "Your father is a powerful man. He's useful to us."

Chiara flinches. "But I don't want to marry any of you."

Maybe not, but a woman in her position doesn't get to choose her husband. She doesn't get the luxury of a love match. She'll perform her duty and say thank you for the privilege of serving her family and her husband.

My daughters, when I have them, will be raised to understand this from birth. This seventeen-year-old girl needs to be taught a lesson.

I reach out and stroke my thumb over her cheek. "What a night you've had. This must be so hard for you."

She looks up in surprise, and her face softens. "Um, yes. It's been a strange day."

I go to an outdoor five-seater sofa nestled between some palm trees and sit down. "The others will screw with you for fun. I don't do that."

"That's reassuring. I like to know where I stand."

She gazes at me boldly, without even calling me *Mr. Ferragamo* or *sir*. Such lack of discipline. A proper mafia daughter wouldn't dare behave this way around the man she's hoping to marry. Her mother at least seems to know her place.

I pat the sofa cushion next to me. "Come here. I don't bite."

"I want to go inside."

I sigh. "This is an opportunity, Chiara. Behaving like a child won't get you anywhere.

She hesitates, and then sits down, but not where I indicated. She's two feet out of reach. It takes all my willpower not to grab her by the hair and drag her closer, and growl in her face. *You sit where I tell you, and if you disobey me one more time, I'll make you regret it for the rest of your life.*

I force my shoulders against the back of the sofa to appear relaxed, extending my arm along the seat. "You seem tense, *bambina*. Relax. I only want to talk to you." I make my voice deep and affectionate. *There, there, little girl. Did the bad men scare you?*

"Are you a criminal?" she asks. "I know inside you said you weren't, but I just want to understand what's happening tonight."

Her insolence knows no bounds. I stare at her for a full minute, watching the light reflected off the water moving over her face. "Yes. But it's business, not pleasure. I'll follow the law until it gets in my way."

"How often does it get in your way?"

All the fucking time. "Now and then."

Chiara watches me with a straight back, her eyes luminous. She has a surprising amount of poise for a seventeen-year-old girl. Like she thinks she's going to get out of this. That she's going to say no, she won't marry any of us, and we and her father will leave her be.

So much confidence. So very stupid.

Adjusting the slender watch on her wrist, she says, "Thank you for your honesty."

You trusting little fool. Did you not listen to a word Vinicius said? "Games are for children."

"Are you all good friends?"

She's trying to figure us out. How she might play us against each other. "We've known each other for a long time."

Our lives are so closely knitted into each other's that it would be impossible to separate them. I know each of them even better than I know myself. We have something stronger than friendship. Stronger than ambition, or blood.

Loyalty.

We learned the hard way that we're stronger together, and we always will be. Chiara will learn in time what that means for her, to be at the behest of all of us.

"How old are you?"

"Thirty-four."

"Older than the others. I guess they're around twenty-eight or so?"

"Give or take a year."

Chiara draws a little closer to me. "I don't imagine you'd want to marry me. I'm still in school. Schoolgirls must be so annoying to grown men." She flashes me a smile and tucks a strand of her hair behind her ear.

This is an unexpected surprise. She's trying to charm me.

"Is there any way you could speak to my father about how ridiculous this is? I feel like he might listen to another man even if he won't listen to me. Being promised to much older strangers when I'm only seventeen…"

She gives a little shiver. Quite the actress, this one.

"You're scared, *bambina*?"

She looks up at me with those big, doll-like eyes, and nods.

"Do you know what I do?" I ask her.

Chiara hesitates, seeming surprised by my change of subject. "You run nightclubs."

"And?"

"And...strip clubs." Even saying that makes her blush. "Why do you ask?"

I shake my head, as if to say, *No reason.* The little idiot knows what I do and yet hasn't realized that I have beautiful women trying to twist me around their little fingers all day long.

I turn a little toward her, mirroring her body language and resting my temple against my fist. "And what do you do?"

"What do you mean?"

I smile at her. "It's not a trick. Who are you? What makes you happy?"

"Well," she begins slowly, "I'm still in school, so that takes up most of my time. I'm not sure what else you'd like to know. Please don't take offence to this, but you're twice my age and I don't think there's much we have in common."

"It's a warm night. You're a beautiful girl. Humor me."

Chiara glances down into her lap and then up at me through her lashes. A jolt goes through me. Fuck, that was cute. She's putting it on, trying to seem even more innocent than she is without realizing it's the most enticing thing she could do for me. If she does this in front of Scava he'll eat her alive. That would be a shame, as there'd be nothing left for the rest of us.

"What would you like to know?"

"What's it like being the mayor's daughter?"

She smiles in relief. "Oh, that. I can talk about that. I don't remember *not* being the mayor's daughter. Dad's been Mayor of Coldlake since I was five years old. Most of the time I don't notice it unless Dad's campaigning and he needs Mom and me with him on stage with him at rallies, or when someone recognizes me in the street. Or if someone starts acting differently when they find out my name."

"Different how?"

She wrinkles her nose. "Sucking up, mostly. Flattering me because they want something. I don't like to be treated differently just because of who I am."

Don't worry, *bambina*. We'll treat you exactly how you deserve.

The next election is next year, not long after Chiara turns eighteen. Mayor Romano will undoubtedly want our help influencing people how to vote. I wonder if he realizes his daughter won't be all we'll ask for in exchange.

She won't be a wife. She'll be our hostage. If he doesn't do what he's told, he'll get her back in pieces.

"Your father's a determined man. It's going to be difficult for you to change his mind."

"Just about impossible," she agrees, nodding her head.

"You need someone to protect you."

Chiara stops nodding, and I can see her mind racing. *Protector* is too much like *husband*.

"A friend," I offer with a smile, and she relaxes once more.

Yes, aren't I warm and approachable. Don't I make you feel safe in this big, scary world? I reach out and tuck a strand of hair behind her ear. "The others gave you a birthday present. I've got something for you too, and it's better than diamonds. Better than advice."

"Oh? What is it?"

I crook my finger, beckoning her closer. She doesn't want to approach, but I take a quick glance around as if I'm worried about us being overheard. The idea that what I'm about to say is just for her and not the others is too enticing, and Chiara slides in closer. She's right next to me now and I can appreciate the beauty of her face and the swell of her breasts in her delicate white gown. It will take weeks of correction to turn Chiara into a proper Ferragamo woman once she's mine. I can't wait another year while she develops more bad habits.

I reach for her hand, and puzzled, she places hers in mine, probably expecting me to give it a pat or slip a bracelet onto her wrist.

Instead, I grip her hand so tight that she gasps and pull her across my lap. She's splayed over my thighs before she can even yelp and I hold her in place with a hand on her lower back.

"What are you doing? Let me go!"

I grab the skirt of her dress and drag it up. Chiara starts fighting, but it's not getting her anywhere. She's wearing a small, flesh-colored G-string with her dress that accentuates the plump curves of her ass.

Chiara inhales, preparing to call for help.

I grab her hair, pulling it tight in my fist. "If you scream, I'll make you fucking sorry. Have you forgotten who we are, Chiara? Do you think we're here to spoil you, like your parents? Or remind you gently about your duty? We kill people for merely inconveniencing us. You're lucky you're still seventeen because otherwise, you'd already be fucking dead."

"Please let me go. I didn't do anything," she whispers, her voice shaking with unshed tears.

"You talk back. You disrespect your parents. You disrespect us most of all." I let go of her hair, flex my hand, and raise it. I'm going to enjoy this. Her tender ass is plump and bright in the darkness.

Chiara twists around and looks up at me. "What are you *doing*?"

"Reminding you of your duty. Your loyalty is to your father for now, but soon it will be to us. When you become my wife, I'll expect you to obey my orders without question."

I land a hard spank on her ass. Chiara yelps, and my hand tingles. There's a perfect red handprint on her ass, and her thighs are spread as she struggles to get away from me.

Beneath her, my cock thickens. The urge to keep going is strong. I want to make her a panting, crying mess and hear her swear to anything I ask for just to make it end. All I crave in this second is that heavenly sight.

But she's not my wife.

Not my wife *yet*.

I release her, and she slithers from my lap onto the ground at my feet. "That's just a taste of what you deserve. By your eighteenth birthday, you better have learned what it means to take your place by our sides. Whichever one of us marries you, we all expect the same obedience."

I stand up and straighten my tie, glancing toward the dining room. I wonder if anyone's bothered to serve the main course.

Chiara sits at my feet, her chiffon gown pooling over my leather shoes. Her head's down and her shoulders are shaking.

Pathetic. I barely touched her.

"We all have different ways of making you obey. You think I've humiliated you, but this is nothing compared to what the others are capable of. I sincerely hope you've learned your lesson tonight. Happy birthday, Chiara."

CHAPTER FIVE

LORENZO

Chiara Romano sits in a crumpled heap, staring at Cassius as he strides back into the house. I've watched her from the shadows as she's talked with and been defeated by each of the others in turn. Cassius seems to have destroyed her.

Get up. Don't be broken, I urge her silently.

I haven't had my fun yet.

Vinicius joins me in the shadows. "Cassius looks pleased with himself. I told her not to trust anyone, but she wouldn't listen. Now look at her."

We watch Chiara take a deep breath and slowly get to her feet.

"He went too easy on her," I sneer. "She's not even crying."

"When was the last time you had a woman and she wasn't crying or expecting to be paid?"

I bare my teeth at the darkness. "I don't pay for pussy. Now fuck off. I want to wish Miss Romano a happy birthday."

"She's not your wife yet, remember that," he says sharply, grasping my arm.

Don't fuck the virgin, he means, because she's not mine to ruin. I pull out of his grip. She's mine for the next thirty minutes, and I can't make any promises. Things might get out of hand.

I step out of the darkness and walk the perimeter of the swimming pool toward Chiara. She's got her head down and she's sniffling as she walks, and I can tell she's halfway to bursting into tears.

Perfect. I'll barely need to do a thing to have her sobbing.

Chiara stops short, and her gaze travels from my feet all the way up to my face. "Have you come to make a fool of me, too?" she whispers.

I regard her in silence. It won't be useful to me to have the mayor in my pocket. I know that's what the other three are looking forward to, but what I do doesn't require contracts and permits, and I fix my own problems.

Chiara takes a shaky breath. "Whatever you do, whatever you say, I'm not going to fall for it. Your friends have shown me what cold bastards you all are, and you seem like the worst."

There isn't much I can do with a wife, either. She can't smuggle things across borders for me once she bears the Scava name. I can't make any money off her because everyone will be too scared to touch what's mine.

"I know you all think that I'm some spoiled princess who needs to be taught my place in the world," Chiara continues. "That I'm not as clever or important as I thought I was."

The only thing she'll be useful for is to bear my children. Three should be enough, and then I'll have to kill her. She's too weak and disobedient to risk having her taint them.

"Do you want to know what I was thinking when I was getting ready tonight? One more year. One more year and then I'll be free to begin my life."

At least she's got a pretty face and she's small enough to be pinned down with one hand. I'll enjoy having a little fun with Chiara.

Her brow wrinkles in confusion. "Do you have a present for me? Some piece of advice, or a warning to do as I'm told?"

The fuck I do. The only presents I give are bullets to the head. She's got diamonds around that chokeable throat of hers. Those are from Salvatore. A mistrustful look in her eyes. That'll be because of Vinicius. And one of her hands keep straying to her ass, courtesy of Cassius. A pre-emptive strike. I've always liked his style.

Now, what do I have for this spoiled, naïve princess to make her birthday night complete?

"Say something, please. You're scaring me."

I tilt my head the other way. I haven't even done anything yet.

I take a step toward her, and fear flickers over her face. "I'm the most dangerous of them all. Do you know why?"

Chiara walks slowly backward as I approach, shaking her head.

"Because I don't want anything from your father, or from you," I say softly. "I just like to win. Once I marry you, I'll probably slit your throat on our wedding night."

Her back hits the wall of the house and her eyes are huge in the darkness.

I keep coming until my body is nearly touching hers. "Your blood all over the rose petals on the bed. What a pretty sight that will be."

Chiara tries to dart away, but I grab her shoulder, turn her around and slam her against the wall, holding her there with one hand. "You thought you could seduce Salvatore. Bargain with Vinicius. Manipulate Cassius. They let you play with them for a little while because it amused them."

I lean closer with every word until my lips are against her ear. "But I don't. Play. Games."

"You're crazy," she whispers.

People say that to me all the time. What they really mean is I can't be controlled, and that's fucking terrifying to them.

I smile against her ear. "If that's what you need to tell yourself. Either way, don't bother trying to charm me. You'd have more success with a piece of frozen metal."

"All right, I won't. Just let me go, please. I'm only seventeen."

Like that will make me merciful toward her after I watched her try to scheme and manipulate her way through tonight. If she wants to act like a tricky little bitch, then she'll be treated like one. "I don't want to. Be a good girl and let me have my birthday present, and you won't have to see my face for another year and a week."

"*Your* birthday present? What do you want?"

I glance down her body and say softly, "Good question."

I grab a handful of her skirt and pull it up.

"No, don't, *please*—"

I pull a zip tie from my pocket and pin her wrists behind her. I tried doing this the easy way. She can't be good, so I'll have to make her. She struggles in my grip but she's not going anywhere. A moment later I have the tie around her wrists and pulled it tight.

Chiara starts to whimper. With my free hand, I reach inside my jacket and draw my knife, showing it to her. That shuts her up. The pointed blade glistens in the moonlight and she freezes at the sight.

"How much blood you shed is up to you. If you scream for help, I'll kill anyone who tries to rescue you and make you watch. Would you like to see your mother die tonight, or are you going to calm the fuck down?"

Chiara doesn't move, doesn't speak. Her cheek is pressed against the wall and her eyes are wide. Much better. I pull up her dress again.

I'm not going to do anything. I just want to look at her.

Probably.

It depends how much she tries to fight me. There's a fading red handprint on her ass, courtesy of Cassius. Fuck, she's got a cute little body. The sight of her and the scent of her fear is making me hard.

I grasp her G-string, slice through the straps, and pull it free while Chiara chokes out a protest.

"What do we have here?" I murmur, holding the scraps of her underwear aloft and examining them in the dim light. There's a dark, wet spot where the fabric has been nestled against her pussy.

I show her the underwear, my thumb moving over the slippery patch, and put my lips close to her ear. "Is that for me? Or for one of the others? Who turned you into a slippery mess while you were pretending to be a sheltered, naïve Catholic girl who's so *scared*, so *confused* by all these bad men?"

"Please, don't," she whimpers, shaking her head, her face creasing like she's going to cry.

Oh, please cry. Making horny girls cry is my favorite thing.

"Do you like bad men, Chiara? Was it me who made you wet? Please say it was me." I run my tongue up the shell of her ear, and she shivers against me. That ass of hers rubbing against my cock nearly sends me over the edge. I have only a tenuous grasp on control, and she's about to shatter it. I press the flat of the knife under her chin and growl, "Wriggle like that again and I'll fuck you right now while everyone in this house listens to you scream."

Chiara pants softly, her whole body rigid as she tries desperately to keep still.

I flip the knife in my hand and shove the hilt between her thighs. Her bare pussy is right there as I stroke the handle back and forth across her lips. So wet, so ready for me to shove it inside her.

"Or did you get wet for all of us? Is that what you want, Chiara, for us to line up and fuck you, one after another? I'll go last. Do you think you'll still be struggling by the time it's my turn?"

Horrified, she squeezes her eyes shut. Bet she wishes now that she never asked me to speak.

"Why are you even here? You obviously hate me."

Hate? To feel hate, you have to be able to love. I run my eyes down her quivering body. I like them innocent and trembling, but the innocent and trembling ones never want me.

"We're not doing it to you, idiot. We're doing it to him."

"My father? But aren't you all friends?"

"There aren't friends in our world. There are only allies and enemies, and the two can switch places at a moment's notice. The mayor wants us as allies, but we don't like to be used, Chiara. He has to be taught a lesson, and it's more fun for us to make him suffer by making you suffer."

"But...but he thinks you want to be allies," she says in a small voice.

I laugh softly. "So you're fucked, aren't you? Think of it this way. It doesn't matter what happens next. You were fucked the moment we stepped foot in this house."

I put my lips against her ear as I speak softly, twisting the hilt of my knife against her pussy. "You're getting your juices all over my knife, Chiara. When you go to school and confess to your priest, make sure you tell him what a very bad man did to you, and just how much you loved it."

I grip the knife harder and increase the pressure, watching her eyes widen as the hilt just presses between her lips.

"Happy fucking birthday."

CHAPTER SIX

CHIARA

Lorenzo's weight against my back and the knife hilt pressing on my bare privates vanish at the same time. The searing heat from his body lifts and I listen to his footsteps recede. I stay where I am, huddled against the wall. There's a *shhhk* sound, like a knife being shoved back into a holster.

Then silence.

Minutes pass, and I don't dare move or open my eyes. I'm naked beneath my dress. Naked and—how did it happen?—wet. I see again my G-string in Lorenzo's big hand with its tattooed fingers, his thumb rubbing slowly over the slippery patch. One of these tyrannical men turned me on while they were threatening and tricking me. But which one? Salvatore as he was putting diamonds around my throat and choking me? Vinicius with his smooth-talking trickery? Cassius with his indulgent concern and fiery threats? Or—please God, no—Lorenzo's sadistic depravity? As I remember each man, I can't discern any difference in my feelings toward them. Whatever crazy reaction my body had, I hate them all.

In the distance I hear a deep, nasty laugh. Lorenzo as he tells the others what he just did to me? What if they all come back and do what he threatened they would do?

One after another.

I push away from the wall and look desperately around. My hands are fastened painfully tight behind my back and every movement makes them burn. I'm totally defenseless. On my left is a staircase leading down to the kitchen. I head for them with a stifled sob, knowing that there's safety at the bottom. People who love me. People who'll protect me.

Don't cry.

Don't you dare cry.

Familiar voices reach my ears as I make my way downstairs. Stephan, who chauffeurs and serves dinner. Violette, who cleans the house.

"…lined up like they were judging her. It was awful."

"And on her birthday, too. The poor girl is only seventeen."

I stagger down the last few steps and into the arms of a comforting, floury woman in an apron. Francesca, our cook. "Do you think that the mayor—Chiara!"

The horrified expression on her face is the last straw, and a sob rises up my throat. These people are my friends. They've always been kind to Mom and me and looked out for me when I was little, especially Francesca. She's nearly sixty and the lines on her face are as comforting as they are familiar.

She pats my back as I press my face into her shoulder. I refuse to go to pieces over what happened tonight. It's what those horrible men want, so I hold my breath and grit my teeth against the tears.

"Stephan, are her hands tied? Cut her free."

Stephan finds a pair of scissors and cuts the zip tie. I pull away from Francesca and gaze down at my shaking hands through blurry eyes.

Violette touches my arm, her brow pinched with worry. "Chiara, what's happened to you? Was it one of these men?"

I open my mouth to tell them all what happened tonight and what my father intends for me, but before I can say a word, Lorenzo's seething threat comes back to me.

If you scream for help, I'll kill anyone who tries to rescue you and make you watch.

My throat convulses. The other three are probably just as ruthless and won't try to stop him.

"Nothing. I'm fine. I…"

Three doubtful, worried faces stare back at me. There isn't anyone who can help me right now. I just have to make it through tonight, and then Mom and I will have a year to find a way out of this mess.

I glance at the clock and see that it's just past eleven. Dad told me I'd be promised to one of these men tonight. I just want to hide down here in the basement kitchen with people who are kind to me.

"Chiara," Francesca says, reaching out to pat my hair. "Did one of those men hurt you?"

"Of course they hurt her!" Stephan exclaims, brandishing the broken zip tie. "Look at her. Look at *this*. We have to do something."

His face is a mask of fury. If he goes upstairs to face them he'll be torn to pieces.

"Nothing happened. Don't worry about me." They don't believe me, but they don't have to as long as they stay down here. I can't let them put themselves in danger for me.

High on the wall, the clock ticks out the passing seconds.

Tick tock.

Violette glances nervously at the others. "Did you recognize that huge, dark-haired man? He owns all the strip clubs in the city. The girls who work there end up dead if they whisper even one word about what they see and hear."

Francesca nods. "That's Cassius Ferragamo. The fair-haired man, the good-looking one—I swear that's Vinicius Angeli. He was arrested for money laundering last year, and then they just let him go."

"And the other two—" Violette begins.

"Salvatore Fiore and Lorenzo Scava," I whisper.

They all stare at me, doubtlessly wondering why four such men were invited to my birthday party. Working for the Mayor of Coldlake requires discretion and I've never heard the three of them gossip about the important men and women Dad entertains. There are sometimes celebrities who visit and occasionally the governor of the state. They could lose their jobs if Dad thinks they're being indiscreet, but I can feel them itching to ask me what happened tonight.

I'm more concerned about their lives than their jobs. The longer I stay down here, the more I'm putting them in danger.

I back away from them. "Thank you. I'm fine now, don't worry about me."

The smile I force onto my face feels brittle and they watch me head for the stairs and go up into the house. The hall is paneled with dark wood and the lights are low. There are voices coming from the dining room. Deep, male voices talking rapidly.

I can't face anyone yet. I go into the nearby bathroom and lock the door.

In the mirror, my face is pale and tense and mascara has blurred beneath my eyes. I sit on the closed toilet and swipe beneath my eyes with wet tissue, trying to make sense of everything that's happened tonight.

The men who occupy the seedy underbelly of Coldlake are supposed to be Dad's enemies. I was on stage with him at his campaign rallies three years ago and he spoke about being a law-and-order mayor and being tough on crime. The people cheered when they heard that. Coldlake is prosperous and safe for the most part, but there are dangerous places, too. Dangerous people. Among the big, flashy stories in the news about a new park opening or a business achievement award, there are short paragraphs about missing people and unsolved murders. Money going missing from retirement funds and shops being burned to the ground. No city is perfect and there's no such thing as zero crime anywhere, but I always believed that Coldlake was a better city than most. Is that because it is, or because I've been told that, over and over?

I stare around at the marble tiles and vanity. The gold taps on the sink and art on the walls. Isn't it strange that we can afford such a big house and expensive lifestyle on Dad's salary? I've never thought about it before. I reach up and pull the tiara from my hair, turning it this way and that in the light. Dad gave it to me this morning. I assumed that the sparkling stones were cubic zirconia. Imitation diamonds. In my reflection, the diamonds around my neck sparkle with as much luster as the ones set into the tiara.

Dad can't afford a diamond tiara. He shouldn't be *able* to afford a diamond tiara.

This house. All that we possess. Our lives weren't built with hard work, but with lies.

"Dad, what have you done?" I whisper, the tiara dropping from my fingers.

I have to find Dad and tell him that he's out of his depth. These men can't be controlled. They're forces of nature, and he's not as powerful as he thinks he is.

I slip out of the bathroom, my heart pounding, and edge down the hallway. The voices from the dining room are louder now, and I can hear Dad's voice among the four men's. There's an ornate Venetian clock standing against the wall, brought to the United States by my great-grandfather. I huddle in its shadow, the *tick tock* of the mechanism drowning out whatever's being said. If I can just make it to midnight without being promised…

It's a stupid thought. Even if I hide until dawn, there's nothing stopping the men from coming back tomorrow night, and the night after, and the night after that until they get what they want.

I don't want to know what they're saying about me.

I can't do this.

Why is this happening?

These four men could be blackmailing Dad somehow, and he thinks he's got no choice but to appease them by marrying me to one of them. Maybe he's too ashamed to tell Mom and me the truth, but I'll never be ashamed of him if he's honest. Honesty and transparency are the most important things. That's what Dad's always said.

I place my hand on the cool wood of the clock and peer around it. I can see the door to the dining room from here, but no one who's inside.

Suddenly, heavy footsteps approach and a voice grows louder. "...business to attend to and then we can finish this. Excuse me."

Dad appears in the doorway and heads upstairs without noticing me. His face is serious and he seems confident and at ease, but after so many years in office and training himself to appear self-assured, it's impossible to tell what he's really thinking.

Now's my chance. I'll follow him upstairs and beg him to call this whole arrangement off. Once he hears what his so-called friends have done to me, he'll have them thrown from this house. Mom and I have always been at his side and the people of Coldlake trust us. If we speak out alongside Dad about whatever he's suffered at the hands of these men, we'll be able to overcome all their lies.

As I approach the staircase, I hear a voice that turns my whole body to ice.

"I won't let you have her."

Mom, in the dining room.

She's with them.

Alone.

Mom speaks clearly but there's a tremor in her voice, as if she's summoned up the very last of her strength to confront this pack of demons. "Any of you."

There's a deep, rich laugh in response. Cassius' laugh. In his accented voice, he asks, "And who are you to stand in our way?"

"Chiara's mother," she exclaims, her voice stronger. "I don't know what my husband has promised you all, but the deal is off."

"He's promised us his daughter and we will have her." Salvatore's arrogant tone. "You have no idea of the pain we will rain down on your family if you dare to defy us."

Taut silence stretches. I rest my hand against the wall by the door. I can't see any of them, but I can picture my painfully thin and distressed mother standing up to those men all on her own. Behind me, the clock ticks closer and closer to midnight.

Tick tock.

A strange sound reaches my ears over the clock.

Shhhk. Shhhk. Shhhk.

Lorenzo's knife, as if he's flicking it in and out of its holster. That goddamn knife. Mom's always been deathly afraid of weapons of any sort. I have to go in there and put a stop to this.

"Pain?" Mom suddenly cries, and I freeze, pressing a hand over my racing heart. "You think you could cause me more pain than ripping my only child away from me? I have a whole year to find a way to stop you all from getting what you want, and if that fails, I'll hide her where you'll never find her. She's not yours, and she never will be."

I can hear the truth in every syllable she utters. She'll do anything and everything to protect me from these men. Tears prickle my eyes as the full force of my mother's love breaks over me.

"You've got a death wish, Mayoress Romano," Vinicius replies, sly as always, but without any of the charm he used on me. How cold he sounds when he's not bothering to manipulate. Almost as cold as Lorenzo.

"I don't care about my own life," Mom spits in revulsion. "If you'd ever loved anything but yourselves, money, and power, you'd know that giving up your life for the one you love is nothing. *Nothing*. But you can't love, can you? You don't know how. You're all despicable. Hateful. Abhorrent. Now get out of my house!"

I hear the garden door slide open and my mother walking away rapidly with a faint sob. She's so much stronger and cleverer than me. I thought I could reason with or persuade these men, but she saw them right away for what they are.

Monsters.

You can't reason with monsters. You can only fight back.

I turn around and walk quickly and silently back down the corridor and around to the staircase leading to the kitchen where there's another door to the garden. As I come out into the night air, Mom's standing on the edge of the pool, her face in her hands and sobbing like her heart will break.

With Mom on my side, I won't be promised to anyone tonight. We'll stand strong together against everyone.

A lone figure in a black suit emerges from the dining room. His head and shoulders are in the shadows and he stands where he is, staring at Mom's back. Anger races through me. They didn't leave the house as she ordered them to, or not all of them, at least. Who has remained, and why must he go on tormenting her?

Tick tock.

I can hear the ticking from out here. How can I hear it from out here? The clock's got into my head, and I can't get the sound out of my ears.

The man steps forward and grasps Mom viciously by the hair, pulling her head back. Her throat arches and her hands fly out as she gasps mid-sob. In his other hand, a wickedly pointed knife gleams in the darkness.

The grandfather clock in the hall begins to chime.

Midnight.

It's midnight and I'm not promised. I've won.

Haven't I?

The knife flashes in the darkness. The clock chimes, heavy and slow. Time's slowing down.

"*No!*"

Someone screams.

I'm running toward my mother. My legs feel like they're in molasses. My lungs are burning as if I've already run a marathon. Blood gouts from Mom's throat as the knife finishes its vicious arc and is brandished in triumph. She falls forward, eyes wide, into the swimming pool.

I run and I run, and she falls slower and slower as the deafening peals of the clock ring out across the garden. So much blood. It's like a fountain down her front. I can't get to her in time. I won't make it.

I fall to my knees at the side of the pool and snatch at the trailing skirt of her dress. The silky black fabric slips through my fingers, and Mom plunges headfirst into the pool, her arms flung wide.

The water blooms red. Mom bobs face down in the water, blood billowing from her throat in a hideous stain.

"*Mom.*"

I try to throw myself in after her, but a hand grabs a fistful of the back of my dress and holds me. I flail in his grip, sobbing and screaming, my tears falling onto a pair of black leather dress shoes. He's clutching a knife with blood dripping from the point.

Lorenzo's knife. The same one he's been taunting me with all evening.

My breath comes faster and faster. I don't want to look, but I have to know which one of these monsters did it.

Who will I hate for the rest of my life?

Who will I destroy for killing what I love?

Mom's blood continues to turn the swimming pool red and her black dress spreads out around her. I look up.

Into his face.

At the man who murdered my mother.

CHAPTER SEVEN

CHIARA

A brush of mascara.

A dab of lipstick.

A lace veil drawn over my hair to cover my face. Light filters through the delicate net and embroidered blossoms. I can see out but the world can't see in.

Dad's waiting for me by the front door in a suit and tie. His gaze travels down over my dress, scrutinizing every fold of fabric, every button. Another man might tell his daughter, *Your mother would be so proud* or *You look beautiful*, but that's not Dad and it never was. Besides, we've barely spoken a word to each other since that night.

Outside, an enormous rental car is idling in the street and the driver helps me inside. I tuck my dress around myself so none of the skirt touches my father. The drive to the church isn't a long one, but we pass down main streets and people peer in and look at us. They all know what today is.

I feel safe inside my veil. The veil is my protection, and I dread the moment *he'll* pull it back and I'll have to look up into his hateful face.

Dad and I walk up the church steps together and into the cavernous, vaulted space. Pale sunshine streams through the stained-glass windows. Organ music fills the air. A huge gold cross dominates the altar.

Hundreds of people are in the pews, and they all turn to look at my slow progress down the aisle at Dad's side.

I try not to look at what awaits me at the far end.

I try not to.

But my eyes are drawn there despite myself, to a shiny black casket heaped with white roses. My insides seize with grief and panic. This is actually happening. I'm burying my mother, my only true protector in this world.

The scent of chlorine and blood fills my nose, each as hateful as the other. Water forces its way down my throat and into my lungs. I can't breathe. I can't *breathe*—

"Chiara. People are staring." Words spoken so low that only I can hear.

Dad pulls me toward the front pew. I grasp the back of the wooden bench and suck in a painful breath. It was better not to feel, it was better not to think about the horror of that night three weeks ago. My mother is here. My mother's cold body that will never embrace me again.

Dad grasps my elbow and forces me to sit down. I see it again, the gash of her slit throat. The eruption of blood. Her slow fall into the swimming pool. An usher hands us both a booklet. *In Loving Memory of Eleonora Mirabella Romano*, with a picture of her smiling face.

I take the booklet in my black gloved hand and lay it in my lap. I twitch my black skirt away from Dad so that nothing of me is touching anything of him. To anyone looking on, they'll see a father and daughter sank in mutual grief, side by side and drawing strength from each other in times of need. It's only how things look that matter to him, not how they really are. He values that over his own wife's life, and his daughter's love and trust. The love between us shattered when he looked the homicide detective in the eye and said, *"I don't know who did it. The coward escaped over the wall while I was trying to save my wife."*

After Mom's body was zipped into a body bag and wheeled away, she lay in the morgue for three weeks while Coldlake Police chased down any leads they could. There wasn't much to go on. No DNA evidence on Mom. No witnesses. No murder weapon. The men disappeared into the night.

No one will pay for the crime of her murder. It's all been smoothed away, like it never happened. Like she never existed.

I haven't shed a tear since that night. Dad's plan will go ahead despite Mom's sacrifice. I'm promised, and her death was for nothing.

I gaze at the casket, the last remnant of her on this earth. She's being buried in a new blue skirt suit I bought for her. As I sorted through her closet, every dress reminded me of Dad. One she wore to dinner with him. One she wore to a campaign rally. Her favorite that she wore to last year's parade, where she sat alongside Dad and smiled and waved to the crowd. Every garment was tainted with the man who wouldn't protect her when she most needed him.

She didn't have to die.

This is all my fault.

The service begins, and after a sermon from the priest and a hymn, Dad gets up to give his eulogy. His face is somber and he seems to have the weight of the world on his shoulders as he casts his eyes around the congregation.

I close my eyes and drown out his voice with memories of Mom. Sitting in her lap at Granny's kitchen table while they chatted about the neighbors and my uncles and aunts, drinking coffee and eating cake. Teaching me how to peel an apple in one long strand. How to pat the kitten she gave me for my fourth birthday. *"Softly, sweetheart. It's only small. Like this."*

She was the gentlest person, and she taught me how to be gentle and move gracefully through the world. Where is the gentleness and grace in my life now?

I open my eyes and turn to gaze at the casket, and a pair of eyes catch mine across the aisle.

My stomach spasms.

My fists clench on my black dress and I scream silently in the back of my throat, lips tightly closed.

He came here.

Here.

How *dare* he.

His lips curve into a smile and he dips his head in greeting, like this is a social event and not my mother's funeral. I hold his gaze, my stomach churning. I don't know if he can see my face through the black veil but I have to be strong even if I know I'm not. Because Mom was strong at the end, wasn't she? She stood up to those monsters all by herself.

The service ends and we all get to our feet. The veil protects me from *him*, and the intrusion of the other mourners. These people didn't know Mom, and they don't know what she sacrificed for me.

Out by the graveside, I watch them weep for her and console my father, and all the while *his* presence is prickling the back of my neck.

The wake is at our home, and I stand in a corner while waiters in white shirts and black bow ties offer silver trays of sandwiches to the hundreds of people that are filling the rooms that Mom so lovingly decorated. They talk about politics and the upcoming election, interest rates and new hotel developments. None of these people are here for Mom. They're here to rub shoulders with Dad and his friends and gossip with each other.

A folded copy of the *Coldlake Tribune* is laying on a side table and I flip it over, wondering what's being said publicly about Mom's murder. It's today's newspaper and the front page is dedicated to "The town's beloved mayoress." Her face smiles out at me, eyes filled with kindness.

My throat burns.

So beloved, that she ended up dead in a swimming pool with her throat slit.

I take a shuddering breath and quickly move my gaze elsewhere, and it catches on a paragraph of text accompanying the image.

…mayoress' death potentially linked to the Black Orchid Murders eight years ago.

I frown. The Black Orchid Murders. Haven't I heard about those? Teenage girls and young women who were brutally killed. I was a child and I don't remember it well, but I think one or more of the women had a black flower shoved down her throat. No one knows who did it. So that's how Dad's going to cover up Mom's murder: pin it on some unknown psychopath and let the case go cold.

I scan the rest of the front page and see my father's name.

Mayor Romano has vowed to begin his reelection campaign against City Hall hopeful Christian Galloway in six months' time. "It's what my wife would have wanted," he stated at a press conference last night. "She loved Coldlake. She died for Coldlake. I will prevail."

"Read me my horoscope, Chiara."

My stomach lurches.

I whirl around at the sound of a deep, mocking voice. He's standing close. So close that I can see the individual shards of blue and green in his eyes, even through the lace of my veil. I haven't wanted to take it off. I don't think I'll ever want to take it off.

"I'm a Sagittarius. November 29th. Do you think the stars say we're compatible?" He smiles, showing a row of strong white teeth.

I look down and realize I'm still gripping the newspaper in my hands, and I throw it aside. When I try to step past him, he grabs my arm.

"I haven't seen my pretty bride's face in weeks." He grasps the edge of the veil and draws it slowly back. I feel like he's stripping me naked. The table is pressing against my back and I can't move away from him, and then I'm looking up at him with nothing between us.

"Ah, there you are," says Salvatore Fiore, a victorious glint in his smile.

"Pleased with yourself because you won?" I ask him.

Salvatore smiles wider and cups my face in his hands. The next thing I know his mouth is descending toward mine, attempting to claim another kiss that I don't want to give him. I turn my face away sharply.

"This is my mother's funeral. Have some respect."

"How can I help myself when my bride is so beautiful?" he murmurs.

I look over his shoulder, expecting to see the other three looming behind him with a collection of smirks and sneers on their faces. I crane my neck as I peer into all corners of the room.

"Where are your friends today?"

The smile dies on Salvatore's face. "Why are you looking for them when I'm standing right in front of you?"

"I was just asking—"

"Then don't," he snarls.

I stare at him, open-mouthed. His mood has changed as quickly as it did the night of my birthday. From polite to murderous in seconds.

"Excuse me." I reach up to my veil to draw it down over my face.

He grasps my wrist. "No. Don't hide that beautiful face away. I'd like to kill every man who looks at you, but I crave to see you even more."

If he were Vinicius I'd accuse him of empty flattery, but I don't know where I stand with Salvatore. He's had me second-guessing everything he's done since that first kiss.

I draw the veil over my face with my other hand. "If I have to marry one of you then I'll remain in mourning."

His bride in black, to despise and destroy, till death do us part.

"Not one of us. *Me*. I'm going to marry you."

I pull my arm from his grasp. I don't know when or how it was decided that I'm going to marry Salvatore. Dad and the four men must have made the arrangement when I was upstairs in bed, paralyzed with grief beneath the blankets.

I wonder how much I'm worth. A few contracts? Building permission for a new skyscraper? Whatever it was, my father will have come out on top. He always does.

"What do the other three think of your arrangement?"

"How about you shut the fuck up about the other three?" he says through his teeth.

I don't understand how he can speak about his friends with so much venom. Unless…they're not friends anymore? Is that it, Salvatore won, but the price was his friends? Dad used me to drive a wedge between four powerful adversaries.

My eyes flick up and down Salvatore's muscular, suited body. "I feel sorry for you. You came to my house so certain of yourselves. You declared to me that you couldn't be bought, and yet look at you. You sold out, and now you're alone."

"That's a sharp tongue you've got for someone who's learned

firsthand the price of disobedience." Salvatore glances meaningfully at my throat.

My knees start to tremble but I clench my fists and remain on my feet through sheer force of will. "You'd throw my mother's murder in my face the day I bury her? I know I'm more useful alive than dead right at this moment. I may as well say what I really feel while I'm still able to."

"Enjoy it while you can. Fifty weeks left, and counting." He gathers up the edge of my veil, puts his lips close to my ear, and murmurs, "For me, it will feel like an age."

His lips find the soft skin behind my ear and he plants a slow kiss there. My future husband lingers where he is, inhaling the scent from my neck. I have fifty weeks to find a way out of this marriage. My mother died to save me from this match. I can't let her sacrifice be for nothing.

Salvatore draws back, his blue-green eyes dark and gleaming. "If you ever need anything, you can count on me. Always."

To do what? I'm in school. My problems are my mother's death, math homework—and *him*.

I stare at his chest through my veil, willing myself not to fall apart in front of him.

And then finally, he's gone.

I plant my palm against the table and take deep, ragged breaths. How dare he come to Mom's wake and gloat over my suffering. I stare around the room and down the hall, peering into the rooms beyond. Dozens of people are standing in groups, eating tiny sandwiches and talking. No one knows the truth about what happened that night except me, Dad, and four dangerous criminals.

I could scream it at the top of my lungs.

Mom was murdered.

Murdered.

And none of you care.

The crowd parts, and I see Dad staring back at me, his expression as grim as his black suit. Did he see me talking to Salvatore? Does he know how much I want to scream to everyone about what happened the night Salvatore, Vinicius, Cassius, and Lorenzo came to my birthday party?

Which of them will kill *me* if I let one word of the truth drop from my lips?

I go and sit up on the second-floor landing, listening to the jumbled conversations downstairs. Every now and then a word floats up to me.

Sometimes it's my name.

Mostly it's Dad's, or *campaign*, or *votes*, or *strategy*.

I don't hear Mom's name. Not even once.

Hours pass, and then the voices start to thin out. Soon there's a little conversation, but mostly the clink of plates and glasses as the catering crew packs up. As dusk falls, even those sounds recede.

I draw the black veil from my hair, leave it on the stairs, and get to my feet. It's the moment I've been anticipating and dreading, the moment Dad and I are finally alone together.

I find him in the empty living room, tapping away on his tablet. I suppose he has lots of emails to catch up on after a day wasted on his wife's funeral. I stand in front of him, rigid with hatred, until he finally looks up.

"Yes, Chiara?" he asks, fingertip poised over the screen.

It's the first time we've talked since he came into my room three days after my mother's death and informed me that I'd be marrying Salvatore.

"A good day's campaigning?" I ask, my throat tight.

I search his face for a hint of the father I once knew. He was always austere and more interested in me intellectually than emotionally, but he was never this cold. Something happened to him these past few months that made him switch off from Mom and me completely.

Now, looking into his eyes is like gazing into a dark abyss.

Dad turns his attention back to his tablet. I dart forward and snatch it away from him. "Why didn't you prepare me for this? Why didn't you prepare Mom? She didn't have to die. You should have *told*—"

Dad's temper suddenly flares and he snatches the tablet from me. "I taught her to do as she was told! I thought she knew her place. Not well enough, apparently. Not when it came to you."

"She *loved* me. You were supposed to love *both* of us and protect us. Nothing you did could have prepared me for this."

"What's done is done. You've had weeks to accept that you're promised to Salvatore Fiore, and you have a year to prepare yourself for the wedding. I'm not rushing you into anything."

I stare at him, unable to believe what I'm hearing. "I could go to the police. What would become of your plans then?"

"Shall I call Salvatore and tell him, or will you?"

I step back and swallow hard.

"I thought so," Dad sneers. "You'd better think long and hard about this world and your place in it. There are consequences if you don't marry Salvatore. If you refuse, what else are you good for?"

I scream and fling myself at him, fists raised to beat his face, his chest, anywhere I can land a hit. He grabs my wrists easily and throws me aside, and I go tumbling to the carpet.

He looms over me. "You'd better learn to behave. In one year, you won't be my problem anymore, and I can assure you, your husband won't spoil you as much as I clearly did. Prepare yourself, Chiara. What happens next is up to you."

"Nothing about this is my decision," I seethe, getting to my feet. "Nothing."

I stay where I am and stare at my father for several silent minutes, watching him work, but I may as well be staring at a brick wall. I'm waiting for some sign of feeling.

Regret.

Humanity.

Mom wasn't the only one who died the night of my seventeenth birthday. It was a turning point for all of us. A threshold of no return, and now there's no way I can reach Dad. To be a human being again he'll have to feel the unimaginable pain of what he's done. Instead, he's chosen to shut down that part of himself forever.

I turn away, wiping tears from my cheeks, and walk slowly upstairs.

I have fifty weeks to find some way out of this marriage and this family. Mom's death won't be for nothing.

I swear it.

CHAPTER EIGHT

CHIARA

"It's too soon, Chiara. I won't let this happen. It's not what your mother would have wanted." Francesca holds me tightly as she sobs. Violette and Stephan hover behind her, their faces shadowed with worry.

I extricate myself carefully from the cook's arms. "I'll be all right, I promise."

The room is filled with the scent of baking bread and there are smudges of flour on Francesca's dove gray dress and white apron.

"But what if something happens to you?" she wails.

"She's right," Stephan says, stepping forward. His body is rigid with anger and his fists are balled. "We can't trust that *bastardo*."

Violette gasps and glances quickly around, as if Dad or even Salvatore himself might have overheard. "Stephan, it's dangerous to talk that way. But he's right, Chiara," she adds, turning to me. "At least here we know you're safe."

I pat Francesca's back comfortingly and ease away from her. "I'll be fine. I want to go back to school."

Two weeks have passed since Mom's funeral, and my grief is still an impossible weight in my heart, but I'll go crazy if I don't get out of this house. Everywhere I look, I'm reminded of Mom. Mom's photo in the living room. The decorations she bought for the hall. Her blood turning the swimming pool a vicious red.

Sniffling, Francesca straightens the collar of my white school shirt and brushes some flour from my black blazer. The red-and-gold St. Osanna Catholic Girls' School crest is stitched over my heart. A pleated skirt brushes a few inches above my knees, and long black socks are pulled up my legs.

"Are you sure?" she asks, and I nod, doing my best to smile for her. "Call us if you change your mind, and Stephan will pick you up."

Stephan nods, but exchanges a look with Violette as Francesca puts snacks into a paper bag for me. They're worried because once I leave this house, I'll be unprotected. Those four men who came to my birthday could do anything they want to me.

Stephan doesn't get it. Those men don't need to wait for me to leave this house. They can do whatever they want to me if Dad lets them, and he's already made it clear he's on their side, not mine.

I take the snacks from Francesca and put them into my schoolbag and say goodbye to everyone.

"You're not saying goodbye to your father?" Francesca asks.

I hesitate, my mouth working. The three of them have noticed the rift between Dad and me, but they've put it down to grief. I have to go on pretending that's all it is or they might end up dead, too.

"I said goodbye to him earlier," I say, and hurry out the door with a wave for them all.

It's a ten-minute walk to St. Osanna and I take deep breaths as I make my way down the tree-lined streets. The routine of putting on my uniform and packing my schoolbag has been soothing. I can't wait to get to class and sit at my desk. Hear the drone of the teachers. Take notes and jot down my homework assignments. Most of all, I want to feel like a small, unimportant cog in an indifferent machine instead of a pawn on a chessboard with fewer and fewer pieces in play.

Leaving just me.

And *him*.

But I don't want to think about Salvatore today. I give my head a shake as I open my locker and get out my books for English. A moment later the bell rings and I hurry to homeroom. Nicole, my best friend, stares at me in shock as I slide into the seat beside hers.

As the teacher calls roll and goes through announcements, Nicole leans closer and whispers, "Why didn't you tell me you were coming back? Are you okay?"

I give her a rueful smile and whisper back, "I'm okay. Sorry I didn't tell you I was coming back today."

As we walk to English class together, Nicole loops an arm around my waist and squeezes me. "I've missed you so much. You must feel like shit. This is all so shitty."

It's shittier than she knows, but my heart feels lighter just being here with her.

"I was so worried about you. You look well, though. You're so brave."

I smile at her. In my mirror this morning, my complexion was gray and my eyes were dull and tired. "I look like crap. But thank you."

"How's your poor dad? He must be devastated."

The smile freezes on my face. I'm saved from answering by crossing the threshold into the classroom where our teacher is already waiting.

I can barely follow the discussion around me about *Hamlet* after missing so many lessons, and my head feels jammed with fog. It's like that in all my morning classes, but I suppose the teachers have decided to go easy on me, seeing as no one chews me out for staring vacantly out the windows.

In between classes I feel the intrusive stares of my classmates, and some of the bolder ones ask blunt questions. Everyone's interested in Mom's unsolved murder, and mumbled sympathies quickly become excuses to probe me for information about the investigation. I hear the phrase *Black Orchid Murders* whispered behind my back more than once. I mutter that I don't know what's happening with the investigation over and over until Nicole sees everyone off.

"What do you know about the Black Orchid Murders?" I ask Nicole as we sit together at lunch.

She scrunches up her face and thinks. "Nothing, really, except they were really gruesome and no one knows who did it. Four girls were killed, and no one knows why. I heard Mom and Dad mention the case the other night. Has it got something to do with your mom?"

I shake my head. "It keeps coming up and I don't know why."

I can't bring myself to search for it online in case I see some horrible crime scene photos or read something that reminds me of what happened on my birthday. I see enough blood and brutality every time I close my eyes.

Nicole chews her lower lip for a moment, and then she drops her voice to a whisper. "Did you really see nothing that night?"

My heart starts to pound. What if I slip up and reveal the truth, and someone else ends up dead because of me?

Nicole mistakes my paralyzed silence as grief. She grabs my hand. "I'm sorry, I'm so insensitive. Forget I asked. You've been through enough."

"I'm okay. I'm still…processing everything and trying not to think about that night too much. Meanwhile, Dad's got a plan."

Nicole smiles. "Your dad always has a plan. I'm glad he's still mayor. Mom and Dad have been worried about him ever since he gave that heartbreaking eulogy."

Yes, didn't he seem devastated.

Nicole opens her sandwich, grimaces, and bites into it.

"He wants me to get married." The words taste disgusting in my mouth.

Nicole stops chewing and her eyes grow round as golf balls. Then she swallows her whole mouthful at once and starts coughing. "Oh, my God. To whom? But you're seventeen. We're in *school*."

I pound her on the back as I try and decide how much to say. Nicole's been my best friend since we were in kindergarten. I can't tell her why, but I have to confide in someone what is happening to me. "I can't say yet. It's complicated. I'm trying to talk Dad out of it but he—he—"

My eyes burn with tears and my throat feels thick.

Nicole takes a mouthful of soda and sits up, and her shock turns to understanding. "It's okay. I get it. He's worried about you. He wants to be sure that someone will take care of you if something happens to him."

I suppose it's only natural Nicole would think that Dad's acting nobly. So many people of Coldlake think of Dad as their hero.

"You're not leaving school or anything, are you? You're not getting married next week?"

"No. Nothing's going to happen until I'm eighteen, and not then, either, if I can help it."

"Oh, phew. It's way too sudden for you to get married. Plus, it's been horrible without you here for the last month. I've missed you so much." She smiles crookedly at me.

"I've missed you, too." I hug Nicole as tight as I can. "I'll tell you everything as soon as I can. I promise."

As I approach the exit at the end of the day, I see that there are two dozen or more girls clustered around the school gate. Their whispers spread like fire.

"He's so hot."

"Is that his car?"

I guess someone's older brother has come to pick her up from school. Boys are such a novelty to us at St. Osanna, that a group of them, or even one really cute boy, can send everyone in a fifty-foot radius a little bit crazy.

I've had enough of that sort of crazy. As the other students jostle against each other to get a better view, I weave my way through them, wincing as my toe is trodden on by a girl jumping up and down and whisper-screaming, "Oh my *God*, he's so sexy! Whose big brother is that?"

I'm almost out the gates when one word stops me in my tracks.

"Chiara." He doesn't even need to raise his voice. It lifts over the crowd and resonates in my ears.

Everyone who was staring at Salvatore turns in unison and stares at me. I grip the strap of my shoulder bag, wishing that a sinkhole would open beneath my feet and swallow me up. I thought I would be safe from him at school. I thought *here*, at least, I could pretend he doesn't exist.

Salvatore has parked a sleek gray Maserati at the front gates and is leaning against it, dressed in a black suit with a gray T-shirt underneath, cut low enough to expose his strong chest muscles. The suit hugs his body like a lover, accentuating the thickness of his biceps and the breadth of his shoulders. The heavy silver watch on his wrist sparkles in the sunlight. He draws one hand out of his pocket and slides his fingers along his freshly shaven jaw.

He smiles, and a shiver goes hroughh the girls around me.

Looking at me but addressing them, he drawls, "Would you mind? I'd like to speak with my fiancée."

Salvatore parts the girls like Moses parting the Red Sea with just his voice, making a path straight to him. All my classmates gawk at me.

And then the whispers start.

"Fiancée? Why didn't she tell us?"

"She's *engaged*?"

"Wait, I think I recognize him."

"Haven't we seen him on the news?"

"*That's Salvatore Fiore.*"

The mood of the crowd changes from surprise to delirious shock. *The* Salvatore Fiore is at our school gates in all his scandalous, bad-boy glory. The expressions on the girls' faces range from envy to confusion to downright disgust.

It's not what you think, I want to scream. *I didn't choose him. I don't WANT him.*

I can feel Salvatore's razor-sharp gaze on me, warning me to play along. I walk slowly toward him, feeling like I'm being led to the gallows.

"What are you doing here?" I whisper when I'm three feet away.

"It's a beautiful day. I've come to take my bride for a drive."

The sun is shining on his handsome face. When he smiles, you could almost believe he's human. I was wary of Cassius and Lorenzo from the moment I saw them, but I was drawn to Salvatore immediately. That kiss he bestowed on my mouth was better than anything I'd felt before. People say that a first kiss is often a let-down, but mine was a little piece of heaven in the arms of a devil.

I remember Lorenzo showing me my wet G-string, humiliating evidence that at least one of those men turned me on. Until he wrapped his hands around my throat and snarled in my ear, I would have been happy to accept that I was attracted to Salvatore.

But not now. Never again. It was some weird fluke that I was turned on.

"Sorry, I have homework."

"My bride doesn't need good grades. I'll take care of anything she needs." He gestures at the open-top sports car, inviting me to get in.

"I'm your bride in forty-eight weeks and not a moment before." Not even then, if I can help it.

I know how to distract him. I glance around the parking lot. "Where are your friends lately?"

Salvatore's face hardens. One moment charming and mellow, the next brimming with malice.

I remember Cassius' words that night. *By your eighteenth birthday, you better have learned what it means to take your place by our sides. Whichever one of us marries you, we all expect the same obedience.*

So much for *us* and *our*.

I lift my chin to project courage that I don't feel. "You seemed like a close-knit group. Did it make the others angry when you won?"

Salvatore's blue-green eyes flicker and the muscles of his jaw tighten. Like what I just said *hurts*.

Can monsters feel pain?

I can guess what happened. Dad wants their help to win the next election, but he also doesn't like four against one, and so he figured out a way to separate one of these powerful men from the others.

With me.

I suppose he used a delicate combination of enticements and

veiled threats on Salvatore. *Marry my daughter, and I'll give you everything the others could never hope to give you. Remember what happened here tonight. I can make things go away—but only for my friends.*

"I hope I'm worth losing all of them," I say with a shrug. The cluster of girls at the gate has drawn the attention of the faculty. Over Salvatore's shoulder, I see the headmistress marching toward us, her focus on Salvatore, equal parts alarm and determination on her face. "The headmistress is coming. You should go."

"Oh, no. Not the headmistress."

Salvatore slides his hands around my waist and dips his head toward mine. It's like someone's thrown a heavy cloak over us as suddenly it's just him and me, his large, scorching hands holding me against him.

Salvatore's mouth descends on mine in a demanding, searing kiss. He captures my lower lip, testing how it yields to his teeth, and then kisses me again. He presses his lips against mine so many times that I feel drunk.

His voice is as dark as midnight when he speaks. "I assure you, you're worth it, Chiara."

The darkness around us lifts, and I'm back at the school gates, breathing hard while Salvatore smirks down at me, my lips tingling.

"Bye, baby," he murmurs, giving my waist a final squeeze and getting into his sports car. He guns the engine, still looking at me, and then roars away in a shower of gravel and dust.

Ms. Brambilla reaches me just as Salvatore turns a corner, her expression outraged. "What is that criminal doing at our school?"

I stare at my feet, my face burning with shame.

"Chiara, I'll speak to your father to let him know that man has been harassing you. It's inconceivable that Salvatore Fiore thinks he can come to this school and molest the mayor's daughter."

I would have preferred that she accuse me of fraternizing with him on school grounds. Hearing her defend me makes me feel even worse.

"Please don't, Ms. Brambilla. He's my—we're, um…" I whisper hoarsely. *Fiancé*. Say fiancé. She's going to find out anyway. Everyone at school will, and the last place that was safe from my terrible future will be tainted.

She rounds on me. "Pardon, Chiara?"

"Nothing. I'm sorry, goodbye."

As I walk home, I feel wetness sliding between my thighs with every step. One kiss and he can do this to me. *One kiss.*

I push the front door open and trudge miserably upstairs. I can still feel Salvatore's body against mine. He's all over me, and so I rip off my clothes and head for the shower. As I catch sight of my damp underwear, I reason that at least I have an answer to Lorenzo's cruel taunt. It was Salvatore who got me in this state on my birthday.

Salvatore, and no one else.

As I walk through the school gates the next morning, no one pays me any attention. My heart lifts. Maybe no one noticed what happened outside the school gates, or they don't care.

I'm riding high on denial when I walk up to Nicole at our lockers and say, "Hey, how did you do on that English essay? I had to rewrite my conclusion four times."

The second her eyes meet mine, I know I've been fooling myself. Surprise flickers over Nicole's face.

Surprise, and fear.

She backs away from me, hands raised, as if I've suddenly pulled a knife on her. As if I'm the dangerous one, not Salvatore.

"Nicole?"

"I'm sorry. Mom and Dad say we're not allowed to be friends anymore."

Nicole's eyes are huge. My best friend of thirteen years is terrified. Even though I already know the answer, I can't help but blurt, "But why?"

She closes her locker and holds her books tight against her chest. "They said if your dad wants you to marry Salvatore Fiore, then it means he's gone bad."

Gone bad. Corrupt.

Plenty of people look up to Salvatore in Coldlake, but plenty of people fear him, too. I take a step toward my friend but she shrinks away as if I've turned into Salvatore himself.

"I don't want to marry him. I'm not *going* to marry him. This isn't my choice and I'm going to find a way out of this. I don't have a plan yet, but maybe you can help me?"

Nicole's expression softens. We always used to help each other out of messes when we were kids. She accidentally let her little brother overhear her saying that Santa wasn't real one Christmas, and I helped her fake a visit from Santa and his reindeer with gnawed carrots and glitter in the driveway. It wasn't sophisticated but it kept the magic alive for the three-year-old boy a little longer.

Helping me call off a wedding to one of the most notorious men in Coldlake is hardly in the same league, but she doesn't need to come up with a perfect solution. I'll settle for her moral support.

Nicole bites her lip, and shakes her head. "Mom and Dad said that if I stay friends with you, I won't be allowed to go to school here anymore. I'm sorry, Chiara." Tears fill her eyes and she turns away, head down, walking fast.

My last true friend in this world.

I look around at the girls who are staring at me, most of whom were standing at the school gate yesterday watching me and Salvatore. Some look scared. Some shocked. Some give me sharp, knowing smiles, and I realize that they must belong to families who are on the side of men like my promised husband. They're the last girls I want as my friends. No one decent will ever want to be my friend again.

I grab my books out of my locker and push past everyone, keeping my head down so my hair hides my face. Until a few weeks ago, I would have said that Coldlake was full of love and respect toward me. Everywhere I went, someone had a smile for me and knew my name. It's taken one vile man's reputation to make me see that I took that respect completely for granted.

The rest of the school day crawls by, with everyone whispering behind their hands as I pass them in the halls. Even the teachers give me fearful looks.

Salvatore Fiore and the mayor's daughter. It's as incongruous as Minnie Mouse marrying Darth Vader.

As soon as the final bell rings, I grab my bag and run for the school gate. There's no sign of Salvatore, but I didn't expect there to be. He already staked his claim and made me notorious in my own school. Job done.

As I walk quickly down the street, I keep my head down so no one can see the tears leaking from my eyes. I wanted one place where I could feel normal, and he's stolen even that from me.

At home I go upstairs and straight to my room, trying to lose myself in my homework. I've got so much to catch up on but it takes all my energy just to concentrate on the words in my biology textbook. Ten minutes later, I realize that I've read the same paragraph over and over without absorbing any of it, and I put down my pen.

An insidious voice at the back of my mind whispers that it doesn't matter if I understand biology or not. The course of my life is already fated. Marriage to Salvatore, and then a lifetime by his side and bearing his children. My mind drifts as I gaze out the window onto the garden. My new home will be just as grand, if not more so, than the one I'm living in right now. I picture myself with a toddler in a pretty dress and another baby in my arms, and my heart twists with longing. I've always wanted children, and for a moment I picture them with Salvatore's blue-green eyes. Any man, even as hard-hearted as Salvatore is, would love such beautiful children, and he'd protect us ruthlessly. Wouldn't he?

A moment later, I come crashing back to earth. They won't be children to him. They'll be pawns in his never-ending quest for power, and I'd be brutally discarded the moment I disagreed with him about what he wanted for our children. Loveless marriages.

Lives of crime, like his.

I gaze at the diagram of photosynthesis and the accompanying text. Suddenly it seems much more interesting than my future, and thirty minutes later I've written half of my science report.

I'm finishing off the concluding paragraph when I hear Dad calling me from downstairs. "Chiara. Can you come here, please?"

A glance at my phone, which tells me it's dinnertime. I've been eating in the kitchen with Francesca ever since Mom was killed. I suppose it was only a matter of time before Dad would want to resume proper meals. Everything in this house has to be proper, and so I pull on a knit dress and some sandals before heading downstairs, my stomach in a snarl.

My anxiety doubles as I see who's standing next to Dad.

Salvatore. Again. I thought that after the kiss that spoiled everything for me at school, he would stay out of my life.

He smiles at me, a cold smile with his lips pressed together.

"Chiara," he murmurs in deep, rich notes. I look away as his gaze travels down my body, and I wish I hadn't worn something so clingy.

I follow them both into the dining room and Salvatore is there to push my chair in, his fingers grazing my bare arm. I've got no appetite as Stephan sets consommé before us all and Dad and Salvatore speak about business.

I let my spoon trail through the clear broth, eyes down, hoping that they've both forgotten that I'm there.

"And how are you, Chiara?"

I look up, and see that Salvatore has finished his soup and is gazing at me with a smirk. Dad goes on eating, his interest in the new turn the conversation has taken is nonexistent.

"I was dumped today."

Bloodlust flares suddenly in Salvatore's eyes. "You have a boyfriend? Who is he? *Has he touched you?*"

If I did have a boyfriend then what might have happened between us is none of his business. The truth is, I've never dated or been touched by anyone except Salvatore and his friends.

I wonder if it would bother him to hear what they did to me. Especially Lorenzo. Humiliation courses through me as I remember the way he showed me my wet G-string and then shoved the hilt of his knife between my thighs. Or maybe they bragged to each other what they did to me. So why is it different if another guy puts his hands on me?

Dad glares at me. "She doesn't have a boyfriend. What are you talking about, Chiara?"

"I'm talking about my best friend. Nicole says her parents don't want us to be friends anymore." I flick my gaze at Salvatore. "Because of him."

Dad's face relaxes into a smile as he cuts through his steak. "Oh, I see."

Salvatore picks up his red wine glass and settles back in his seat. "For a moment there, I thought I'd have to go and spill some blood."

"If I had a boyfriend it would be none of your business."

"My fiancée's private life is all my business. Do I have to come to the school every day and kiss you? I thought once would be enough to spread the message around. You belong to me, and no one else is to touch you."

"The headmistress won't allow it."

A grin spreads over Salvatore's handsome face. "Some old woman in a cardigan isn't going to keep me away from my girl. I'm warning you, Chiara. You kiss some boy or let him get his hands on you, I'll make him wish he'd never been born."

I imagine one of the students from the nearby boys' school going up against Salvatore, and shudder. Right now he's relaxed and sharply dressed in a designer suit, not a lock of rich brown hair out of place, but I have no doubt he can go absolutely feral when he wants to.

I turn to Dad, gripping my knife and fork tight in my fists. "Nicole's parents and people like them are the core of your voter base. Isn't this a sign that you should rethink everything? You could lose the mayorship because of Salvatore."

"There'll be some pearl-clutchers, undoubtedly, but I can lose the De Lucas' votes without any problem."

Salvatore takes a sip of wine. "Losing a few weak-minded idiots is nothing to the number of people that I can persuade to support Mayor Romano. Everyone who works for me, everyone who loves and respects my family, lives on the streets I own, and everyone who's terrified of me will do as I say."

Weak-minded idiots. I hate hearing him talk about Nicole's parents that way. Salvatore might be wrong, but what matters is that Dad believes him.

I eat my dinner in silence and tune out whatever Dad and Salvatore are saying to each other. If my match with Salvatore isn't going to damage Dad's political reputation enough for him to call it off, I still have forty-eight weeks to find another solution.

When dinner is over, Dad says my name. "Chiara. See Salvatore to the door."

I look up and realize that the plates have been cleared away. Wordlessly, I get to my feet and walk out of the room.

I can feel Salvatore following me, but I can't bear to even look at him.

At the door, Salvatore takes my waist in his hands. "Hold your head up. You're a Fiore bride, and we bow to no one."

"I'm not bowing to you. I'm sad. I lost my best friend because of you."

"If she cut you out so easily then she was never truly your friend. You'll make new friends."

"People like you, you mean?"

"Exactly. Better friends." Salvatore moves closer to kiss me, but this time I'm ready for him and I turn my face away.

He stays right where he is, his fingers biting into my waist and fury lighting up his eyes. "Turn back to me."

"No."

I brace for him to grab my chin and force my face back to his. It's the only way he'll ever kiss me again.

"That's the last time you refuse me anything," he seethes, letting me go. "Next time, I'll fucking make you." He strides down the hall, opens the front door, and slams it behind him.

When I turn around, Dad's watching me from the door to the living room. I'm not even angry anymore. Despair and disappointment fill me from head to toe as I go upstairs to my bedroom. He knows what I'd say if I thought there was any point at all in trying to shame him.

If Mom saw you now, she wouldn't recognize you.

On Saturday morning, I'm alone in the house watching TV when the front doorbell rings. We're not expecting anyone, and I don't recognize the person standing on the front step.

I open the door to a breathtakingly beautiful young woman. Her hair is thick and a rich brown, and there's something familiar about her bright blue-green eyes. She smiles, and I see she's holding an orchid with delicate white blooms in a pot.

"Hello, you must be Chiara," she says, without an ounce of self-consciousness. "We haven't met. I'm Ginevra Fiore." She wears a white silk shirt and gray slacks and carries a designer handbag with a chunky gold chain. There's gold jewelry around her throat and in her ears, and her nails are long and painted burgundy.

She pauses, as though this name is supposed to answer all the questions that are flying through my head. Finally, one word sticks.

Fiore.

Those eyes. The shape of her mouth. That air of confidence.

Her smile dims. "Oh, please don't be scared. I just came to give you this and introduce myself. I'm Salvatore's sister."

She puts the orchid into my hands and I stare at the incongruous object. Am I supposed to understand something from this present? "Why the plant?"

"I was sorry to hear about your mother's passing."

Oh, yes, Salvatore must have made it sound so *sad*. "Did your brother tell you to come here?"

Her smile comes back, and this time it's mischievous. "He knows better than to tell me to do anything. He asked me if I wanted to meet you, and I said yes, but that I'd come by myself."

Someone talking back to Salvatore. It sounds incongruous to me, and suddenly I'm curious about her.

"I suppose you can come in." I stand back and gesture inside. I sound ungracious, but Ginevra doesn't seem offended. As she steps over the threshold, she gazes around the entrance hall.

"You have a beautiful home."

"Thanks. Mom did all the decorating." It's a shame that it was with Dad's dirty money. Did she know that he was involved with criminals the whole time? The question has been haunting me since my seventeenth birthday. I've been going over and over her behavior that night and how she seemed in the weeks leading up to my birthday. Her sudden nerves and weight loss, like she was worried about something. Mom was always such a happy woman. Never carefree, but content. I feel instinctively that she didn't discover what Dad was really up to until recently, and it horrified her.

"Chiara?"

I realize I'm still standing with my hand on the open door, and close it behind me. As I lead her through to the lounge, I say, "Sorry. There's so much on my mind lately."

Ginevra's lips press together in sympathy as we sit down on the sofas. She places the orchid on the coffee table. "I understand. It's a lot to deal with all at once, a death in the family and a marriage on the horizon. Our family always does everything at breakneck speed." She holds up her hand and shows me a diamond engagement ring flashing on her finger. "I've only been wearing this for two weeks. The wedding is in two months. I'm freaking out." Her smile is nervous but excited.

I stare at the enormous stone on Ginevra's finger, dread solidifying in my belly. On my eighteenth birthday, I'll be presented with a ring like this. I can already feel it weighing down my hand.

"Is your fiancé a criminal as well?" As soon as the words slip out, I bite my lip.

If Ginevra has taken any offence to what I've said, she doesn't show it. After musing for a moment, she smiles and says, "I suppose in the traditional sense of the word, yes. But there's a lot more to a person than whether they break the law or not, don't you think?"

I bite the inside of my cheek. For me, someone taking a lax approach to right and wrong constitutes a huge part of a person's character.

"Such as how a person treats their family," Ginevra continues. "For the Fiores, we put family first. Always. You're going to be family to me soon, and that means Salvatore and I and everyone else will protect you. All the Fiores will fight to keep you safe, no matter who your enemies are."

But what if my enemy *is* a Fiore?

"So, tell me, what do you think of my brother?"

"I don't think you want me to answer that."

"It's early on. You still have a whole year to get to know each other, and marriage is for the rest of your lives. I met my fiancé the night he put this ring on my finger."

I search Ginevra's beautiful face for any of the resentment I feel, but she seems only happy as she gazes at her ring. "Who chose your husband? Your father?"

She shakes her head. "Dad passed away three years ago. Salvatore's in charge now, and he chose Antonio for me. He and Salvatore have been business associates for many years. He's in Italy right now, but I'm excited for him to return so I can get to know him better."

This must be the sort of woman Salvatore and the others anticipated when they came to my birthday party. Someone who's been raised with the expectation that none of her choices will be her own, and that marriage is a transaction, not for love.

"I thought you said Salvatore wouldn't dare tell you to do anything?"

"He wouldn't. He pointed out all the reasons why Antonio would be an excellent husband for me, and I agreed."

That sounds like telling her what to do. All the same, I can't help but like Ginevra. Her eyes sparkle with intelligence and she's confident as well as warm. She seems genuinely interested in getting to know me, but I have to presume that every word I say to her will get back to her brother.

Maybe that could work in my favor?

"You seem like a kind person," I say slowly. "I wish you every happiness with Antonio, but this isn't the life that I want and Salvatore isn't the husband I'd choose."

Ginevra adjusts the diamond ring on her finger, her face serene. "A year is a long time. Salvatore seems cold sometimes, but he's just protecting himself. He's suffered heartbreak in the past."

"Salvatore's been in love?" I blurt out. Nothing about that man says hearts and flowers to me. More like blood and daggers.

For the first time, sadness flickers over her face. "Not that sort of love. We had a sister between us in age. Ophelia. She was murdered eight years ago. You can't imagine the pain it caused him, knowing that he wasn't able to protect her."

A sister. My grief is a knife in my heart and I pity anyone who's ever felt like this, even Salvatore.

Ginevra gets to her feet and touches the white orchid bloom, which is as luminous as the moon and twice as beautiful. "You'll never forget your mother, but the pain will get easier, I promise. I'll see you soon, I hope."

CHAPTER NINE

SALVATORE

"She doesn't like you one little bit. What on earth did you do to her, Salvatore?"

Ginevra cuts a piece of strawberry tart with her pastry fork, puts it into her mouth, and closes her eyes in bliss. My sister always did love cake.

"To Chiara? I didn't do anything." I take a swallow of black coffee and gaze around at the other customers outside the French patisserie. It's been a week since I sent my sister around to see my promised bride, and I've only just found the time to catch up with her about it. "She doesn't need to like me. She just needs to marry me."

"That's going to be difficult. She doesn't trust you, either."

There's no difficulty. In fact, it's very simple. Chiara will do as she's told or end up like her mother.

Ginevra licks her fork and smiles. "You chose such a wonderful man for me. I want my brother to fall in love, too, and for love, there needs to be trust. Why don't you try getting closer to her?"

"Should I play footsies under the table like you and Antonio?" I drawl. My sister and her fiancé had instant chemistry, which was easy because she's beautiful and he's rich. Antonio is a shrewd and ruthless businessman who understands that his life would be forfeited if he hurt my sister. I'm pleased to hear he's fooled her into thinking he's in love with her. Or maybe he is in love. Who fucking knows.

More importantly, who cares. The essential thing is Ginevra has someone strong to protect her if something happens to me.

Ginevra has another mouthful of tart and chews it thoughtfully. "I'm pleased you're getting married, but why Chiara Romano?"

Chiara Romano. Her face flits across my mind and I recall those big, blue eyes that held mine as she talked back to me at the school gate. How they grew dark and lust-filled as I kissed her. Her curvy body in her school uniform, and then again in that clingy knit dress.

I feel a smile tug at the corner of my mouth. "She's cute."

Ginevra's eyebrows shoot up. "I've never heard you say that about any woman before. Is my big brother in love?"

I clear my throat impatiently. Why the fuck did I say she was cute? Ginevra reads something into every little thing I say. "If you think I'm in love with some schoolgirl, you're mistaken. Her father is useful to me."

But my eyes narrow as I remember Chiara saying she was

dumped over dinner. She better have been telling the truth, that it was a girl who had dumped their friendship. No one is going to touch what's mine.

"How are the wedding plans?" I ask.

My change of subject works and Ginevra begins to recite everything that she has done and still needs to do for her 2.5-million-dollar wedding. The cake alone is costing thirty thousand dollars. I pretended to wince when she came to me with all the bills, but anything for my baby sister. My only baby sister, now. We only have each other, and her special day is going to be lavish.

"I'm finalizing the table settings this weekend. Are your friends really not coming to the wedding?"

"Who?" I ask vaguely.

"Vinicius. Cassius. That other one." A cloud passes behind her eyes and her smile dims.

"Lorenzo Scava?"

"Yes, that psycho," she mutters, pushing her tart around her plate.

"You, better than anyone, know why Lorenzo is the way he is."

Ginevra's eyes drop to her plate and she shrugs. "Maybe I do. Maybe I don't. We all went through the same thing and none of us turned out like he did. Something's wrong in his head."

I sit forward and grasp her wrist. "*No*. We didn't all go through what he went through. He had it far fucking worse."

"I'm sorry, you're right. Please let go."

I ease up my grip and sit back, and Ginevra puts her fork down. Our conversation seems to have ruined her appetite.

"Why are you defending him, anyway? I thought you weren't

friends anymore."

Anger burns through me. I forgot. Again. It's going to take a long time getting used to this new normal. "Can we please change the subject?"

"I was surprised when you introduced me to Antonio. All these years, I expected you to want me to marry one of them."

"No!" I sit up so suddenly and shout, that everyone turns around to stare at us. Ginevra stares, too, her mouth open.

"We had a—we were going to... Never fucking mind," I finish with a growl. Ginevra wouldn't understand. No one would understand what the four of us wanted to do. We didn't even know how we were going to make it work. That's why, four years after we came up with the idea, we never acted on it.

We wanted to, though. We really fucking did.

But we never found the right woman, and now it seems like we never will.

I pinch the bridge of my nose. I think I feel a headache coming on. I get to my feet and throw some bills on the table. "Enjoy your cake."

I put my sunglasses on and start to walk away. Then I turn back, bend down and kiss her cheek. "I'm happy you're happy, Gin. That's all that matters to me."

She gazes up at me with big, worried eyes. "And you? What about your happiness?"

I push my sunglasses up my nose and give her a thin smile. "I'll be happy once I have Mayor Romano in the palm of my hand."

As I walk back to my car, my smile vanishes. Why must women always prod and probe and ask so many fucking questions? How do you *feel*? What do you *want*? Why are you so *angry* all the time, Salvatore? I hope Chiara doesn't develop this bad habit. I'll put up with it from my sister, but not from my bride.

Ginevra's words play on my mind all day as I work. *She doesn't like you one little bit.*

Plenty of women in this town would fucking kill to marry me, despite my reputation. Some of them *because* of my reputation. I remember the two dozen girls standing at the school gate gawking at me, ready to get in my car and hand over their panties if I so much as smiled at them.

And there was Chiara in the middle of them all, reproach and mistrust filling those baby blues. If she hadn't been so rude to me the night of her birthday I wouldn't have lost my temper and clamped my hand around her throat. We started so well, too.

That kiss.

That was a really good kiss. I want my wife to want me. When I put my hands on her, she should burn up under my touch.

I pull on a suit jacket and comb my hair. Well, why don't we start again? Another dinner. Another kiss. I'll show her more of the life she can expect as the woman on my arm, and just how fucking nice I can be.

It's nearly seven when I pull up at Mayor Romano's mansion and knock on the front door. Chiara herself opens it.

She's wearing a printed playsuit with a halter neck and her feet are bare. All her blonde hair is piled up on top of her head in a haphazard bun, and tendrils have escaped and are framing her face.

Yeah, she's fucking cute. Cute girls are trouble.

Just the sort of trouble I crave.

As she sees me standing on her front step, her eyes widen. I bare my teeth at her in a smile. "Miss me, baby?"

Her hand slips down the doorframe and she stands back. "Are you here to see my father? I'll go and get him."

"I'm here to see you." I step past her into the hall and gaze around. It really is a lovely house. My own is bigger, but it's missing that woman's touch.

"What? Why?"

Arguing with me already. I crowd her close to the wall and brace my hands on either side of her head. She smells like vanilla, and those big eyes open wide in surprise as she gazes up at me. Such plush lips she's got. I bet she could learn to give a killer blow job.

"Because I haven't got anything better to do, or because I wanted to see you. Pick one and go upstairs and get dressed. I'm taking you to dinner."

"I'm not going anywhere with you."

"My sister will be there and she wants to see you," I lie. "We're eating at one of my casinos."

"I can't go to a casino. I'm seventeen."

I lean closer and stroke a finger under her chin. "It's my casino, baby. Don't you worry your pretty head about that."

"Someone might recognize my face and you'll be reported to the..." she trails off as my smile widens. People can file a thousand reports, charges, and complaints about me, but no one will stop me from doing whatever I like.

She's opening her mouth to protest some more when there's a

deep voice behind us.

"Please go with Salvatore, Chiara, and stop talking back to him. I didn't raise you to be so disobedient."

I glance over my shoulder at Mayor Romano. He seems more annoyed with his daughter than the six-foot-three man who has her backed against the wall.

As it should be.

Chiara flushes and looks away. I lean down close and whisper in her ear, "Do as Daddy says, baby."

The mayor steps forward. "How are you, Salvatore? All well in the city?"

"All's well in my part of the city."

The mayor grins like the Cheshire cat, but as his gaze lands on his daughter again, the smile is wiped from his face. "What are you still doing here? Go upstairs!"

Chiara ducks out from under my arm.

"Take all the time you need, baby," I call after her, watching her walk up the stairs in those tiny shorts. Damn, that's a cute ass she's got.

I go out into the courtyard and drink a Campari with the mayor while Chiara gets ready. Twenty minutes later, I hear the click of high heels coming toward us, and turn around.

Holy fucking hell.

On her birthday, Chiara looked chaste. In her school uniform she's deliciously cute. Now, she's coming toward me in a black satin dress that clings to her breasts and hips and is slit up her thigh, and she has the attitude and lifted chin of a femme fatale. The look is completed with bold red lipstick.

"Holy fuck," I purr, my teeth sinking into my lower lip. "I could eat you up."

I reach for her and splay my hand on her lower back, drawing her closer, vaguely aware that Mayor Romano has left us alone together out by the pool.

Chiara gazes up at me through her lashes. "I don't want to be recognized tonight, so I dressed differently."

"Sure, baby. Whatever you say." Even if she didn't put on this dress for me, I'm the one who gets to look at her all night. I'm the one who gets to touch her, too. I trace the thin strap of her dress with my forefinger, from her shoulder and down over her collarbone.

Chiara breathes in, her eyes landing on my mouth and growing unfocused.

Mayor Romano appears with a necklace laid over his hand. The diamond necklace I gave Chiara for her seventeenth birthday. "This was in the safe. Salvatore would want you to wear it."

"Allow me." I reach for it, but Chiara takes it quickly from her father and moves inside to a mirror.

"It's fine. I'll do it."

I catch Chiara's eyes in the mirror as she closes the clasp at the nape of her neck. She doesn't trust me with my hands anywhere near her throat. I saunter over to her and run a forefinger down the back of her neck.

"If you're a good girl, then there's no reason for me not to be nice."

"I won't risk it, thank you." She shakes out her hair and looks at herself in the mirror. Then at me.

"We look good together. Come on," I say, reaching for her hand

and drawing her toward the front door.

"Bring my daughter back by eleven, Fiore. It's a school night. And keep your hands to yourself."

"Of course, Mayor. Good night."

A car is waiting by the curb; not my car, but a black Bentley with a driver, and I get into the back seat with Chiara. She adjusts the straps of her satin dress and straightens her skirt, and I gaze at her, drinking her in.

All mine tonight.

Already she's surprised me with how strong she's been since her mother's murder right in front of her eyes. Let's find out what this girl is made of.

As the car pulls away from the curb, I slide closer and palm her waist. "You look beautiful. Good enough to eat."

Her eyes flick up to mine. "I'm not on the menu."

Always reaching for defiance first. Silly girl should know better by now and try to charm me. Or just give in. I trail my forefinger up the middle of her chest, across the diamonds at her throat, and down her arm. "Did you like Ginevra's diamond ring? I'll be getting you one just like it."

"No, thank you," she says, her voice breathy. As my fingers slide up her leg beneath her skirt, she grabs my hand. "Stop that. You heard what my father said."

"Diamonds look good on you, baby." I nip her throat with my teeth. "I'll get you something big and sparkly to wear on your finger when we're engaged, so that everyone knows your mine."

Chiara's breath hitches and her eyes flutter closed. I inhale sharply through my nostrils at the sight. Fuck, she's so turned on already. Lorenzo said her panties were soaking when he cut them off her.

"I don't know if I can wait a whole year to get my hands on you. You won't tell Daddy if I make you come, will you?" I slide my hand from the outside of her thigh to the inside.

Chiara's eyes fly open. She puts both palms against my chest and shoves. "Don't even think about it. Keep your hands to yourself."

I laugh and let her push me back on the leather seat. "It's you who's going to be squirming until you get home."

Her cheeks are stained red and her lips are parted. "I'm not squirming."

"Do you use your fingers to make yourself come, or have you got a vibe?"

"Is that all you can think about?"

"There are a hundred things on my mind, most of them unpleasant. Some of them downright vicious. When I'm with you, I want to forget about every single one."

Her lower lip softens as I move closer to claim her mouth. From our first kiss, I could taste something special about this girl. She'll be downright dirty in bed by the time I get her into mine.

"Tell—tell me about the casino you're taking me to."

I pause, my mouth an inch from hers. "You really want to know about my work, or are you trying to distract me from kissing you?"

Chiara sucks the pillow of her lower lip into her mouth, nibbles it briefly and then releases it. She doesn't mean it as a come-on. She's gathering her thoughts, but my balls tighten and I groan deep in my chest. She shouldn't do that when I'm this close to her, she's wearing that ridiculously hot dress and her curls are tumbling around her shoulders.

"Yes."

"Then look out there." She turns toward the window and I slide my arm around her waist and put my lips close to her ear. "Do you remember which buildings are mine?"

The city lights paint colors on her beautiful face. All the casinos in Coldlake line the north end of the main strip, which is lit up white, yellow, pink, and blue with flashing lights, neon playing cards, and jets of water from ornate fountains.

"That one," she says, pointing at a silver-and-white skyscraper as we glide by, and then turns to look back the way we came at another. "That one."

The Bentley turns into the Grand Plaza Hotel and sweeps around the circular drive to pull up at the main entrance. The tiles are white marble, and the front entrance is shining glass and gold. All the bellhops wear the same cream-and-gold livery, and inside, a huge crystal chandelier hangs over the lobby.

"And this one," Chiara finishes, gazing inside.

"Very good."

We get out of the Bentley and I hold out my hand. Chiara takes it without thinking as she stares around at all the people in evening dresses and the flashing lights and colors. As we stroll through the lobby, I watch people watching us. Most people around here know who I am, and I can tell they're wondering who this beautiful and vaguely familiar blonde is on my arm. They've seen Chiara at events and on TV, but always looking so demure. They don't recognize this bombshell.

I take Chiara upstairs to the member-only casino where the restaurant overlooks the casino floor.

"We'll have a bottle of Dom Perignon," I tell the waiter as we sit down. The table overlooks the private blackjack and craps tables, where men in tuxedos and women in long dresses and dripping with jewels are busy handing over their money to me.

I reach for her hand again. "See how nice I am when you're good?"

Chiara seems to realize she's letting me touch her and pulls away. "I'm not *being good*. I'm trying to prevent my throat from being slit like my mother's was."

"And I thought my charm was starting to work on you. What are you hungry for?" I ask, flipping the menu open. "Lobster? Salmon? Caviar?"

She eyes the menu in bewilderment. "I don't know. We never eat at places like these. Dad wants us to be seen at local businesses because it's good for votes."

When the waiter comes back and pours the champagne, I order for us. I push the champagne glass closer to her, smiling. "You're with me. It's all right."

Chiara gazes at me, around the restaurant, down at herself, then to my surprise, she reaches for the flute and takes a sip.

My smile widens. So much for the rules when she's tempted by something she wants. "Does my bride have champagne tastes?"

Chiara swallows, hesitates, and takes another sip. "It's strange, but I don't hate it."

"Like me?" I ask, smiling at her.

She pretends I didn't say that. "This place seems legitimate. Everyone in this city knows you run casinos. So…"

"So?"

"So, what's the trick? You make most of your money illegally, don't you?"

"The trick is…" I lower my voice and lean toward Chiara. She's so curious that she leans toward me, too. "The trick is I don't tell anyone how I make my money, and I admit to nothing."

Chiara sits back and takes another sip of her champagne, watching me with narrowed eyes. Suspicious little cat.

One of the senior casino managers comes to the table and asks to speak to me, and I can tell from his face that it's not something for Chiara's ears.

We draw away from the table, and he tells me, "We've discovered a pair of card counters in the main casino. They're from out of town."

My jaw tightens. Card counting isn't illegal, but it's against the unwritten laws of every casino that belongs to me. Counters keep track of the cards that have been dealt in blackjack and bet high when they know a deck is stacked in their favor. Some counters work in pairs or groups to disguise what they're up to. One person counts, and then another joins a game and receives a signal if they should bet high.

Out of the corner of my eye I see Chiara wave to a waiter and place an order.

If these assholes were from Coldlake, I'd kill them for their sheer fucking stupidity. Out-of-towners can take a message back to where they came from.

No one steals from me and gets away with it.

"Give them their winnings. Then escort them out back and break their legs."

"Yes, sir." He nods and slips away to do what he's told. Or rather, he'll find two of the biggest security guards in the place to do it for him.

I walk to the mezzanine rail and gaze around at the players below. The people who come to my casino are welcome to try their luck, but in the end, the house always wins.

When I turn back to Chiara, I see that she's upending a shot glass into her mouth, and she swallows and makes a disgusted face. A second empty shot glass is at her elbow.

I stride over, snatch the glass from her hand and sniff it. "Tequila?"

Chiara sticks out her tongue and gags. "It's *horrible*. I want another one."

I was gone for two fucking minutes and she's doing shots? She raises her hand to signal for the waiter but I push it down.

"You've had enough. Drink some water." I take away her champagne flute and set her water glass in front of her.

"But I want tequila."

"Why do you want tequila?"

She shrugs. "I don't know. The champagne was making my insides feel warm and bubbly and suddenly I wasn't thinking so much about...about everything."

I study her face carefully as I sit down. Her cheeks are thinner than they were on her seventeenth birthday and there are dark smudges beneath her eyes.

I pick up my champagne and take a large gulp. "What have you got to worry about?"

"Everything."

"Don't be. I worry about things so you don't have to."

"But it's you who worries me."

As I gaze at her, I see Ophelia in the curve of her cheek. The long line of her throat. Ophelia loved to talk back to me and tease me. She's the only one who ever dared.

A soft, feminine voice whispers in my ear. *Hasn't she suffered enough?*

Chiara leans her chin on her hand and gazes at me, her big blue eyes slightly unfocused. "You're really cute, you know that?"

"Yes."

She rolls her eyes. "Of course you do. All your money and looks, and you have to be a criminal. Why?"

Chiara's other hand is on the table and I reach out and take it. She must be really drunk because she lets me. I hold her slender wrist in my hand and gaze at the delicate traceries of her veins. "Because people are envious and bloodthirsty and they will always try and take what you have."

"So you take first?"

Always. If my enemy hasn't protected what's theirs, then they don't deserve what they possess.

"You're wicked, you know that?"

"And you're beautiful. For a spoiled princess."

"Maybe in your world I'm spoiled because I was loved and free and told I could be anything I wanted to be. In my world I'm lucky. I *was* lucky." Her face falls and I watch despair wash over her. "I promised myself I wouldn't cry. I just wanted to forget for a while, but I can't forget her. She loved me. I was *loved*. You probably don't know what that feels like."

Chiara breathes in sharply, and I realize my hand has tightened viciously on her wrist. "Don't make assumptions about me if you like your blood inside your veins."

"Ow. Okay, okay." She stares at her wrist in my grip. Clearly her inhibitions have been lowered because a moment later she asks, "Do you mean your sister loved you? The one who died?"

I'm so shocked that I loosen my grip. For fuck's sake. I sent Ginevra around to Chiara to soften her up for me, not spill our family secrets.

"There's no shhhame in it," Chiara says, slurring slightly. "Maybe I'd like you better iffyou acted human sometimes."

"How am I meant to take you home in this state?"

"Inwhatssstate? I'mfine."

I should get her into my car and make her drink Cokes until she sobers up. I pull her to her feet and walk her across the floor, but her knees keep buckling beneath her, so I scoop her up in my arms and carry her through the casino to the elevator.

"Hey! Put me down. I'm *fine*."

Heads turn to stare at the woman who's yelling at the top of her lungs.

"The mayor's daughter is drawing so much attention to herself in my casino. I hope this doesn't get back to her father."

Chiara claps a hand over her lips, her eyes widening. She whispers around her fingers, "Dad will be angry if he finds out that I'm drunk in a casino."

"We won't tell him, baby."

"But he'll find out. I don't know who he is anymore. Since Mom—" She breaks off, her eyes filling with panic and tears. "I'm going to die, aren't I?"

"Shh," I say, my lips against her temple. "That's the tequila talking."

"Liar," she whispers, her eyes glistening. "Women who don't do as they're told by men like you end up dead."

I get her out to the Bentley and pour her into the back seat. Well, this is a fucking train wreck. I should have kept a closer eye on her.

"Take us to the Maxim," I tell the driver. It takes Chiara a moment to raise her head and realize what I've said. Tears have spilled down her face and there are black mascara tracks on her cheeks.

"The Maxim Hotel? You're not taking me home? Don't try any funny business, mister." She wags an admonishing finger in my face.

Drunk Chiara seems like she'll start a fight with her father or fall apart if I deposit her back at home in this state. This is my fault, so she's mine until she sobers up.

Fifteen minutes later we pull up at the Maxim Grand Hotel at the other end of town. Out front is an enormous white marble fountain. Every fifteen minutes, water shoots out of hundreds of jets, lit up by colored lights.

The perfect drunk-girl distraction.

I help Chiara out of the car and perch her on the edge of the fountain. I stand back and watch her dangling her fingers in the water, gazing at the colors as the lights change. There's something strange about this tableau that I can't put my finger on.

Then I realize what it is.

Chiara's smiling.

I don't think I've seen her smile before.

A moment later, water shoots into the air behind her in a great rush, lit up in yellow, turquoise, and pink. There's a gasp from the crowd, and Chiara lifts her head and laughs. The spray makes rainbows in the air around her and her bare skin is burnished in jewel tones.

A moment later, her gaze shifts to my face, and I feel a lurch as the full force of her smile slams into my chest. I wait for her smile to dim as she remembers who I am, but she merely raises her eyes to the water jets above her head as if inviting me to share in her delight.

Suddenly, I remember why I brought her here, and I can't fucking breathe. Ophelia. The last time I saw her was sitting right where Chiara is now.

Saw her *alive*.

I saw her plenty after she was dead.

My fists clench at my sides. Chiara's smiling and watching the fountain jets, pushing damp strands of her hair back from her face. The image glitches in my mind and becomes blood red. I try to hold back the graphic images from pouring into my brain but it's like trying to hold back a tsunami with a chain-link fence.

The corners of her mouth slit with razor blades in a grotesque smile. Dead, staring eyes. Her nipples slashed. Her stomach cut open and her intestines dragged out in fat, shiny ribbons. The black and bloodied petals of a flower, just glimpsed among the broken teeth in her mouth.

Chiara goes on smiling and reaches out to run her fingers through a jet of water. There were black mascara tracks on Ophelia's cheeks too, as she grinned the permanent grin that had been cut into her face.

I hear footsteps behind me. Several sets of feet, and deep voices. The voices fall silent and the feet slow to a stop.

Chiara looks past me, and the smile dies on her face.

"You've been making her cry, Salvatore." A deep, sly, familiar voice. Vinicius.

I turn and see all three of them. My former friends all dressed in suits. I presume that they've just come out of the Maxim, which has one of the few casinos in the city that I don't own. Vinicius will have been needing his fix.

"Tequila has been making her cry. I've been kissing it better."

Chiara grasps the edge of the fountain. Her feet gather beneath her and her shoulders clench. Her breathing comes faster as she looks at Vinicius, Cassius, and Lorenzo.

Don't be afraid, baby. I won't let them anywhere near you.

"*Bambina*," rumbles a deep voice. Cassius is circling around me and watching Chiara like a hawk. He holds out his hand to her. "There's been a mistake. Come here and we can talk about it."

She stares at his hand like it's a snake that's going to bite her.

I step closer to my promised bride. "Don't even think about it."

But Cassius wants to do nothing but think about it. "If he ever scares you or does anything you don't like, I'm here. I'm nothing like him." He jerks his chin at me.

Chiara's gaze flickers among the three men and comes to rest on Lorenzo, the only one who hasn't spoken. He's staring at her with naked hunger in his eyes. It's that dress she's wearing. That clingy, black satin dress that hugs her hips and her tits like we only dream of doing. Our sweet virgin, looking like sex.

My sweet virgin.

"Back off," I say to my former friends. "I won't tell you again."

I loop an arm around Chiara's waist and haul her to her feet. We're walking toward my car when Lorenzo steps in front of us.

"Has he fucked you yet?"

Chiara stares at him in revulsion. "I'm *seventeen*, asshole."

Lorenzo's eyes open mockingly wide. "Oh, Salvatore wouldn't want to break the law, would he?"

Vinicius strolls closer to the fountain as if he's suddenly interested in the water, but his manner is too casual. I feel Cassius pressing in our other side. Three wolves, circling closer.

I try to guide Chiara to my car, but she pulls out of my grasp and rounds on them, brimming with drunk-girl anger. "Why do you guys even care about that?"

Vinicius smiles a pointed smile. "Isn't it obvious? We want it for ourselves."

"It? My virginity? Don't be disgusting. It's not some trophy you can hang on the wall! It's my body and…" she trails off, her inebriated mind stumbling onto another possibility. "Actually, yes, Salvatore has screwed me a dozen times. You can all just go home."

"Beautiful girls shouldn't tell ugly lies," Cassius says. He's close enough to reach out and touch her. I can see his hand lifting toward her cheek.

I pull Chiara closer and wrap an arm around her waist, giving the others a look of gloating.

She's mine.

So back off.

"Chiara couldn't wait to dress up for me tonight, could you, baby? Doesn't she look delicious? Excuse me, I have to take my bride home."

Cassius' jaw is tight with fury. Even Vinicius has dropped his perennial smirk as he watches me walk Chiara away from them.

Lorenzo's eyes are narrowed and his head turns slowly as he watches our progress. "Better keep a close eye on her, Fiore. You don't want anything to happen to her between now and your wedding."

"Go fuck yourself, Lorenzo. If you lay a finger on her I'll cut off your hands."

I help Chiara into the car, and slam the door closed behind us. As the driver pulls away, Chiara sits rigid on the seat beside me, staring straight ahead. She seems like she's sobered up at last.

"You all right, baby? There's no need to be afraid. I would never let them touch you."

Tears fill her eyes and fall down her face. Tequila tears?

"Seeing them all again reminds me of that night. The moment when—"

No, tears of grief and pain as she remembers her mother's throat being slit right in front of her. I watch her with teeth gritted, torn between pulling her into my arms and telling her to toughen the fuck up.

In this life we all see things we wish we hadn't.

I take her inside her house, meaning to see that she gets safely up the stairs and then leave. Chiara turns to me in the hall and stares at me, her eyes huge in the darkness.

"Your three friends. Ex-friends. Do you think they meant what they said?"

"I'll kill them if they lay one finger on you, that's a fucking promise."

Chiara steps closer. "You would kill for me?"

I stare at her, wondering at her sudden change in mood. Mentions of death and violence have always had her shrinking away from me. "Is that what you want, baby? I thought you'd want me to be sweet with you. Treat you gently and make you feel like a princess."

She shakes her head. "I've been treated like a princess all my life, and look where it's gotten me. I want to know if you'll kill someone if I ask you."

Hatred and determination are burning in her eyes.

"Who do you want me to kill, baby?"

Chiara places her hands against my chest. Her beautiful face is raised to mine like she's begging for a kiss, and the whisper falls from her lips like a word of love.

"Dad."

CHAPTER TEN

CHIARA

Dad. He's the one who deserves to die.

I see him again, stepping out of the house clutching Lorenzo's knife in his grip and approaching Mom as she stood by the side of the pool and wept.

She never even saw him coming.

With four ruthless men in the house, Dad was the one to kill her.

I step closer to Salvatore, and automatically, my hands smooth up his chest to wrap around his neck. It's dangerous to ask a man like Salvatore for anything, but he's promised to protect me like a husband, and this is what I want from him.

It's the *only* thing I want.

"Please kill Dad for me," I whisper. "I have no way to pay you other than with what Dad's already offered you, but if you do this for me then I…" I falter over promising him the one thing that I can offer that he cares about. "I…"

I can do this. For Mom's sake. I swallow hard.

"I'll marry you without…resisting. I'll do what you want."

Salvatore's eyes narrow. "You're going to do that anyway. Don't bargain with what's already mine."

He doesn't understand. I'm not just talking about what happens between us on paper.

I step a little closer until I'm pressed tight against his chest, and my heart starts to pound. I'm just acting, trying to convince him to do what I desperately need him to do, but the line between pretense and reality is razor thin.

"But the *way* I'll be yours, doesn't that matter to you? Wouldn't you rather have me willingly when the time comes? Wouldn't you rather I—"

Wanted you.

Desired you.

"Wouldn't you rather I was grateful to you?"

I'm promising him more than my virginity if he kills my father. I'll make it good for him. I'll make him believe I'm enthusiastic about letting him take me to bed. It shouldn't be too difficult. Salvatore is one of the most handsome men I've ever met. Even now, standing in his arms with murder on my mind, my heart is pounding against his chest.

Salvatore laughs softly. "Baby, you think you won't want me on our wedding night? You think you'll have to fake anything?" He ducks his head and puts his lips against my ear. "I could make you come right here with a few words and one finger, and there's nothing you could do to stop me. Pin you with one arm against my body and drive my hand down into your panties. Rub your clit fast while I whisper what a horny girl you are for your husband-to-be."

Heat ripples up my body and my eyes nearly flutter closed. I've never not reacted to Salvatore when he's touched me. Just his lips against my ear are enough to make my knees weak.

"Please," I whisper, and then realize it sounds like I'm begging him to do just that. "Please do this one thing for me. I'll never ask you for anything again."

He's killed people before, I'm sure. What's one more?

A sepulchral voice speaks from the shadows. "My own daughter."

I turn and see Dad walking slowly down the hall toward us. My arms drop from Salvatore's neck as pure hatred fills my heart.

"My own daughter would betray me like this. There's a special place in hell for children who try to destroy their parents."

"What about husbands who kill their wives?" I seethe.

Dad gives a humorless laugh. "I doubt it. Wife-killing is so common it's barely even a crime anymore. I'm sure you'll find out the same thing in time if you don't learn your place."

Dead in the pool like Mom.

Dad glances at Salvatore and back at me. "You little slut, trying to use your body to bargain for vengeance."

My chest feels so tight it's hard to breathe. Dad heard everything Salvatore and I were saying to each other. I want to crumple up and die. "If I had a gun or knew how to do it, I'd—"

Salvatore grabs a fistful of my hair and yanks my face until it's upturned toward his. "*Don't.*"

His eyes are boring into mine, but he doesn't look angry. He looks alarmed.

I grab his wrist and claw him with my nails, yelling at him to let me go. I wrest my hair from his grip.

"*My mother!*" I scream at Dad, chest heaving. "You killed my mother. You should be rotting in jail for what you've done."

I've lost all self-control. The world has turned red and I want nothing more than to watch Dad bleed. To make him die, or at the very least make him hurt as much as I'm hurting.

I hurl myself at Dad, screaming, and he lifts his hand and strikes me across the face. I go flying off to one side, my vision black and my eyes stinging. I find myself on my knees, my palms pressed against the tiles.

"Get out of here, Salvatore. I need to discipline my daughter."

"No." Salvatore steps in front of Dad, and for a moment I think it's to protect me. "She's going to be my wife. *I'll* discipline her."

Salvatore grasps my upper arm and yanks me to my feet. He marches me over to the living room and slams the door behind us.

"Get your hands off me," I pant, struggling in his grip. He grasps my other arm and shoves me against the wall, and pushes his furious face into mine.

"What the fuck do you think you're playing at?" he seethes.

"Let me *go.*"

Salvatore slams his palm against the wall, right by my head, and roars in my face, "The next thing I hit will be you if you don't *shut the fuck up*."

I flinch and stop struggling.

"You're threatening the man who can end your life and wash his hands of guilt like *that*. Did you learn nothing the night of your seventeenth birthday?"

"I hate him," I sob. "I hate him so much. He got away with murder. You don't know what it's like, seeing him walking around this town after what he did to Mom."

"Sure, I don't know what that's like," he growls.

Oh, yes. His murdered sister and the crime still unsolved. He doesn't know who killed her but it must still hurt. His heart must ache for her, day and night.

"If you're going to be my husband, shouldn't you be protecting me from him?"

"I don't have to do anything, you little idiot. Do you think I owe you any favors? Do you think I've got nothing better to do than fret about one unpunished murder? Your mother should have known better."

"Why? Why should she have known better? She was the mayor's wife, not a mafia wife."

"Don't kid yourself. Your father may not have been a criminal when she married him, but I doubt she was so stupid that she didn't guess that all the pretty things in her life cost more than his salary."

"Then should I have seen it? I never realized there was anything dangerous about my father until that night."

"I don't know. Should you?" Salvatore gives me a challenging look, and then steps back and rakes a hand through his hair. "It's pointless beating yourself up about what you did and didn't realize. Your mom did her best to protect you from what she knew. That was a fucking stupid thing to do."

His words are a punch in the gut. My mother was stupid for loving me like she did? "You know what? I hate you almost as much as Dad."

"No kidding." For a moment his eyes are bleak. Despite his cruel words, some part of him feels sorry for me. It must be a very small part, though, as a moment later, his expression hardens. "This is your life, Chiara. You want something changed, you fix it yourself." He grabs me by the shoulders and shakes me. "Grow the fuck up. Harden up. Do what needs to be done and don't fucking cry about it."

My head pounds as he shakes me and I try and fight him off. "You're an asshole."

"Yeah, I am, but your destiny is to be surrounded by men like me, so learn from this moment. You'll thank me later if I'm not there to protect you."

I suck in a startled breath. What does that mean? Salvatore's going to abandon me? Or he could be killed. He's got enough enemies.

I get a sudden, vivid picture of someone slitting his throat in front of me like Dad slit Mom's. It could happen. It could even be *likely*. I wrap my arms around my stomach and moan. I can't do this. I'm not strong enough.

Salvatore grasps my chin and makes me look at him, but not in an unkind way. "Listen to me, Chiara. You're tougher than you think you are." With his other arm, he gathers me closer to him. He even smiles a little. "Did you know, I expected you to scream or faint the moment I kissed you on your birthday."

Not kiss him back. Not stare him down when he pulled away to show him I couldn't be intimidated even though my stomach was churning.

His mouth slants over mine, and I taste salt on his lips. Salt from my tears. His rich, masculine scent washes over me, and I find myself breathing harder as his tongue moves against mine. His hand slides up into my hair and cradles my head as he kisses me.

"You like my kisses, Chiara?" he murmurs, his lips brushing over mine. "Maybe I'm an asshole, but I want you to live. So fucking kiss me so I know you're still breathing."

I do as he demands, opening my lips and pressing them over his.

I'm so crazy for wanting him.

Or I'm just crazy with wanting him.

We're both breathing hard when he breaks away. "Now go out there and apologize to your father, and make it good or I really will punish you."

I take a step toward the door and then turn back. "After we're married, will you kill him for me?"

Salvatore puts his hand in his pockets and leans against the wall, smiling broadly. The devil's own smile, bright and dazzling. "I can promise you this, Chiara. Anyone hurts my woman, I'll make them bleed."

Which doesn't mean yes.

I shouldn't feel disappointed when I know Salvatore is only marrying me because I'm the mayor's daughter. The mayor's *virgin* daughter. "And if I'm not a virgin anymore by the time our wedding comes around? Will you still marry me then?"

The smile drops from his face and his eyes turn black. "What are you talking about?"

They all seem so obsessed with my virginity. It makes me wish I'd lost it years ago.

"Let's get one thing straight. This," he says, grasping my throat with one hand and pushing the satin of my dress between my legs and cupping my pussy with the other, "is mine, and don't you fucking forget it. Now, do as you're told."

He releases me with a push and I go out into the hall where my father is waiting. He has a nasty, expectant expression and I want nothing more than to scream and try to hit him again.

"I'm sorry I asked Salvatore to harm you," I say, forcing the hateful words over my lips. Dad doesn't react. He just goes on staring at me.

I glance at Salvatore and he makes a *go on* gesture.

My mouth fills with an acrid taste. "I respect your authority in this house. I'll be an obedient daughter from now on."

Dad glances at Salvatore and drawls, "Nice work, Fiore. You pulled my daughter right back into line."

"It's what I do," Salvatore replies, and his smirk prickles up my spine. They're talking about me like I'm a naughty child.

Anger surges through me so strong that I can feel my ankles trembling in my high heels. Before I can fall apart in front of these two hateful men, I turn and walk up the stairs and into the solitude of my bedroom.

I grab a pillow off my bed and scream into it until I can't breathe. I want him dead. I want him *dead*. It's obscene that he gets to walk around smiling and living while Mom lays butchered in a cold grave. No one cares that her killer roams free. Not the police, not the people of Coldlake who professed to love their mayoress so much, and not Salvatore Fiore, who gets exactly what he wants now that Mom's not standing in his way.

Salvatore's not going to get what he wants if I have anything to say about it, and neither is Dad.

I take off my makeup with a cotton pad and give my teeth a swift brush before crawling into bed and hauling the covers up over my head. I want to give in to a long bout of angry sobbing. I can feel the tears crowding at the back of my throat, ready to burst forth in a great storm of pain. For Mom. For myself.

But tears don't solve anything. I can't expect anyone to fix my life for me. I swallow them down, and use their pain to hone my focus.

I can't reason with people who are power-hungry and ruthless, and I can't offer something that they could easily take for themselves. Salvatore has power, and knows how to leverage it. I just have to discover my own power, and then use it to get what I want.

One month later

"So I told Mr. Spears, if he doesn't let me do extra *extra* credit, then my father will come down to this school. That changed his mind."

With a glossy acrylic nail, Rosaline cracks open a can of diet soda and takes a sip.

The other two girls nod approvingly and tell Rosaline that she's absolutely right to fight for her grades when it's her future on the line.

As I take a bite out of my tuna sandwich, I notice someone staring at me from across the cafeteria.

Nicole. Her expression is a mix of longing and apprehension. We haven't talked since she dumped me as a friend. She glances at the girls I'm sitting with, and her lips press together with disapproval.

I chew with difficulty and swallow the bite of sandwich. I didn't set out to make new friends. Rosaline, Sophia, and Candace gravitated toward me. Welcomed me. Took away my crushing loneliness. I always thought of them as smart girls, but too edgy for me. They talk back to teachers and will shred anyone in the halls who bumps into them or dares to catcall them in the street.

They're tough. These days, I respect that.

Rosaline is the daughter of the head croupier at Salvatore's biggest casino. Sophia's mom is head of PR for his restaurants, and Candace's father is a financial manager at one of Salvatore's companies.

"I should see Mr. Spears about extra credit as well," I mutter, putting my sandwich down. Thinking about my grades and why they're so awful this year has made me lose my appetite.

The three of them tell me that's a good idea and start brainstorming how to persuade all my teachers to give me extra work to bump up my grades, which makes me smile. They're all beautiful, and they're whip-smart and competitive about grades and colleges. I think I would have let my brain turn to mush and given up at school if it weren't for them.

Lunch ends, and we all hurry off to our different classes. I sit beside Sophia in Italian class as we fill out verb worksheets. My pen writes automatically but my mind is drifting. For a member of the mafia, Salvatore has a strong corporate presence. So does Cassius. Vinicius and Lorenzo, who knows what the hell those two get up to. I suppose that's what makes Salvatore so successful. He has a veneer of legitimacy, which makes him untouchable. There are many people in this city who are afraid of him, but many more who respect and admire him.

After school, the four of us grab our bags and head out the school gates. As we walk through the parking lot, I notice a boy leaning against a black Cadillac Escalade in a leather jacket with his arms folded, watching us.

No, watching me. And smiling.

A faint smile, but it lights up his hazel eyes. He's eighteen or nineteen from the look of him, with high cheekbones and rumpled hair. As he notices me gazing back, he smiles wider, and dimples appear in his cheeks.

"Damn, he's cute as hell," Rosaline murmurs, slowing her pace as she stares at the boy. "I wonder who he is."

The moment we slow down, the boy pushes away from his car and strolls toward us. He comes to a stop right in front of me. "Hey. What's your name?"

I can feel the three girls bristling at my sides. Not with jealousy that he's talking to me, but with protectiveness.

"She's spoken for," Sophia immediately says.

The boy grins and pushes his fingers through his thick hair.

"Spoken for? What is this, the Dark Ages?"

Considering how my marriage has been arranged, he's not far off.

This boy is smiling at me like he expects us all to fall at his feet and worship his handsome face. But I've seen handsome. I've *kissed* handsome. As cute as this boy is, he's got nothing on Salvatore Fiore, and even if he was the hottest boy on the planet, I don't need the trouble of another massive ego connected to a charming smile laying waste to my life.

Besides, if this boy touched me, Salvatore would probably have him killed.

I grasp Rosaline's arm and start dragging her away. "Sorry, we have to go. We all have homework."

"I'm Griffin," the boy calls after me. "Have a lovely afternoon, ladies."

Five minutes later, we're walking along the street when a gray Maserati pulls up next to us. The top is down and a man in a suit, black shirt, and sunglasses gazes at me, his handsome face a blank mask.

My stomach rebounds around inside me. Salvatore. Does he know that I've been talking to a boy? How *could* he know? An internal radar that goes off when a member of the opposite sex dares to talk to me?

Then he smiles and the sun glints off his white teeth and burnishes his tan throat. "Hey, baby."

A ripple of surprise and delight goes through the girls I'm with. They absolutely adore Salvatore. Candace calls out, "Hello, Mr. Fiore. What a beautiful day it is."

She's not flirting, but I supposed she thinks it's prudent to be friendly to her dad's boss.

"Yes, it is, Candace," Salvatore replies, looking only at me. "I saw four beautiful girls while I was on the way to a meeting and I couldn't help but stop and say hello. I've been busy lately, baby. I'm sorry."

The news is full of a money laundering scandal that involves one of Salvatore's CEOs. I suppose he's been working to keep the man out of jail.

"Yes, I read all about it," I reply, not smiling back.

"Your father's been helping me smooth everything over. The mayor is such a generous man. I'll talk to you later, Chiara. Bye, girls."

My father. A wave of disgust goes through me. With one last smile for me, he steps on the gas and roars away. The girls gaze after him and then turn back to me.

"Damn, you're an ice queen," Rosaline tells me, but her tone is admiring. "If Mr. Fiore was my fiancé I would have jumped right into that car."

"I wouldn't have bothered to open the door," Sophia jokes.

"You're playing it right, though," Candace tells me as we all keep walking. "A man like Salvatore loves to be teased. Holding him at arm's length is only going to make him crazier about you."

"Not always at arm's length. It's wise to let him stake his claim in public once or twice," Rosaline points out with a smile, and I know she's referring to the time Salvatore showed up at school and kissed me at the school gate.

Is that what I'm doing, making Salvatore crazier about me by being cold to him? I suppose it could be his fantasy, his untouchable bride who only melts for him in private. I don't want to melt for

Salvatore, so I'll just have to be careful never to be alone with him.

I glance at the three girls. "Can I ask you guys something? Are you saving yourself for marriage?"

Candace immediately says yes, and that's no surprise. Of the three of them, she's the most uptight and ambitious, and she's open with the fact that she wants a husband from high up in Salvatore's organization. She even has a scrapbook with photos of every eligible bachelor under forty who works for Salvatore and earns more than two hundred thousand dollars a year. One of them was married last week, and she crossed out his picture with red pen, tears running down her face.

"I lost my V-card last summer," Rosaline says with a shrug. "I want to get good at sex before I meet my future husband. Besides, sex is fun."

"Right now, I'm keeping it," Sophia says, "but when I get a proper boyfriend I'll give it away so damn fast."

"I'm thinking of losing it." It would be the solution to all my problems, wouldn't it? Salvatore won't want to marry me if I've already given his coveted prize to another man. The other three mafia men are just as virginity obsessed. I could be free of all of them at once.

"You think you want to lose it?" Rosaline asks. "You better make up your mind before suggesting it to Mr. Fiore. He's so hot for you he'll jump you like *that*." She snaps her fingers.

"Not with Salvatore. With someone else."

The three of them stare at me, scandalized. Then Sophia bursts out laughing. "You could try, but Mr. Fiore wouldn't let it happen."

"Do you remember when he dragged Ginevra out of a restaurant last year because she was on a date with Adriano Montessori?" Candace says, her eyes shining. "The pictures were everywhere online. He was like a tiger."

Montessori is an infamous playboy with a reputation of going through every socialite in Coldlake. Seducing Ginevra Fiore would have been his crowning glory.

The three of them discuss Salvatore's bouts of brotherly overprotectiveness over the years, until Rosaline says to me, "Anyway, our point is, when it comes to family pride, Mr. Fiore is an unstoppable force. He's not going to allow anyone unworthy to get their hands on his sister *or* his fiancée."

Candace stares at me, baffled. "Why would you even want to give it to someone else when you're marrying Mr. Fiore?"

I shrug and mutter vaguely about having reasons.

Rosaline's words ring in my ear for the next week. *When it comes to family pride, Mr. Fiore is an unstoppable force.* With pride that strong, surely me having sex with another boy would wound Salvatore so much that he would break off our engagement?

As if he's trying to stay upmost in my mind, the boy in the black leather jacket, Griffin, crosses my path again. On Sunday morning he's in the line behind me in my favorite café, buying coffee, and he smiles at me when I notice him.

The following Wednesday evening I'm jogging in the park when I spot a familiar figure on the tennis courts. Griffin, wearing black shorts and a tight black T-shirt. As I jog past, he waves at me, a yellow tennis ball clutched in his fingers. There are tattoos decorating his forearms and more on his biceps.

On Saturday afternoon I'm studying in the public library when someone carrying a stack of books slides into the seat next to mine. Right next to mine, when there are half a dozen free tables nearby.

I look up, and I'm only mildly surprised to see it's Griffin. He pretends to be absorbed in his reading but a smile is glimmering around his mouth. When he finally "notices" me staring at him, he leans his chin on his fist and grins lazily at me. "Oh, hey. Fancy seeing you here."

"Are you following me? This is getting creepy."

Griffin laughs and shakes his head. "No. But, okay, full confession. I see you around a lot but you never notice me. I thought I'd try making you notice me. I think you're cute and I can't get you out of my mind."

He gazes deep into my eyes, and smiles. If Salvatore looked at me like that, I'd probably feel a tug on my insides and hear a voice whispering to tilt my mouth up to his. But he's not Salvatore so that smile just leaves me cold.

Griffin is playing with fire, flirting with me in public, and I don't want to get anyone beaten up or killed. I turn a page in my book. "You should stay away from me, for your own sake. My fiancé is crazy."

Griffin laughs softly. "Salvatore Fiore doesn't scare me."

"He should," I say, highlighting a line in my notes.

Griffin leans over and covers my hand with his big one. His voice is low and his lips are close to my ear. "Want to get out of here?"

His voice is thick with suggestion. This is what I've been waiting for, isn't it? A sign I should sleep with some other boy and get Salvatore off my back. I glance up at Griffin. He's cute enough, I guess. He's got a great body, but I don't feel anything when he touches me. His hand on mine doesn't cause fire to ripple through my veins.

But that's a good thing, right? I don't want to want Griffin. I just need a boy, any boy, to rid me of my pesky virginity.

And yet the idea of kissing Griffin gives me the creeps. Salvatore and his ex-friends seem to have left indelible ownership on my body. I can remember vividly every place they touched me, and it didn't feel wrong.

Except for Lorenzo. That felt insane.

Griffin picks up a pen and writes a number in my notebook before getting to his feet. "Call me," he says, and walks away.

I watch him go, worrying at my lip with my teeth. My life has turned into a game of chess as I try to think three steps ahead. It will never be over unless I find some way to win.

Later that week, I stay after school for an extra chemistry class with a handful of other students. The school is deserted as I walk out the gates. The parking lot is almost empty except for a handful of teachers' cars.

And a black Cadillac Escalade.

The driver's side door opens and Griffin gets out, looking like any high school girl's wet dream in that black leather jacket and faded jeans. He waits for me by the open door, one eyebrow raised.

Enough messing about. In or out?

I take a tighter hold of my backpack and walk slowly toward him. "Want to go get a soda?" he asks when I'm a few feet away.

It's not soda he's thinking about. If I get in that car, he's going to take me to his place and we're going to have sex, and that will be that. All my problems over in one afternoon.

"Uh, sure," I whisper, and go around to the passenger side door and get in. I'm really doing this. I'm going to give my V-card away to some boy I don't know so my mafia fiancé will dump me and I can be free.

This is crazy.

But the alternative, marrying Salvatore, is unbearable.

I expect Griffin to make small talk as we drive, or to be flirty and charming like he's always been, but all he says as we get onto the main road is, "My place is on the other side of the city."

The emptiness of his words makes unease wash over me. At least Salvatore makes me feel precious and coveted as he's controlling every moment of my life. I push away thoughts of Salvatore and try to ignore the sick feeling in my belly.

While we're stopped at the lights, I stare out the open window, my arms folded tightly. I just hope the deed itself doesn't feel too awful, or Griffin doesn't make it awful by being cold and callous. I cringe, and my courage evaporates.

I don't want this, and I open my mouth to tell Griffin I've changed my mind.

That's when I notice that the man in the next car over is staring at me. It's a huge white SUV, spotlessly clean and expensive-looking. The person sitting in the driver's seat is a bear of a man in a white business shirt that's pulled tight around his biceps and fitted across his shoulders. He has a neat dark beard and his muscled forearms are dusted with black hair.

If we both reached out, we're close enough to hold hands. I feel a jolt as I recognize him. Cassius Ferragamo has one severe black eyebrow raised at me. His gaze slides over to the driver, and his other brow rises to join it.

My heart lodges guiltily in my throat, as if it's Salvatore himself who's caught me with another man and not one of his estranged best friends.

He opens his mouth to say something, and in that moment the lights change. Griffin guns the engines and we shoot forward.

I take a few deep breaths, and then glance out the window. Cassius' white SUV isn't there. A blue Ford is in its place. I'm about to relax when I glance into the side mirror.

Cassius is *following* us.

He's on the phone and his expression is grim. I can't tell what he's saying but I have a horrible feeling it's got something to do with me.

A few minutes later, Cassius hangs up and Griffin turns onto the freeway. I stare into the wing mirror, hoping that the white SUV peels away, but Cassius stays dead on our ass.

Maybe it's just a coincidence. This is the busiest freeway in the city and it's entirely possible that Cassius is just—

"What is that asshole doing?" Griffin's squinting into the rearview mirror.

I turn around and look behind us, wondering if Cassius is flashing his headlights. A few hundred yards down the road, an obnoxiously red Ferrari is weaving through traffic, speeding and swerving like a race car driver. It takes the car just a few minutes to catch up with us and pull into the lane next to Cassius.

I recognize the handsome face behind the sunglasses. Vinicius Angeli.

What the hell is going on?

"You like Ferraris or something?" Griffin asks, clearly puzzled by the way I'm still twisted in my seat and staring out the back window.

I'm about to turn around and try to pretend there aren't two mafia bosses on our tail when I see a black, militaristic Mercedes-Benz G-Class 4WD tearing up the slip lane next to the freeway, about to merge into traffic.

Oh *no*.

I have a sinking feeling who's driving such an aggressive-looking car. The driver of the Merc jerks the steering wheel and pulls across two lanes of rush-hour traffic, causing half a dozen people to slam on the brakes and sound their horns.

"Is he crazy?" Griffin mutters.

Not crazy. Insane.

Behind the wheel of the Merc, Lorenzo Scava catches my gaze, points at Griffin, and then draws his finger across his throat.

That guy? He's dead.

"Why do you even care who I'm with?" I moan under my breath.

"What?" Griffin asks.

I turn to Griffin and grab his arm. "I've changed my mind. Take the next exit and drop me off somewhere crowded and leave…quickly."

These three men might hurt me, or they might not, but they will *definitely* hurt Griffin if I don't get him out of this.

"My place isn't far." He switches the radio on.

"No, I'm serious, you need to—"

"I love this song," Griffin says, turning the radio up and tapping his fingers on the steering wheel.

A few minutes later, Griffin pulls off the freeway into a distinctively sketchy part of the city. It doesn't seem like a fun place to be left stranded without a ride, but I don't care as long as Griffin can get out of here unscathed.

He presses a few buttons on his steering wheel and says, "Call Jax."

A moment later, a number being called cuts across the music. When the call is picked up, Griffin says, "Jax? It's me. I'll be there in ten minutes."

A deep male voice without any inflection replies, "Dope."

Then he hangs up.

"Who's Jax?" I ask.

Griffin stares straight ahead and doesn't answer.

I take another look around at the buildings we're passing. Run-down warehouses and chain link fences. Rottweilers on rope leashes. Houses with boarded-up windows.

"Griffin? Where exactly is your place?"

"Chill, would you? You're jumpier than all those drivers on the free—" Griffin trails off as he glances in his rearview mirror and sees the same white SUV stuck to his bumper. Behind it is the red Ferrari. Behind that is the black Merc that nearly caused a pile-up.

Griffin's furious eyes snap to mine. "Did you call them? Where the fuck is your phone?"

"It's in my bag. I've just been sitting here the whole time."

"Then what the fuck are your friends doing here?" he snarls, hands gripping the steering wheel.

"They're not my friends. They're not even my fiancé's friends. I told you to let me out and go, so pull over!"

Griffin ignores me and speeds up. Cassius' white SUV pulls into oncoming traffic and races up beside us. He tries to cut in front of the Escalade but Griffin twists the wheel savagely and we swerve into a side street. I grip the handle above my window and gasp a prayer.

The other three follow in a squeal of rubber, Cassius in the lead. Lorenzo's black Merc turns down a side street and disappears.

I suppose it's too much to hope that he's going home.

I lean down for my bag and pull out my phone, intending to call Salvatore. He might have a meltdown when he finds out what I planned to do, but at least he'll protect me from whatever the hell is about to go down.

Griffin grabs my phone and shoves it inside his jacket. "No, you fucking don't."

"Give that back. I'm trying to save your life."

"Shut up," he growls, his eyes darting around the streets as we drive way too fast.

"Those guys following us?" I say. "They don't want you. They want me. Stop the car and let me out and they won't follow you. *Stop the car, Griffin!*" I'm screaming at the top of my lungs but he's ignoring me.

Lorenzo's 4WD races out of an intersection in front of us, and Griffin swears and slams on the brakes. I shoot forward and the seat belt digs painfully into my throat. We stop just a few inches short of slamming into the Merc.

Griffin tries to put the car into reverse, but Vinicius' Ferrari is right behind us, and then Cassius pulls up beside Griffin's door. The enormous Italian man jumps out of his car, his shoulders bunched and his eyes black with fury.

Griffin is scrambling around behind his seat and I see the flash of a metal barrel. A split second later I realize what it is.

"*He's got a—*"

Before I can finish the sentence, Cassius has yanked the door open and grabbed Griffin by the lapels of his leather jacket. I lunge for the gun and smack it out of Griffin's hand, and it goes skittering into the footwell.

I jump out of the car and race around to the men. "Let him go, please. This is a horrible mistake."

Cassius ignores me and drags Griffin out of the car. Vinicius frisks Griffin for weapons and Lorenzo's got a gun in his hand. I look desperately around for something or someone to make this insanity stop, but the street is deserted.

Cassius begins dragging Griffin down a driveway toward a warehouse. "Chiara, get in my car and lock yourself in."

With these three acting like Griffin is the Unabomber and Griffin making weird phone calls and grabbing guns? No chance.

I follow the three men and a twisting, swearing Griffin into the empty lot of a deserted warehouse. Cassius throws Griffin to the ground and the three of them start kicking him. In the stomach. In the kidneys. In the head. Vicious kicks that have Griffin groaning in pain.

I run forward and grab Cassius' arm. "What are you doing? You're going to kill him. Stop it!"

Cassius pushes me off and lands a kick between Griffin's shoulder blades, who grunts in agony.

"*Stop that. All of you. He didn't do anything!*" I push my way between Cassius and Lorenzo, prepared to throw myself down on top of Griffin in an attempt to shield him with my body. If they're going to kick him then they can kick me, too.

Cassius wraps his arms around me and hauls me out of the fray. Feet off the ground and thrashing in Cassius' grip, I watch the other two continue with the beating. "You pricks! Leave him alone. I was just in the car with him. Why do you care when you don't even know who he is?"

"We know exactly who he is," Cassius growls in my ear, "and what he planned to do to you."

"It's just my virginity," I scream. "Who cares? It's mine to do what the hell I want with. This was my idea!"

The other two stop kicking Griffin. The boy alternates between gasping for breath and coughing his lungs out, blood dripping from a split lip and gashed eyebrow.

Boy. Griffin is a *boy*. The other three are grown men. I knew they could be despicable, but this is on a whole other level.

Cassius loosens his arms and lets me slide down his chest until my feet touch the ground, but he doesn't let me go. Griffin rolls onto his side and tries to push himself up. Lorenzo puts his foot on Griffin's neck and shoves him back down.

Keeping Griffin prisoner with his boot, Lorenzo takes his phone out of his jeans and makes a call. "Hey, fuckface, we found someone about to get his greasy hands all over your girl. Want to have some fun?"

I guess Salvatore is *fuckface* now. I feel sick at the thought of the kind of "fun" these men could have with someone they've already beaten half to death.

Lorenzo holds the phone away from his ear and winces. "Quit shouting at me. Get off at exit twenty-three. We're at the old, tinned food factory over on Pond—" He glances at the screen and grins. "He hung up. I think he's on his way."

He leans down closer to Griffin, an insane glint in his eye, and points at me. "That girl's fiancé is on his way. Any last words before we pull all your teeth out with rusty pliers and shove them up your ass?"

Griffin tries to speak but Lorenzo grinds his boot into Griffin's throat, making him wheeze.

"Stop that! He can't breathe."

Lorenzo glares at me like he's thinking about choking the life out of me next. "Bring her here. I want to talk to our princess."

Their princess. I'm not theirs.

Cassius forces me closer to Lorenzo. I try to fight but Cassius holds me against his chest as easily as a child holds a doll.

Lorenzo dips his face close to mine and snarls, "If you were looking to get gang-raped by a bunch of criminals, you should have called us."

My blood pounds hard in my ears. "What are you talking about?"

Lorenzo pulls that hateful knife out of his jacket and leans down to Griffin.

"No—" I start to say, thinking he's going to stab Griffin with it, but he grasps the sleeve of Griffin's leather jacket and slashes it open.

He straightens up and points to a tattoo on the boy's forearm. "He's a Geak, you fucking moron. Do you know what they do to women when they want to send a message to the man who owns them?"

"No one owns me," I say automatically, but I'm staring at the gothic letter G inked into Griffin's arm. I was never close enough to Griffin when his arms were bare, but would I have recognized this tattoo for what it is? I barely know anything about the Geaks except that they're a gang that's sometimes mentioned in the news.

Jax. That was the name of the person Griffin called. "Who else is in the Geaks?"

"A bunch of lowlife scum," Vinicius replies.

"*Names*," I demand.

"It's not like we're mutuals on fucking Instagram," Lorenzo growls. "He's got a Geak tattoo on his arm. What more do you want?"

"All I know is they're led by a guy called Jax," Vinicius says.

I suddenly feel like Lorenzo is leaning on my windpipe. Jax. That deadpan voice on the phone. Griffin was taking me to him.

"Is that enough proof, princess? How about this?" Lorenzo raises his foot from Griffin's throat. "How many of your buddies has Mayor Romano put in prison?"

"Seven," Griffin rasps, his eyes full of hate as he glares at me. "This cunt deserves to be fucked with a broken bottle in every ho—"

Lorenzo draws his foot back and kicks Griffin viciously in the head. I stare at the boy as he writhes on the bloodied concrete.

Slowly, Cassius releases me and places his hands on my shoulders. "*Bambina*. Go back to my car while we take care of this. You shouldn't watch."

The last thing I want is to watch them torture someone to death, but I need to understand.

"Griffin, you were really going to…" I can't bring myself to repeat the horrible things he spewed, "hurt me just because some of your friends were put in prison? I didn't do anything to you or them. I can't control who the courts convict."

"This isn't about you, you stupid bitch," Griffin wheezes, spitting blood.

"So why bring me into it?"

Lorenzo answers for him. "It's about your father. Right now, you belong to him and you're fair game for anyone who wants revenge against the Mayor of Coldlake. Killing you is punishing him. Later, you'll be targeted by anyone who wants revenge against Salvatore. That's why we—" He breaks off and glances at the others, and then growls, "Never fucking mind. Go back to Cassius' car. We won't tell you again."

The sound of an engine roars along the street and a vehicle screeches to a halt. A car door slams, and then a tall, broad-shouldered figure in a dark suit comes stalking across the lot with murder in his eyes.

No one speaks. Even Griffin has stopped moving.

Salvatore stops a few feet away and glares at each of his former friends. At me. At the bloodied boy lying on the concrete. And finally, the ornate G inked into his arm.

His hands curl into fists and he growls, "How did this happen?"

Vinicius is the one to speak up. "Your promised bride sought to do something about her virginity with a cute, harmless boy who's been, what?" He glances at me. "Walking you home from school?"

I wince. Oh, Jesus Christ. I thought Vinicius, Cassius, and Lorenzo were following me because I dared to get into a car with a strange boy, when they were actually freaking out because I was in a car with a Geak, someone they knew wanted me dead in the most horrific way. They saved me, and now everyone knows about my humiliating plan.

"He—Griffin—has been following me. We spoke a few times, and today he was waiting at school for me."

"You've been stalking her?" Salvatore snarls at Griffin.

I wait for all four of the men to give me looks of loathing for being so stupid, and for attempting to have sex with a complete stranger, but all their venom is reserved for Griffin.

"Get him on his feet," Salvatore says. Vinicius and Lorenzo haul Griffin up by his armpits as Salvatore takes his jacket off and rolls his sleeves back to his elbows. He takes his time about it, but his jaw is flexing like crazy.

Cassius stays close to me with his hands on my shoulders, his bulk a solid, almost comforting, presence.

Griffin can barely put weight on his own feet but he glares at Salvatore through a fringe of bloodied hair. He knows what's coming, but he's not crying or begging for his life.

My future husband steps closer to Griffin and then, without warning, punches him in the gut. The boy would collapse if it weren't for the other two holding him upright. Salvatore goes on punching the boy with both fists, a slow, methodical, and brutal beating all over his torso and face. I can't look away. Every sickening crunch and groan pierces my mind.

Griffin vomits, blood and half-digested food spattering on the broken concrete. Vinicius and Lorenzo finally let him drop.

"Do you want to do the honors?" Vinicius asks Salvatore, drawing a gun out from the back of his pants and aiming it at Griffin's head.

"Do whatever you want with him," Salvatore mutters, massaging his bruised knuckles. "Just see that he ends up dead."

Vinicius glances at me, as if asking for my opinion about what should become of my would-be rapist.

Then he smiles.

Vinicius is always charming, and so blindingly handsome that you couldn't possibly believe that anything ugly or gruesome could ever happen because of him.

He pulls the trigger. The shot explodes in my ears and in Griffin's skull. A hole is blasted out the back of his head and blood, bone fragments, and slimy, scrambled-egg-like lumps spatter over the concrete.

I stare at the lumps until I realize it's Griffin's brains. A wave of nausea rolls up my body.

The night of my seventeenth birthday, I didn't believe that Vinicius was dangerous, and I'm still being fooled by his angelic looks. All four of these men are violent devils with handsome faces, powerful bodies and tailored clothes. They warned me they were dangerous, but I didn't believe them.

My priest once gave a sermon on how the devil himself can appear beautiful, for Lucifer was an angel before he fell from grace. Beauty is deceptive, and a handsome face can hide a multitude of horrors.

CHAPTER ELEVEN

SALVATORE

"Ah, I wasn't done having fun." Lorenzo pushes his bloodied fingers through his hair and smiles at the mess that was the Geak piece of shit.

Chiara is doubled over, her hands pressed against her knees as she struggles to control her breathing.

I glance at the other three, who have drawn together opposite Chiara and me. Them and us. I put my hand on Chiara's back. "Say thank you to my former friends. It's because of them you're untouched."

Chiara slowly pulls herself upright. She's deathly pale and her eyes are hollow, but she suddenly looks furious. "Untouched?

Untouched? Are you kidding me?"

"What are you talking about? What did that piece of shit do to you?"

"I'm talking about the night of my birthday and what your *friends* did then."

Lorenzo laughs. "Quit whining. It's not like you had anything shoved between your legs, princess."

Chiara glares at Lorenzo, who smirks back.

"Fuck you," she whispers at the blond man. "You never told him, did you?"

I stride forward and grab Lorenzo by the collar. "Told me what? What did you do to her?"

Lorenzo snatches his knife from inside his jacket and holds the pointy end against my ribs, growling, "Back off, pretty boy."

I let go of him slowly, teeth grit, and turn to my future bride. "What's he talking about?"

She nods at Vinicius. "He wasn't too bad. He just kissed me and slid his hand up my leg. He was worse," she adds, turning to Cassius. "He pulled my dress up and spanked me. But *him*." Chiara gazes at Lorenzo with an expression full of loathing. "He tied my hands behind my back, pushed me against a wall and said disgusting things to me. Then he ripped my underwear off and shoved the hilt of his knife between my legs like he was going to…you know what."

I go back to Chiara and put my hand on her shoulder, but she angrily shrugs me off.

"And you were just as bad! You choked me with your bare hands because I dared to talk back to you. I'm grateful I didn't get raped with broken bottles and killed because my father put some gangsters in prison, but expressing gratitude to these three assholes sticks in my throat. And you know what? So does saying thank you to you, Salvatore."

Silence falls across the lot. There's a pinch of regret in Cassius' face, but Lorenzo just looks bored and Vinicius is preoccupied with his hair.

"I'm sorry," I finally mutter.

Chiara looks up. "Sorry for what, exactly?"

Not for what we did. I'm sorry that I never explained why. "On your birthday, we did what we had to do. We walk into every unknown situation and establish ourselves fast as the most dangerous men in the room. That way no one challenges us. This is how we stay successful. This is how we stay *alive*."

"But I wasn't going to hurt you! I was just trying to celebrate my birthday. The four of you knew you were coming to meet a seventeen-year-old girl. There was no reason for you all to scare the living daylights out of me."

"We were coming to arrange a business deal," Vinicius says, from the other side of the bleeding corpse. "The deal involved the most powerful man in Coldlake and his daughter who's been wrapped up in cotton wool her whole life. We needed to make it clear to your family who we are and what we're about."

I turn toward Chiara and put my hands on her shoulders. "Forget about them. This is between you and me. For my part in how we terrorized you that night, I'm sorry. I lost my temper. I assumed you were a spoiled brat and so I treated you like one, but I see now that you were just scared."

I stare deep into her eyes. Come on, baby. We understand each other better now.

Chiara sniffs and doesn't say anything. Then she pulls away from me and bends down over the Geak's corpse. Gingerly, with her thumb and finger, she lifts his leather jacket and fishes out her phone.

The screen is shattered, and Chiara's shoulders slump. "Will one of you please call me a taxi?"

"Sure, call a taxi to a murder scene," Lorenzo mutters.

"Then I'll walk," she seethes at him.

I grasp her hand. "I'm taking you home. Come on."

We head for my car but Cassius steps in front of us. His white shirt is spattered with blood and his eyes are only for Chiara. "*Bambina*, there's danger at every turn in this city. Sometimes three is better than one. Have a think about that."

"Fuck off, Cassius," I growl. "I can protect my woman on my own."

The three of them could have finished the Geak off by themselves, but they called me because they wanted to rub my nose in the fact that they saved my bride from being raped while I had no idea where she was.

"Sure, you could have," Cassius sneers. "Enjoy kissing your bride, who's all in one piece and just as beautiful as she always was, thanks to us. You're welcome, you *cazzo di merda*."

Dick-faced piece of shit.

"*Cazzo sì*." I put my fingers under my chin and flick them at Cassius, telling him to get fucked. "Come on, Chiara."

We walk out to the jumble of cars on the deserted street and get into my Maserati. By now, the sun has gone down and dusk has set in. Mayor Romano must be wondering where his daughter is. He's going to take one look at Chiara's ashen face and know that something went down.

When we reach her house I take her inside, hoping I can distract the mayor while she slips upstairs.

No such luck. He comes charging down the hall the moment we get inside. "Where have you been? I've been calling you for hours."

"Apologies, Mayor Romano. I should have informed you that I was seeing Chiara today."

"Don't lie for her, Fiore. The school rang to say they saw Chiara getting into a black Escalade. Where was she?" He grabs Chiara by the arm and shakes her. "Where were you?"

I try and step between them. "Leave my fiancée alone."

"She's not your fiancée yet, and she never will be if you lie to my face."

Chiara seems calm. Too calm. She regards her father with hollow eyes. "I was going home with a boy to get rid of my virginity. You're all so obsessed with it and I didn't want it anymore. It turned out he was in a gang and he and his friends all wanted to rape and murder me because of you. Good night."

Chiara tries to walk away from her father but he yanks her back, and she stumbles. My blood pressure goes through the roof seeing him hurt her.

"You were doing *what*?" he roars. "How could you act like such a slut?"

The rape and murder part doesn't interest Mayor Romano. Just the virginity part.

Chiara's face transforms in disgust. "Do you think I'm scared of you? You've already taken everything from me that I love. Shout all you like. I won't hear you."

"Stay right there," he growls, and pulls out his phone. He makes a call to someone and arranges something they seem to have already discussed.

"Yes, tonight. Now." The mayor hangs up. "You can go, Fiore. Thank you for bringing my daughter home."

"What was that call about?" Chiara asks.

"You've disobeyed me for the last time. I'm having a tracker put on you so you can't run off again."

"What do you mean, put a tracker on me?"

"A chip. Something implanted so you can't take it off and run away again."

A chip implanted. I grit my teeth against all the things I want to shout and the punch that I desperately want to land right in the middle of Mayor Romano's face.

"That's disgusting. I won't let you," Chiara tells her father.

"You don't have a choice."

Lost for words, Chiara turns to me.

I shake my head. There's nothing I can do. "I warned you to obey your father, but you didn't listen to me. Now, you'll suffer the consequences."

"You cold bastard," she whispers.

I seal my heart off from her words. I'm cold. I feel nothing. I care about nothing but myself. What happens here tonight has nothing to do with me.

I lunge for the front door handle, stalk down the front path toward my car, and get in. I go to start the engine, but I can't do it. If she's going to suffer, then I should sit here and suffer with her.

Ten minutes later, an SUV pulls up and a man in a white coat with two men escorting him get out, and they go inside Mayor Romano's house.

Then the screaming starts.

She's lucky. It could easily have been her life tonight if the others hadn't found her.

But it doesn't feel lucky as she screams and screams, and then the house falls ominously silent. Either they've bound and gagged her or drugged her.

A few more minutes pass, and then the doctor and his escort leave the house and drive away. I lean my head against the steering wheel, fantasizing about kicking the front door down and beating the mayor to death. Why did I stay? I was just opening myself up to the agony of sitting out here like a powerless moron while someone hurts her.

I grab my phone and make a call. "One day, I'll fucking kill him."

"Who?" asks the voice on the other end.

"Mayor Romano. Chiara disobeyed him, and he put a chip in her so he can track her wherever she goes. He wasn't gentle about it, either."

There's silence on the other end of the line, and I know what they're thinking. I'm the one who decided he wants to play house with the Mayor of Coldlake's most prized possession. At least it was a chip and not a bullet in her head.

I pinch the bridge of my nose and try to dispel the memory of Chiara's screams. "There's the other plan."

But maybe I've ruined the chances of that plan succeeding before it could even occur to me.

The voice on the other end hesitates. "Yes, I've been wondering if that's crossed your mind. How could the two work at once? We can't sacrifice one for the other."

But what if there's a way to have both? I try and force the two ideas together but can't see a way to make them fit.

"The wedding's soon. I'll focus on that. Talk to you tomorrow." I hang up and start the car. Ginevra's wedding is in just three weeks and my sister is radiant with excitement and love.

And Chiara?

I envision her walking down the aisle of the church toward me, dressed in white, her beautiful face just glimpsed through her veil and her eyes full of pure hatred.

***

"You may now kiss the bride."

At the front of the church, Antonio sweeps Ginevra into his arms and presses his mouth to hers. All around me, people break into applause and smiles for the happy couple.

Beside me, Chiara's face is blank and she stares straight ahead. Her hands remain folded in her lap and she's as closed off as she was the day of her mother's funeral. When I kissed her cheek in greeting, she wouldn't even look at me.

The deal is unfolding the way it needs to, but I couldn't predict how the girl in the center of this was going to throw a whole toolbox worth of spanners into it. I could call the whole thing off and go back to the other three…

But this is the only way for me to get what I want. I've waited years. I can't wait any longer.

At the reception, Chiara eats a little of her dinner and sips water. She doesn't say a word to me until it's time for the couple's first dance. Antonio leads Ginevra around the dance floor, and Chiara finally speaks.

"What happened when Ginevra first met Antonio?"

"Ginevra always knew I'd arrange her marriage for her. There was a dinner at home and I told her the man who'd be her husband was coming. She was a little scared, but mostly she was excited. When she and Antonio saw each other, they were…" I recall the impulsive kiss I gave Chiara when we first met. "Instantly attracted to each other. That first kiss will tell you everything."

Chiara is silent for a long time. "I'm happy for her. She's found a kind man who'll love and protect her."

"He's not kind. He's violent and dangerous, but that doesn't mean he won't love and protect *her*." I reach for Chiara's hand and thread my fingers through hers. For a moment she lets me, her face softening.

Then she takes a shuddering breath and pulls away from me. "Then she's wrong to accept the love and protection of a man like that. He could turn on her at any moment."

"Chiara!"

Chiara turns around at the sound of her name, just as something comes hurtling toward her. She catches it automatically, and her face falls as she realizes what she's done. She turns the object in her hands slowly until it's the right way up.

The pale yellow and white blooms of Ginevra's bridal bouquet.

Ginevra smiles broadly at my promised bride. "You're next."

CHAPTER TWELVE

CHIARA

TEN MONTHS LATER

"Yes, yes, yes," Candace breathes, her face alight with wonder. "The satin. The lace. It's *perfect*."

I glance between her face and mine in the floor-to-ceiling mirrors. We're standing on the plush cream carpet of Coldlake's most prestigious bridal boutique. Sophia and a store assistant are fanning out my skirt while Candace flutters about us in excitement. Anyone would think she was the one getting married. Come to think of it, she should be the one marrying Salvatore. Her family practically worships him.

Rosaline is reclined on a chaise lounge in a cloud of lilac tulle and sipping free champagne. I guess no one cares that we're all barely or not quite eighteen when I'm marrying Salvatore Fiore. All three girls are wearing their bridesmaid gowns, midi dresses in pastel colors. This is the final fitting before the wedding next week.

"Babe, you look amazing," Rosaline says after another mouthful of champagne. "Mr. Fiore is going to fall even harder the moment he lays eyes on you."

Only I know that Salvatore can't stand to look at me. He made all the wedding arrangements, including choosing this dress, without even one phone call to me. I suspect that Ginevra made most of the decisions as she's been the one coming to see me, radiantly happy with her six-month baby bump.

"Is Mr. Fiore excited?" Sophia asks.

A pang goes through me. I swallow, feeling strangely desolate as I confess, "I don't know. I haven't seen him in months."

Ten months, to be exact. I haven't seen Salvatore in the flesh since Ginevra's wedding. I suppose he was so disgusted that I was going to give my virginity away to a stranger that he can't bear to be near me. At first I was so angry with him that I didn't care, but as the months dragged on…

I missed him.

I shouldn't yearn for Salvatore Fiore, or search for him in the news or in expensive cars as they drive by. But I do.

Candace nods in sympathy. "I've heard he's fiendishly busy. Don't take it personally."

Rosaline screws up her nose. "Are you serious? How can she not take it personally? What a dick."

Everyone turns to her with shocked expressions, including the store assistant. Sophia strides over, snatches the glass of champagne from Rosaline and pours it into a potted plant.

"Hey! I was drinking that."

"You've had enough."

I take one last look at myself in the mirror, my nerves in a snarl. I suppose it's normal to feel nervous before a wedding, but there's nothing normal about my marriage to one of the most notorious men in Coldlake. There's nothing normal about the almost indetectable lump in the back of my neck, either. Ten months later, the humiliation still burns.

How I hate my father. Once I'm married, I'm never going to speak to him or look at him again.

"I'll have everything sent around to your home tomorrow," the assistant tells me with a smile. "And happy birthday for tomorrow, Miss Romano."

My stomach lurches as the girls kiss me goodbye and I get into the waiting car alone. I'm not allowed to go anywhere unless it's with the driver that Dad pays for. I'm dreading my birthday tomorrow. One whole year since Mom was killed, and it's beginning to feel like she never existed. It's rare that anyone talks about her to me. If Dad skates close to the subject then I feel like I'm going to throw up.

My hatred for Dad *burns*.

As the sun sets on another awful day, I pace around and around the house, my head full of last year and my heart in turmoil. The evening is warm and my restlessness is making moisture bead on my top lip. I don't know how I'm going to sleep at all tonight. All I can picture is Salvatore's fists as he beat that Geak to death. I wish I were strong so I could sink my fist into Dad's stomach and watch the color drain from his face.

Then suddenly, Salvatore's there.

He strides across the dining room toward me, looking as breathtaking as he did the very first time I laid eyes on him. I open my mouth to speak. Before I can utter a word, he takes my face between his hands and his lips descend on mine in a hungry kiss. There's only Salvatore, and I'm breathing him into my heart and opening my mouth so he can taste me.

He pulls away and whispers against my mouth. "I couldn't stay away. I kept thinking about what happened last year."

So many things happened last year. "What were you thinking about?"

Salvatore frowns, puzzled by why I'm puzzled. "Your mom. I know it didn't happen until tomorrow, but today must be just as hard for you."

Tears sting my eyes and I throw my arms around his neck. My heart gives a painful, grateful double-thump. When Ophelia died, was everyone reluctant to speak her name, too? Does he feel the anniversary of the moment of her death drawing nearer every year?

"This day last year was my last happy day with her," I whisper.

Salvatore strokes my hair and kisses behind my ear. I glance at the clock on the wall. Nearly thirty minutes past eleven.

Tick tock.

I draw back from him, but keep my arms around his neck. "Can you get me out of here for an hour? I don't care where, but I don't want to be here when—" But my throat locks up.

When the minute hand ticks over and it's finally my birthday.

Salvatore strokes my cheek with the backs of his fingers. "Of course, baby."

Taking a firm grip on my hand, he starts walking toward the front door and calls out to my father, "We'll be back in an hour, Mayor Romano."

Dad appears in the hallway wearing a frown. "At this hour?"

"Chiara wants some fresh air."

He doesn't look happy but he glances at his watch and goes back into the lounge. "One hour, Fiore."

Wherever we go, Dad will be able to track our movements online by following the blue dot on his computer or phone screen. Sometimes when I'm out I swear I can feel the pressure of his hateful gaze.

In Salvatore's car, we drive in silence for several minutes, and then he reaches out to take my hand. "Where would you like to go?"

"Anywhere. I don't care."

We only have an hour so it's not like we can go far. Salvatore takes a left on a street that winds up into the Lincoln Hills. It's an old part of town and the houses are huge and expensive and the streets are quiet, especially this late at night. He parks at the top at the lookout over the city.

He cuts the engine and turns to me. I can just make out his face in the darkness.

"Salvatore, why have you been avoiding me?"

He touches my face. "I thought it would be easier, but it's not."

"Can I ask what you think of me?"

"I think you're going to be a troublesome wife." But he's smiling as he says it.

It's more deflection than answer, but I don't push him because I only asked the question so I can answer it. "You're not who I would have chosen as a husband. This isn't the life I would choose for myself, but here we are. If you believe you're worthy of it, I think I could grow to love you."

He raises one eyebrow, as if the idea of not being worthy of something has never occurred to him. "Worthy?"

"You're full of fear. Full of hate. Full of ambition. There isn't room for love in your heart with all that crowded inside."

A shadow slips over his expression, but he seems to shake it off and gives me a charming smile. "Baby, you're worried about my heart?"

He kisses me, and slides a hand up my sundress. His questing fingers brush my inner thighs.

"Salvatore. I'm still seventeen."

"You little goody-goody. You're only seventeen for…seven more minutes." Salvatore glances at the clock and then slides one strap of my dress down and then the other. "We'll be officially engaged tomorrow. You'll be my wife in one week." He leans down and sucks one of my nipples into his mouth, and then the other.

I can't find it in me to resist when his touch is sending fireworks through me.

He scoops my breasts together and runs his tongue across them both. "Fuck, baby. You're soft as butter. What were we talking about?"

My eyes are closed, I have one hand braced against the roof of his car and my heels are lifting off the floor. I have no idea.

He tests one of my nipples with his teeth. "Oh, yes. You becoming my wife. You will honor the Fiore name when it becomes yours. You will be obedient. Respectful. Beautiful." He sucks my nipple slowly and then lets it go. "But that last one will be easy for you, won't it, baby?"

Obedient. Respectful. Beautiful. Oh, piss off. "If I want to lie around in sweats with tangled hair and talk back to you after we're married, then I will."

He tugs my dress down to my waist and pushes my thighs apart. I glance out the windows at the surrounding park. There are no other cars. No movement.

"There's only one way this goes," he says, sliding two fingers against my clit over my underwear. "You'll be my wife and do as I say."

He slides down with his fingers, and then up with his nails. They scrape over the wet fabric, the vibrations coursing through me.

"And if I—*ahhh*." I open one eye and peer at the dash. "It's still five minutes to midnight."

Salvatore grasps my underwear and pulls them down my legs. "Fuck midnight. I want to feel your pussy."

When he starts circling my clit I let my legs fall open and give in. I've made myself come thinking about Salvatore, more than once. I crave to know what the real thing feels like.

"And if I don't do as you say?" I pant.

"I gave you a taste of the man I can be when I lose my temper on your last birthday. You never have to see that man again. It's your choice."

"I'm not going to live in fear of you."

"Chiara, if you keep talking back, I will fucking ruin your orgasm," he growls through his teeth.

Ruin my orgasm? What does that even mean? "I'm not scared of you."

"You should be." Salvatore rubs my clit in firm circles, exactly the right pressure and tempo to have me panting and seeing stars. I press my fist against the car ceiling and give in to what he's doing, suddenly not caring if there are a hundred people staring in at me with my legs splayed open and my breasts bare.

"Screw you," I moan. Just as my head tips back and the warm, golden sensations start to cascade through me, Salvatore takes his fingers away.

My deep breathing becomes a strangled cry. I was so close. My hand dives toward my clit but Salvatore grabs my wrist in an iron grip.

"Why did you—" I screw my eyes up tight and groan as the powerful orgasm that he was about to unleash on me warps into something harsh and unsatisfying and fizzles out. "That feels *horr*—"

Smack.

"Ow!" My eyes fly open. To add insult to ruined orgasm, Salvatore just spanked my pussy. I struggle to close my legs but he won't let me, and spanks me again.

"What the hell! Stop that."

"Happy birthday, baby."

He keeps spanking my pussy and it makes wet, smacking sounds. He's not hitting me hard but I'm over-sensitized and tender and every smack makes my body jerk in the car seat.

"Stop that—it's not—you're too—*Salvatore!*" Smack. Smack. Smack.

"I'm too what? Too mean? Too cruel? This is the man you're marrying. Get used to him."

Smack.

My frustrated orgasm is loitering deep in my core, and each strike of his fingers perversely makes it grow. I *won't* come like this, while he's being such an asshole. I won't give him the satisfaction of punishing me and then witnessing how much I *like it*.

I glare into his blue-green eyes, only to find him smiling wickedly back at me. I'm trapped and there's nowhere for me to go as he keeps smacking me. Nowhere for the sensations in my clit to go as they gather rapidly and infuriatingly into a—

"*Fuck you, Salvatore*," I scream, and come harder than I ever have in my life.

I collapse back against the seat, gasping for breath. Salvatore finally releases me and I look down at myself. Naked from the waist up. Dress rucked up to my hips. Underwear gone, exposing me. And to top it all off, my insides are red-raw from the way he's scrambled them with his fucked-up dirty talk and cruel fingers.

Salvatore kisses me hard and then starts the engine. "Damn, you're incredible, baby. I can't wait to marry you."

"Oh, Chiara. Your mother would be so proud. It's exactly what she would have done." Francesca turns away from the decorated dining table and regards me with misty eyes.

It's not exactly how Mom would have done it. The napkins and table centerpiece are in white and pale blue, not black and gold like my father prefers. It's the way she would have *wanted* it, and that's what's important.

"Thank you. I'm going to miss you so much." I wrap my arms around the old cook and squeeze her tight. The only things I'll miss about this house are the reminders of my mother, and Francesca, Violette, and Stephan. Maybe once I'm settled in Salvatore's house I can hire these three so there are some familiar faces around me.

In Salvatore's house. As Salvatore's wife. My future is rushing toward me at breakneck speed.

Francesca kisses my cheek and leaves me standing by the dining table. A few minutes later, Dad joins me, wearing his tuxedo. I'm dressed in baby blue, which was my mother's favorite color. Dad glances at the knee-length dress and his mouth thins into an unpleasant line, but he doesn't say anything.

We wait in silence for Salvatore's arrival. Soon Dad will be rid of me, and then he and Salvatore can indulge in whatever cozy business and crime adventures they want to go on together.

There's a knock at the door, and we hear Violette open it. For a moment I think I hear four sets of feet coming down the hall, but it's merely an echo in my mind. Salvatore and Salvatore alone comes through the door, tall and broad-shouldered in his suit, his hair swept back and a cocky smile on his lips.

A smile just for me.

He looks only at me as he walks across the room, takes me in his arms, and kisses me like I really am the reason he's here.

Dad and Salvatore do most of the talking over dinner. They discuss the guest list for the wedding, and it sounds like every important person in Coldlake will be there to watch me walk down the aisle. Dad's expression is brimming with delight as he recites names and I can almost see the votes stacking up inside his head.

When the meal is over, we all stand up and Salvatore takes my hand. Turning to Dad, he says, "Will you give Chiara and I a moment? I have something for her."

Salvatore leads me into the lounge and closes the door. We're standing in the middle of the carpet, and he reaches into his pocket and pulls out a black velvet box. He opens it, revealing a platinum engagement ring with an enormous emerald-cut diamond, surrounded by a cluster of smaller diamonds.

Salvatore grasps my left hand and slides the diamond onto my ring finger. "Now, the whole world will know you belong to me."

I turn my hand this way and that, watching the diamond sparkle. I hear again Salvatore's footsteps coming down the hall tonight. There was something strange about the way they sounded.

Hollow.

They sounded hollow, and alone.

"You've been played and you don't even realize it."

Salvatore's gaze narrows. "Excuse me?"

"It's so obvious that even naïve, stupid little me can see it. You think you've won, but really, you've lost. The four of you together were a threat to my father's power. At least the other three have stuck together. You've been peeled off from the herd and now Dad's going to use you however he wants."

"Is that so?" Salvatore asks, his voice quiet and dangerous. "If you're so clever, how is it you're poking me like a bear when there's no one here to protect you from me?"

"I didn't say I was clever. I said I was stupid."

"So you did. After what I warned you about last night, I have to agree with you." He grabs me by the throat and squeezes, anger sparking in his eyes. "I'm starting to think you mouth off because making me angry makes you wet."

He puts his hand on my shoulder and shoves me to my knees. Maybe he's right. Or maybe I'll learn to be afraid of him, but right now, all I'm anticipating is what he'll do next.

Salvatore grips the hair at the back of my head. "I've been obsessed with your mouth from the moment I saw you. Now open up and show me what it can do."

There's a bulge at the front of his pants and I reach up and touch him. So, that's what he feels like, thick and hard beneath the layers of fabric. I rub him back and forth, watching the pleasure flicker over his face. "Is this how you're going to shut me up for telling the truth? By shoving your cock in my mouth?"

"It's worth a fucking try." He unzips his pants, grips his cock and draws it out. With his other hand he pulls my hair, making me gasp. As soon as my mouth is open, he shoves himself inside.

"Let me tell you something," he growls, pumping his hips back and forth and making me gag. "If you wanted out of this marriage, you would have found a way by now."

I try to pull away so I can argue with him but he holds me tighter and fucks deeper.

"That's it, suck. Open your throat. You're a prisoner and you always will be. Not because I'm making you a prisoner. Because you *want* to be one."

I fight him harder but his grip on my hair is merciless. All I can do is focus on my breathing as tears leak from my eyes.

"God, I can't wait to hold you down and fuck you when you're as angry as this. I bet you're so…fucking…delicious." With each word he thrusts further into my mouth, and then he groans and his cock spasms. My mouth is flooded with his cum and I swallow him down before I choke.

He squeezes my throat and growls, "You're beautiful like your mother, and you're going to end up like her, too. That mouth of yours is going to be the end of you."

He lets me go, and I fall in a heap on the floor with my hand over my mouth, feeling like he's struck me across the face.

"Fuck you," I whisper, my shoulders shaking.

"I thought we were dishing out hard truths," he growls, tucking his shirt back in his pants and zipping them up. He smooths his hair and his jacket and casts one last look at me. "Goodbye, Chiara. I'll see you at the wedding."

I feel Mom's presence hovering over me, and her heart is breaking. This is what she died for, to see me brought to my knees by a man who can be crueler even than my murderous father.

I stare at the diamond ring on my finger. He'll see me at the wedding?

Over my dead body.

I get to my feet and wipe the tears from my face. As the front door slams, I walk out into the hall and downstairs to the kitchen. I've let most of this year pass in a blur of fear and confusion, but it's not too late to thwart Dad and Salvatore. I can defy them even with a chip in my neck and just a week until the wedding date.

Salvatore's given me one last chance.

Francesca, Stephan, and Violette look up in surprise as I burst into the kitchen.

The old cook wipes her hands on her apron and comes toward me. "Chiara? What's wrong?"

I pull my engagement ring off and hold it up, looking between all three of them. "I need to get a message to someone. Will any of you help me?"

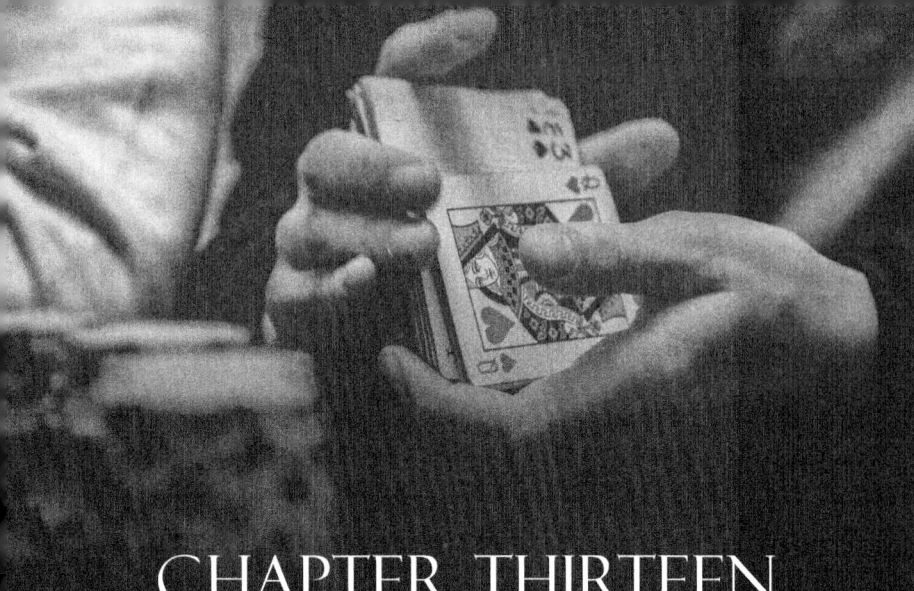

CHAPTER THIRTEEN

VINICIUS

"I need to see Mr. Ferragamo. The matter is urgent."

As I pass the young man leaning over the front desk practically begging to see Cassius, the concierge nods to me. He presses a button to call the elevator which will take me up to Cassius' penthouse.

"Please, just call Mr. Ferragamo and tell him I have a letter for him," the man pleads.

I keep walking, half listening to the exchange. Some random man isn't going to be able to speak with Cassius. I wonder what made him think he could.

"I'm sorry, who are you?" asks the concierge.

"It doesn't matter who I am, but if I don't see him then I fear what Mr. Fiore will do to her."

Fiore? Salvatore Fiore? And who's "her"? I slow to a stop. Then I turn around. It could be nothing, but I always enjoy making other people's business my business. You never know what you might find out.

"Who is the message from?" asks the concierge, who's rapidly losing his patience.

"I can't say, but it's very important that I speak to Mr. Ferragamo."

I stroll closer to this messenger and tap him on his shoulder. "Excuse me, I couldn't help but overhear. Is it possible that your mistress is a beautiful little blonde, about this tall?" I hold up my hand at chest height.

The man stares at me. "You're Vinicius Angeli, aren't you? A friend of Mr. Ferragamo's?"

I smile at him, showing him my teeth. "His best friend. How may I help you?"

The man glances around the lobby and then pulls me aside and whispers, "Miss Romano has a message for Mr. Ferragamo. It's a matter of life and death."

I smile broadly at him. "Say no more. I'll escort you up to the penthouse myself."

As we walk toward the elevator that the concierge called for me, I pull out my phone and make a call. "Come to Cassius' penthouse, now."

"Why the fuck—" begins an irate-sounding Lorenzo, but I hang up on him. The messenger gives me a puzzled glance but seems reluctant to question me when I seem to be giving him the one thing he wants.

As soon as the elevator doors close and we start to rise, I reach out and hit the emergency stop. "I'll take that message."

The man's eyes widen. "No, it's for Mr. Ferragamo. My instructions were to give it only to him."

The smile drops from my face. "I'm sorry. I didn't catch your name."

"Stephan. Stephan Russo."

"Stephan, did no one ever show you a map of this city? A *real* map of this city. Right at this moment we're standing on the slice that belongs to my dear friend Cassius Ferragamo, and he…"

I pinch the bridge of my nose. Normally I enjoy using nothing but a few words to get what I want. It's a game, watching the way color drains from someone's face without me needing to skirt anywhere close to a threat, but right now, the game doesn't feel fun. The message this man is holding has something to do with Chiara Romano and my patience has vaporized.

I hold out my hand. "Give me the message or I'll knock your fucking teeth out."

Stephan scrambles to do as I say, and he places an envelope and a black velvet box into my palm.

"Thank you," I say, and restart the elevator. I give the letter a cursory glance and shove it in my pocket, and then turn my attention to the velvet box. Inside is an exquisite diamond engagement ring, fit for a princess.

Or Coldlake's equivalent of a princess, Miss Chiara Romano.

"Salvatore always did have excellent taste in jewelry."

Stephan stares in horror as I put the ring back into the box and slip it into my pocket. "But—"

I pat his shoulder. "Don't get overexcited. I'll hang on to these, and you can give your message to Mr. Ferragamo."

"The letter *is* the message," he protests.

The elevator pings and opens directly into the penthouse. Cassius looks up from the sofa where he's reading on his tablet and raises his dark brows. He was expecting to see me, but he wasn't expecting our guest.

"Lorenzo's on his way. This man has something for us."

Stephan starts to say that his message is for Mr. Ferragamo, but Cassius closes his tablet and speaks over him.

"Why is Scava coming here?"

"I told you why. I'll have a vodka. Anything for you?" I ask, turning to Stephan, who shakes his head.

Scowling, Cassius disappears into the next room and comes back a moment later with two Grey Goose vodkas on the rocks. It's always Grey Goose at Cassius' penthouse and at his clubs. I take a mouthful, watching Stephan stare around at the enormous interior and the view of Coldlake through the floor-to-ceiling windows.

Five minutes later, the elevator doors slide open and Lorenzo strides in wearing a vicious glare and a white T-shirt spattered with blood. "I was in the middle of something."

Lorenzo's always in the middle of something. The man doesn't know how to relax. I nod at his shirt. "Who died?"

"No one yet, so fucking get on with it."

"Vodka?"

"*I said get on with it.*"

I look at Stephan. "Go on. Tell them what you told me about Chiara Romano."

At the sound of her name, the other two stop scowling and perk up. Lorenzo's tattooed arms have been crossed tightly over his bloodied chest, but now they loosen.

Stephan steps closer to Cassius. "Mr. Ferragamo, I came here tonight with a very important message from Miss Romano. She said I should only deliver it to you."

"It's Miss Romano's birthday today, isn't it?" Cassius murmurs, peering at the ice in his glass. He knows it's her birthday. Last year on this day we all met the blonde beauty, and at the end of the night we watched as her mother was murdered.

Cassius was the one who was covered in blood that night. There was blood and pool water all over Chiara, and he was the one to grab her when she tried to jump into the swimming pool after her mother. He walked her away from the edge of the pool and stayed close to her, fearing she might try it again.

Chiara was eerily calm. Shaking slightly, but totally silent.

We listened as Mayor Romano called the police and told them that he'd just found his wife dead in the swimming pool. Then he told the four of us to leave.

Chiara grabbed hold of Cassius, the man who'd awkwardly tried to comfort her after her father had just slit her mother's throat, and started screaming hysterically. "*Don't leave me. Don't leave me here alone with him.*"

Cassius prized her fingers from his arm and pushed her away. We all left before the police could arrive, Chiara's sobs echoing through the house. Standing by our cars, the four of us looked at each other, and at the bloody water soaking Cassius' shirt, and I knew we were thinking of the same four people.

Amalia.

Evelina.

Sienna.

And Ophelia.

"That was fucked up," Cassius seethed. He got into his SUV, slammed the door, and roared away.

Now here we are on the anniversary of that night, and Chiara Romano has something for us.

"Yes, it's her birthday," Stephan confirms. "Mr. Fiore came for dinner, and then after, Miss Romano had me come here with a message."

"Well, where is it?" Cassius snaps.

"Mr. Angeli took it from me in the elevator."

I take a mouthful of vodka. "I'm sorry?"

"The message, and the ring. You took them from me in the elevator."

"What ring?"

Stephan's face drains of color. "Miss Romano's ring. It's there, in your jacket."

I frown and put my hand in my pocket, and draw out the velvet box. "Oh, you mean this? I'd forgotten about this."

I throw the box across the room to Cassius, who catches it with a glare. Screwing with people is a habit I have no intention of breaking.

Cassius opens the box and nods appreciatively at the diamond ring. Then he shows it to Lorenzo and me.

I smile broadly. "An engagement ring, for us."

"No one's ever proposed to me before," Lorenzo says, and even Cassius laughs.

"The ring is for Mr. Ferragamo," Stephan points out, more confused than ever. "And you need to read the letter. I don't think she intended—"

Cassius speak over him. "When it comes to Miss Romano, anything that she gives one of us is for all of us."

Stephan's baffled expression tells me he doesn't understand, but it doesn't matter. He doesn't need to.

"Give him the letter," Stephan says to me.

"The what?"

The poor man is practically in tears. "The letter, the letter! You have her letter."

I push him toward the elevator. "It's time for you to go. Say thank you to your mistress for us. It really is a lovely present, and so thoughtful considering it's her birthday."

Stephan is still protesting when the elevator doors slide closed.

I turn to Cassius. "I've got the letter, but do we really care what it says?"

Cassius takes a thoughtful sip of vodka and gazes out the window at the night. A moment later, he holds out his hand, and I give it to him.

He reads it, and then crumples the letter into a ball with his fist and throws it aside. It bounces on the rug and skitters under the sofa.

"No, we don't care."

Lorenzo takes my vodka from me and drains the glass. Suddenly, he doesn't seem interested in hurrying off to whatever blood-soaked activity he left behind.

He pins us with his electric blue gaze. "We know what we're going to do, don't we?"

I nod slowly. "We do. But when, and how?"

Cassius glances into his glass and heads for the kitchen. "More vodka. I think we're going to need the bottle."

CHAPTER FOURTEEN

CHIARA

I blink, and suddenly I'm staring at the reflection of myself in an expensive satin wedding dress, my hair pinned up and my face carefully accented with makeup.

That's what it feels like, anyway. The morning of my wedding has dawned and my bridesmaids are here in their pastel gowns. I've spent the last night I ever will under this roof, and tonight Salvatore will carry me over the threshold into his home.

"I have to sit down." I collapse onto the end of the bed and put my head between my knees.

Candace rubs my back. "Nerves, poor thing."

It's not nerves. It's humiliation and disappointment that I've been rejected by the one man in the city I thought would help me.

If he ever scares you or does anything you don't like, I'm here. I'm nothing like him.

Bambina, *there's danger at every turn in this city. Sometimes three is better than one. Have a think about that.*

Cassius Ferragamo is full of shit. Was a four-million-dollar engagement ring not incentive enough to help me when he offered on two separate occasions to be my knight in shining armor? The first time was at the fountain the night I got drunk on tequila shots and he saw the tearstains on my face. He knew how cruel Salvatore could be. The second was at the deserted warehouse the night I was nearly raped and murdered.

But it was neither of those occasions that made me reach out to him a week ago. It was what he did exactly one year earlier on my seventeenth, right after Mom was murdered. I lost it completely, screaming and crying and grabbing the person nearest me and begging them not to leave me alone with Mom's murderer.

That man was Cassius Ferragamo.

As I sobbed hysterically and begged him not to go, he murmured words only I could hear. *I'm sorry, I can't help you tonight. You have to wait. I promise I'll be back.*

He would help me, but not yet.

And I believed him.

I take a deep breath and sit up. It's just another hard lesson I had to learn. Fathers are murderers, fiancés are cruel, and knights in shining armor will take your four-million-dollar diamond ring and run. I know it's a four-million-dollar ring because that's what my father bellowed at me when I told him I lost it.

You lost Salvatore Fiore's four-million-dollar engagement ring?

I can only imagine what he would have said if I told him the truth. *Actually, I used it to bribe Salvatore's former best friend to smuggle me out of the country, and he ignored me.*

I pull the lace veil over my face and let my bridesmaids escort me downstairs to Dad and the waiting wedding car.

Before I get inside, I turn around and look at the house that was my home for seventeen years, and my prison for one. For a second I think I see the outline of someone standing in one of the upstairs windows, her face in shadow.

I'm sorry, Mom. You died for nothing.

At the church, I stand in the vestibule next to Dad, bouquet in hand, while Rosaline, Sophia, and Candace spread out the train of my wedding gown. Organ music plays from within.

There's a sudden, loud bang from inside the church and voices rise in confusion.

"Wait here," Dad says, and pushes through the doors. I only get a quick look inside but people are milling about, and I wonder if something's fallen over inside the church. Is that smoke drifting through the air?

My bridesmaids gasp in shock and hurry forward to see for themselves. As the door closes behind them, I feel the air pressure change around me. I whirl around and see that two tall figures dressed head to toe in black and wearing black ski masks are looming over me.

The taller of the two men in black smiles, and I recognize those deep brown eyes. "*Bambina*. I told you I'd be back."

I asked Cassius Ferragamo for help, but as he bears down on me, the black sweater he's wearing stretched tight across his chest and his leather gloved hands poised to grab me, he knows this isn't the help I was hoping for.

But he's doing it anyway.

I brandish my bouquet of flowers like a weapon. "Get away from me!"

I back away, toward the door into the church. There's a leaner man next to him, almost as tall, that has to be Vinicius. My high heel catches the edge of a tile, and I stumble. The satin dress drags across the floor, weighing me down.

From inside the church, I hear Dad yell, "*You*. What are you doing here?"

There are shrieks and shouts of alarm from within the church and the sound of pounding feet. Cassius scoops me up in his arms like I'm nothing just as Lorenzo Scava, dressed in black combat pants and a polo, shoves open the door and is framed against the huge gold cross at the far end of the aisle. Soft light from the stained-glass window falls across his powerful shoulders.

He's got his ski mask pulled up, revealing his face. As he sees me pinned against Cassius, his mouth curves into a triumphant smile that freezes my blood.

Over his shoulder I see Salvatore standing at the altar at the far end of the church. He sees me in Cassius' arms.

His mouth falls open in horror. And he starts to run.

Seeing the fear on his face, my heart lurches. I've made a huge mistake. I should never have asked Salvatore's enemies for help. My three assailants pause just long enough to give my groom, Dad, and everyone inside the church a clear view of what they're doing, and then they start to run outside, taking me with them.

"Salvatore!" I scream as Lorenzo lets go of the heavy door and it starts to close. My fiancé is running as fast as he can toward me, an expression of horror and fury on his face. He's not going to make it in time. I know it before I even finish screaming his name.

Lorenzo's black Mercedes 4WD is waiting by the curb, all the doors open, and Cassius bundles me into the back seat. I stare desperately out the window with my hands pressed against the glass as Salvatore bursts out of the doors. He's so far away, but he runs as fast as he can, arms pumping.

Lorenzo throws the car keys to Vinicius and gets in on my other side. "You drive. I need to check her over."

All the doors slam, Vinicius steps on the gas and we roar away from the church. My throat burns with despair as we accelerate away and Salvatore becomes smaller and smaller until he finally gives up.

Cassius is holding me tight against him and I wrench myself from side to side. "Let go of me. Don't touch me!"

Lorenzo grasps my wrist and wrenches me around to face him. "Where's the GPS device?"

The microchip. The little piece of silicone in the back of my neck that I've hated for the past ten months is actually going to do me some good.

"No answer, princess? Then we're doing this the hard way. Cassius, hold her arms." Lorenzo pulls off my shoes and starts to feel his way up my calves while Cassius holds my wrists with a vise-like grip. I struggle with all my strength but it does me no good. My bridal bouquet slips from my fingers and falls to the floor of the car.

"Nothing here," Lorenzo mutters. He reaches beneath my skirt and I try to kick him in the gut. He grabs my ankle and pins it against the seat with his hip.

"Get your hands off me!"

Lorenzo ignores me, takes hold of one of my stockings and rips it off my leg. "Want to keep fighting me, princess? I'm going for your panties next."

"I'll kill you," I seethe. He knows it's an empty threat as much as I do.

Lorenzo pulls out his knife. "This dress is coming off. Keep fighting me, and you'll have me carving chunks off your body as well."

My eyes latch onto that knife. It looks evil in his grip, the honed edge glinting with malice.

I shrink back against Cassius' chest. "Please, don't."

"Then tell me where it is," he growls, grabbing my chin and forcing me to look at him.

There's something preternatural in his cold blue gaze, like he can see right to my soul.

"It's in the back of my neck," I mutter. "How do you even know about that?"

"I've got eyes and ears all over this town." Lorenzo puts the knife away, sits forward, and reaches for me. Cassius' chest is as hard as a plank of wood against my back as Lorenzo strokes my nape, a mocking smile on his lips. They come dangerously close to mine. "It would be a shame not to kiss the bride on her wedding day."

"Fuck you," I whisper.

"Not right now, I'm busy." His fingers press and prod until he finds the tiny lump on the back of my neck. "I can feel it. Vinicius, take us to the compound. I can't do this here."

Vinicius turns the wheel. "On my way."

Lorenzo stays where he is, face too close to mine. Crowded between the two men, I can feel both their hearts pounding. "I asked Cassius to help me, not all of you to kidnap me on my wedding day."

Lorenzo wraps his hands around my waist. Tight. Possessive. "We are helping. You're welcome, princess."

From the front seat, Vinicius laughs.

Cassius digs inside a pocket and pulls out my diamond engagement ring on the tip of his forefinger. He holds it up to the light. "We've never been proposed to before. So romantic, *bambina*. We accept."

He takes my hand and forces the ring back onto my finger. I stare at it, my mouth going dry. "That's *not* why I sent you the ring. Didn't you read my letter? I wanted Cassius to get me out of the country. Just Cassius. This has nothing to do with the rest of you."

Vinicius pulls off his ski mask as he drives. "When you ask for assistance from men like us, you don't get to be picky about how you get it."

I'm pressed even tighter between the two men as we veer onto the freeway and Lorenzo's weight crushes me against Cassius. They keep me pinned between them the whole drive.

Ten minutes or so later, we pull up to a property with high concrete walls. A heavy black gate opens, revealing several men in black combat gear holding on to snarling German shepherds. Vinicius turns the car into the property and I get a glimpse of a large and imposing house before we're speeding into an underground garage.

Will Dad and Salvatore be able to find me down here? The signal probably won't even work, and even if it does, Lorenzo is going to smash the tracker as soon as he cuts it out of my neck.

Vinicius parks in a bay and Cassius gets out, scoops me up in his arms, and carries me. Lorenzo leads the way down a long concrete hallway and then through a door. I'm put down just inside, shoved forward, and the door is slammed behind me.

I stare around the room, my blood roaring in my ears. There are stainless-steel tables, medical lamps, and shelves of glass and plastic bottles. The floor slopes down toward drains. It's a cross between a morgue and an operating room, and it's giving me a huge case of the creeps. I'm alone in here with the most dangerous man I've ever met.

Lorenzo snaps black latex gloves on over his tattooed hands and points to one of the metal tables, which is roughly human-sized. "Sit."

I back away, not daring to take my eyes off him. "Don't you dare come near me, you psycho."

Lorenzo gives me a sly smile. "Trust me. I'm a doctor."

"You're joking. Someone gave you a medical degree?"

He goes to a glass-fronted cabinet and places things on a metal tray. A vial of liquid. A hypodermic needle. Gauze. A kidney dish and, most terrifying of all, a scalpel. "Oh, I didn't bother with the exams."

"Then how do you know what you're doing?" What the hell *is* he doing?

He places the tray down, sticks the hypodermic needle in the vial and draws back clear fluid. Then he advances on me, brandishing the needle. "I guess we'll find out. Give me your arm."

I back away around the room, my feet bare on the cold concrete and the satin dress dragging across the floor. "Not in a million years."

"Listen, moron. I'll happily cut you without an anesthetic, but Cassius asked me to play nice. So, give me your arm."

"What is that? I'm allergic to about a thousand things." I'm allergic to nothing, but he doesn't know that.

Lorenzo's gaze narrows, but he keeps coming. "It's a local anesthetic. What medications are you allergic to?"

"Anesthetics. All of them."

The longer I stall, the better chance Dad and Salvatore have of finding me, but what miserable choices these are. Stay kidnapped for God knows what purpose, or go home and marry my despicable fiancé.

Better the devil I know, I guess.

Lorenzo shakes his head. "I don't have time for this. I've got EpiPens if you go into shock. Give me your fucking arm."

"If you think I'm letting you stick me with anything—"

Lorenzo holds up his fist. "Two choices. I punch you in the face until you pass out, or you start cooperating. Either way, I'm sticking you with this needle."

He will punch me. I can see it in his eyes. So much for the Hippocratic Oath, first, do no harm. Maybe they only make you swear that if you pass your exams.

"Fine," I mutter, and hold out my arm.

"Sit on the table. I'm not catching you if you faint."

It creeps me out to go anywhere near his horrible metal tables but I clamber up onto one and perch on the edge. Lorenzo grasps my wrist and pulls a rubber tourniquet around my upper arm.

"Pump your fist open and closed. Let's see those pretty veins."

I do as I'm told and a thick blue vein stands out at the bend of my elbow. I watch him closely, eyeing the needle in his black gloved hand. His blue eyes are burning bright.

"Most people don't watch this part," he says, hovering the needle over my arm.

I've never been afraid of needles or blood and I want to see exactly what this psycho is doing to me. "I'll watch every little thing you do to me, *doctor*."

As the needle slips into my vein and he depresses the plunger, something occurs to me. "If the chip is in the back of my neck, why are you putting a local anesthetic in my bloodstream? Shouldn't it go in my neck?"

Lorenzo doesn't look at me as he tosses the hypodermic aside. "No kidding, idiot."

My mouth falls open in horror. "Wait, what did you—" A second later, dizziness washes over me. I stare at Lorenzo while he smirks coldly at me and watches me fall in a heap on the table. I wait to pass out, but I don't. I try to sit up but my arms are numb and heavy.

I'm wide awake.

I just can't move.

Lorenzo hoists my legs up onto the table, braces his hands on either side of my head and gives me an evil smile.

My mouth works. I can still move my jaw, but my tongue feels thick. "What are you doing to me?"

Lorenzo lifts my hand and then lets it drop with a thud. "Apparently, whatever the fuck I want."

Anger and despair overwhelm me. I stopped fighting for one second. Just one second. Why did I ever believe he was telling the truth? Tears fill my eyes and run down my temples.

Lorenzo leans over me and licks one of the tearstains, and says softly, "The other two want to play with you, but I knew you were worthless the night I met you. If it were up to me, I wouldn't bother taking this chip out. I'd drive you out to the desert and use you as target practice, and then let Salvatore find your body. I'd give you a head start so I could chase you. Maybe you'd live. But probably you wouldn't. Then we'd see how many deals he can make with your father behind our backs."

I see it burning in his eyes: his desire for revenge for losing to Salvatore, and he's going to get it in pounds of my flesh.

Footsteps sound along the corridor outside and Cassius opens the door. In a cold, flat voice, he asks, "Have you got that chip out of her yet?"

"It's coming," Lorenzo calls back without moving, and the door slams closed again.

More tears leak from the corners of my eyes. "Do you always do what the others tell you to do? You're like a trained dog."

As quick as a snake, Lorenzo slaps me across the face, turning my head to one side. Pain blossoms in my cheek and I can't turn my head back.

"Mouthy little bitch. We'll see how long that lasts," he growls.

I can hear him clanging around with various instruments. The next thing I know he's rolled me onto my side and he's holding a scalpel in front of my face. "I was going to use this to get that chip out of your neck, but seeing as you have a poisonous mouth, I'll use…" He switches the scalpel with what he has in his other hand. It's a much bigger blade, but it's not the honed edge that makes my heart pound.

It's Lorenzo's knife. *That* knife. The one Dad used to kill Mom.

"You don't like that, do you?"

"Please don't," I whimper.

"It's too late for please. Next time, don't be a bitch."

I can feel Lorenzo's fingers on the back of my neck, and then a pulling at my skin with something sharp. I can't feel any physical pain as he cuts into me, but I want to curl up and die, the pain in my heart is so overwhelming.

"There it is. Jensen!" Lorenzo suddenly roars, and another door opens on the other side of the room. A man wearing motorcycle leathers comes over to the table and Lorenzo passes him the chip. "Take this for a ride about the city for a few hours and then dump it in the lake."

"Yes, boss." Jensen tucks the chip into his pocket, takes a bored glance at the bleeding girl in the wedding dress, and heads out.

Lorenzo wipes something cold over the back of my neck and slaps on some gauze. Then he rolls me onto my back. "What a waste of time. You'd better hope you keep the other two amused because as soon as they're bored, I'll slit your throat."

He doesn't look at me as he tidies up his medical equipment and his face is a blank, inhuman mask. Now that his "fun" is over, he's switched off completely.

I stare at his back, filled with hatred over what he's done to me, my hands curling into angry fists.

My hands.

I can move them.

"Lorenzo," I call, but he ignores me. "Can I ask you a question?"

He pulls off his black latex gloves with a snap and doesn't bother turning around. I stare at his muscular back, hatred threading every vein of my body.

"That night. My seventeenth birthday. Did you hand him your knife?"

The knife that killed my mother. Did Lorenzo give it to my father, or did Dad take it from him?

Lorenzo freezes and raises his head. I can't see his face, but I can hear the cruel smile in his voice as he says, "What do you think?"

I grab the scalpel lying in the kidney dish like a dagger, lurch to my unsteady feet and bring it down between his shoulder blades with a scream.

Lorenzo whips around and grabs my wrist. The scalpel blade is an inch from his cheek.

"Let me go! *I hate you.*" I grapple in his grip but he's too strong.

"Don't attack if you don't know you'll kill," he growls, and sinks his teeth into the fleshy part of my forearm.

I scream in pain and the scalpel falls from my fingers.

Lorenzo goes on biting me, his eyes filled with rage and his jaw locked around my arm. I go on screaming, expecting it will bring the others running, but the door stays closed. He could be killing me and they don't care.

I'm on the verge of passing out from the pain when Lorenzo releases me. I fall into a heap at his feet, my legs like rubber from the drugs.

The scalpel is lying a foot away on the concrete and Lorenzo bends down and snatches it up. Twisting the glinting object in front of my face, he seethes, "The fuck is this? Don't stab with a scalpel. Steal it, hide it, and creep into my room at night and slash my throat." He jabs a forefinger deep into the side of my neck. "Right here. You feel that? That's the jugular vein, two centimeters in. Cut that with this little blade and I'll be unconscious within a minute. Even if I get my hands around your throat, I'll pass out before I can strangle you to death."

Lorenzo's hand slips around my throat. He stares at my lips, which I've bitten until they're swollen this past hour. He runs the pad of his thumb over the indentations from my teeth as if he's fascinated by them. As if each one is precious. His thumb swipes across my lips again and I pant against his touch, struggling to breathe as he grips my throat. Lorenzo's cold, pale cheeks darken. Reddening with blood.

He stands up suddenly and throws aside the scalpel, as if disgusted I haven't tried to kill him properly.

"Vinicius, Cassius!" he roars at the door. "Get this fucking idiot out of my sight."

A moment later, Vinicius is bending over me and hauling me

to my feet. He'll answer this asshole's orders and not my screams. Before I can say a word, he slaps a piece of duct tape over my mouth and covers my head with a pillowcase. He tries to walk me out of the room but thanks to Lorenzo's drugs I can't walk properly, so he hoists me over his shoulder like I'm a sack of potatoes.

I'm slung into the back of a car and we're on the move again. I try to count the turns and the passing minutes, but my head is spinning and the back of my neck stings. The car is parked, and someone helps me walk.

The ground beneath my feet lurches, and a moment later my ears pop. We're in an elevator and we're going up. It takes a long time so I assume this must be a skyscraper. My heart leaps. A skyscraper is full of people and security.

I'm led out of the elevator and across carpeted floors. Someone pulls the pillowcase from my head. Vinicius. He rips the duct tape from my mouth without looking me in the eye. We're in a bedroom. I open my mouth to ask him what's happening, but he leaves, slamming the door behind him.

I turn around slowly. A bed. A chest of drawers. A small bathroom through a door. The windows are floor to ceiling along one wall and I hurry over, wondering if there's any way I could signal to someone. I recognize from the buildings that we're in downtown Coldlake, but there's nothing close enough for me to hope to signal to someone for help. I can make out people far below on the street, and they crawl like ants, oblivious to me far above them.

Beyond the door to my room, I can't hear anything. Either the men have left, or they're in some distant part of the apartment.

We're so high up that I suppose this could be a penthouse. Cassius' apartment, or maybe Vinicius'? The horrible place they took me to first was probably Lorenzo's.

I sink down onto the bed, feeling my wedding dress crumple around me. There are twelve purple and red teeth marks on my arm, six at the top and six at the bottom, a grisly reminder that if I'm going to try and kill one of these men, I better know that I'll succeed.

After a while, the adrenalin hyping me up ebbs away, and I realize how uncomfortable I am in my wedding dress. I go over to the drawers and start going through them. There are sweaters. Joggers. T-shirts. Denim shorts. Socks. Underwear. All in roughly my size, so I know they planned this. No shoes, I notice. There's nothing in this room that could help me run away or be used as a weapon, unless I want to try strangling one of the men to death with my panties. I don't think I'd get far, though.

I shed my wedding dress and bridal lingerie and pull on underwear, a T-shirt, and some joggers.

Then I go to the window and stare out. I wonder what Dad and Salvatore are doing. Running around town after Jensen on his motorcycle, I suppose. The last thing I want is to be kept captive here, but I can't bring myself to wish that I'll be rescued by them, either.

I think of my bridesmaids, and how terrified they must be for me, and I realize that I've grown attached to Rosaline, Candace, and Sophia. They've been there for me this year while I've struggled to make sense of this unfamiliar world. I wish they were here now, if only so I could hear them curse out Cassius, Vinicius, and Lorenzo for stealing me from their beloved Salvatore.

Hours later, I get up and go to the bathroom. My stomach rumbles and my eyes burn with exhaustion. I drink from the tap to fill my belly and splash water onto my face.

It's getting dark outside, and so I crawl into bed and pull the covers up over my head. There's only silence around me, and it's deafening. I don't know how I'm going to relax when I don't know if someone's going to charge into my room and take me to another location or do something even worse.

But somehow, after laying still for a long time, I fall asleep.

When I wake up, the light in the room has changed. It's morning, and sunshine is streaming through the window. I sit up and listen, but hear nothing. My stomach growls, sounding loud in the silence.

I use the bathroom and drink more water, and then my eyes land on the door handle. Is that door actually locked, or did I just assume it was?

I try the door and it opens easily. I stare at the hallway beyond, frozen with shock. That's crazy, and I feel stupid for not trying the door last night.

I'm greeted with more silence, so I start edging along the carpet, poised to run if anyone jumps out at me. The hall opens into a huge, sunny living room with expensive modern furniture in neutral colors.

The apartment is filled with the sort of silence and stillness that tells me I'm alone, but I search every room that I can get into just the same. A few doors are locked, but otherwise I'm free to roam the penthouse. The elevator doesn't respond when I press the button, but I never expected it would. If there are stairs, then the door to reach them is locked.

Seeing as I can't escape, I turn to my next pressing need: food.

The kitchen is huge, but there's nothing in the refrigerator except sparkling water, and nothing in the freezer except for Grey Goose vodka. Cassius must eat out all the time. The apartment feels like it belongs to the big, dark-haired Italian man.

I find two biscotti in a box by the coffee machine and eat the rock-hard pieces, chasing them down with some sparkling water. I consider the vodka briefly, but since my misadventures with tequila, I haven't touched alcohol. Now doesn't seem the best time to start again.

I spend the rest of the day wandering around the apartment, trying to fathom what I'm doing here and learning more about the man who's holding me captive. Cassius has a taste for modern art prints and history books.

It's growing dark outside when a rushing sound fills the air, like something big getting closer and closer. I'm lying on one of the sofas with a bottle of sparkling water and staring at the glittering lights of the city, when suddenly the elevator pings and the doors slide open. I glimpse more than one man as I jump to my feet.

Shit. Shit. Shit.

There's a bathroom halfway down the corridor and as it's closer than "my" room, I dive inside just as Cassius calls, "Chiara? Come here."

"Screw you," I mutter, and slam the door behind me. My heart is racing so fast that it feels like it's going to explode out of my chest. I can hear them out there, talking, Cassius and at least two others.

The back of my neck prickles and I realize it's the Band-Aid that Lorenzo stuck over the cut he gave me. I prod at it for a moment, and then peel it off.

I'm standing with my back to the mirror trying to peer over my shoulder at my own neck when the door slams open, and I nearly jump out of my skin. Lorenzo glares at me from the doorway, and then sees the bandage with dried blood on it in my hand.

"What are you doing with that?" he snaps.

"Trying to see how badly you cut me, you psycho."

He turns me around, grabs my hair in his fist and pulls it up, inspecting the mark. I watch his reflection in the mirror as he peers at me. The hard line of his jaw. That narrowed blue gaze. The ink decorating his fingers that disappears into his sleeves. If he has tattooed hands then he must have tattoos everywhere. All over his body.

"You made a mess of me, didn't you?" I accuse.

"It's healing fine. What are you so worried about?"

His bare hand is on the nape of my neck and he's standing so close I can feel the heat from his body. I wish my skin would crawl where he's touching me, not tingle.

"I'm worried because you butchered me with a hunting knife!"

A cold smile spreads over his face and he strokes the nape of my neck as he meets my eyes in the mirror. The tingles become a jolt. "Such a little drama queen. I barely touched you." Lorenzo lets me go. "Get the fuck out there. I've got shit to do tonight."

He pushes me out of the bathroom and toward the lounge where I can hear the rustle of paper bags and Cassius and Vinicius talking. I suppose they were all working today, Cassius doing nightclub stuff and Lorenzo and Vinicius…I don't know what they get up to. Probably nothing legal.

"What shit to do? What do you do, anyway?"

"Organ harvesting," Lorenzo says, without missing a beat as we walk over to the sofas where Vinicius and Cassius are unpacking boxes of takeout and chopsticks.

I can't tell if Lorenzo's joking or not. The fact that he's got so much medical equipment gives me the creeps.

He palms my lower back like a lover and murmurs, "How are those kidneys of yours? Fully functioning?"

I push his arm away. "Don't touch me, asshole."

"In your dreams, bitch," he replies, and shoves me onto the U-shaped sofa. He sits down as well and I move around it until I'm four feet away from him.

The coffee table is loaded with Chinese takeout boxes and a savory aroma fills the air. My stomach growls in response, and Vinicius smiles as he opens a box and holds it out to me.

"I heard that. Egg roll?"

There are half a dozen golden, fried egg rolls in the box. As hungry as I am, I'm too freaked out to move.

Vinicius shakes the box at me. "Egg roll? No? Suit yourself." He takes one from the box and bites into it. The wrapper crackles and a few flakes fall onto the carpet at his feet, and my mouth waters.

"*Mio Dio*, you're making a mess," Cassius tuts, and shoves a plate at him. Yep, it's definitely Cassius' apartment.

"What am I doing here? What do you all want with me?"

Cassius raises heavy-lidded eyes to me, but turns his attention back to the food. He opens an enormous bag of prawn crackers and empties them into a bowl. I stare at them. I love prawn crackers and the weird way they stick to your tongue. Adjacent to me, Lorenzo eats Singapore noodles straight from the box, his eyes never leaving my face.

Cassius makes up a plate with fried rice, noodles, and chicken stir-fry, adds a pair of chopsticks and holds it out to me.

I stare at the plate, and then at him. I'm supposed to just eat with them like being kidnapped is normal?

"I don't understand what's happening." I point at Lorenzo but keep my gaze locked on Cassius. "You let that bastard molest me and cut me up. I'm not going to sit here and eat Chinese food with you all."

"You are a little stray cat with nowhere to go," he says in his thick accent. "You should be grateful we don't lock you in a cage and throw you scraps."

"What do you mean a stray? You *kidnapped* me."

Vinicius digs in a box of Szechuan chicken with his chopsticks. "We rescued you from a dangerous life. If it weren't for us you'd be married to Salvatore by now."

Sure, they're so altruistic. The reality is they sabotaged my wedding to prevent their ex-friend from getting any advantage over them with my father.

"You didn't want to marry Salvatore and your father would have killed you for disobeying him. Be thankful you're here and eat." Cassius offers me the plate again, but when I don't take it he sits back and starts to eat it himself. He and Vinicius continue their conversation and my stomach growls loudly.

Eat. Just like that, as if everything's fine now. I gaze at the food, recognizing the name of my favorite Chinese restaurants on the boxes. Mom and I used to eat lunch there after a morning of shopping because she loved their soup dumplings so much.

A pang goes through me at the memory, and I find myself looking around for some. "Are there any soup dumplings?"

I don't expect anyone to pay me any attention, but Lorenzo reaches inside a paper bag and pulls out a plastic box steamed up on the inside. I reach for it, but he pulls it out of my reach. I was expecting him to do something like that, though, and I don't react.

"If you really wanted to screw with me, you'd dump them all in the trash. Soup dumplings were my mother's favorite."

He chews for a moment, and then hands them over. "It's no fun when you hand me your torment on a silver platter."

As I peel back the plastic lid, fragrant steam rises around my face and I close my eyes and breathe in the aroma of pork and ginger. Lunch with Mom. No cares except for returning a dress that doesn't fit or wondering if we have enough time for dessert before Mom's next appointment. With a pair of chopsticks, I pick up a dumpling and shove the whole thing into my mouth. As I bite into the soft wrapper and meatball, the broth inside fills my mouth and I close my eyes in bliss. Mom would always order soup dumplings and let me eat some of hers while I tucked into Shanghai fried noodles with sliced beef.

When I open my eyes, all three of the men are staring at me.

"What? I like soup dumplings."

A few minutes later, Cassius stands up to fetch a bottle of wine and glasses and sees I've eaten all the soup dumplings. He pats my cheek as he sits down. "Good girl."

Good girl. I wonder if that's a trick he learned from managing his club girls and strippers, a little bit of praise to keep them in line. To my surprise, he passes me a glass of wine along with the other two, and a bowl of noodles and some fresh chopsticks.

The white wine is cold and smells like apricots. Infinitely more appealing than tequila, and not dry like champagne, so I take a sip.

"How are things at the compound?" Vinicius asks Lorenzo.

"Almost empty. Things are quiet on the streets right now."

The compound. That must be where Lorenzo lives. I keep my eyes on my noodles as I eat and pretend not to listen to their conversation. Sooner or later, I'll hear something that will help me get out of here. An escape route. A bargaining chip. These men are only out for what they can get.

I can feel Lorenzo's sharp gaze on the side of my neck. If I can't find a way out of here soon, I'll probably end up with my throat slit.

"I'm sure you'll have your hands full now that our little guest has been taken," Cassius says.

Lorenzo swears under his breath, as if whatever consequences he and Cassius are envisioning are all my fault.

An hour later, the men are still talking and have opened another bottle of wine. They speak in jargon only they understand and it feels too awkward to go on sitting there. I gather up the leftovers and take them to the refrigerator as an excuse to leave, and then head toward the room I slept in last night.

As I'm passing a door, two hands grab me and drag me into a darkened room. I'm shoved up against a wall. The light from the hall glints on strands of blond hair.

Lorenzo.

"We're on the same page, you and me," he growls, pushing his face close to mine. "Neither of us know what the fuck you're doing here. The other two've had a hard-on for you for the past year. I don't know why they're not getting the hell on with it."

Getting on with screwing me. The night of my seventeenth birthday, Lorenzo seemed as interested in getting into my underwear as the others were. Actually, he's the only one who *did* get into my underwear, ripping it away and sliding the hilt of his knife against me.

"I thought you—" But I stop myself before it sounds like I'm trying to talk him into having sex with me.

"You thought I wanted you too?" He laughs. "I'd rather fuck a rotting corpse than a scrawny virgin like you. You were useless to me once your father decided Salvatore was going to marry you."

His words that night come back to me. *I don't want anything from your father, or from you. I just like to win. Once I marry you, I'll probably slit your throat on our wedding night.*

Lorenzo releases me. "Keep out of my way. Better yet, keep out of my sight."

"Gladly," I fling at him as I shove him away. "The thought of you looking at me, let alone touching me, makes me want to throw up."

I feel his eyes boring into my back as I walk down the hall. I don't know what's worse, Cassius babying me or Lorenzo's venom. At least with Lorenzo I know what to expect. Pure hatred, and a violent end.

The next day I wake up to an empty apartment. I spend the morning trying to find a phone or a device that will let me send an email or log on to my social media, but Cassius has been thorough about removing anything I might access. I watch TV and eat leftover Chinese food, finding it ironic that it's day three of being kidnapped and I'm bored already.

In the afternoon I go back to my room for a nap and sleep for a few hours. It's dark when I wake up and stare at the ceiling. More leftovers and TV, and then back to bed, I suppose? I can't hear any voices in the apartment so I assume the men are out extorting or gambling or beating someone up.

As I walk into the lounge, Cassius enters from the other side, and I suck in a breath. He's fresh from the shower with a white towel knotted low on his hips and he's drying his black curls with another.

His eyes widen as he sees me staring at him, and he slowly lowers his hand.

"*Bambina*. I want to talk to you." He sits down on the sofa and indicates the spot next to him.

I stay where I am, excruciatingly self-conscious about being in the same room as a semi-naked man. Cassius is just so big, and he lounges on the sofa like a king. I try to look everywhere but at him. "Don't you, uh, want to put on some clothes?"

"Sit down."

I remember what happened the last time I sat too close to Cassius, and I perch on a cushion several feet away.

Cassius' dark eyes flicker with annoyance. "Chiara, you're trapped in here with me and I have a nasty temper. Did I say sit there?"

Goddammit. I move a little closer.

As soon as he can reach me, Cassius scoops an arm around my waist and pulls me onto his lap. I sit astride him, my hands pressed against his bare chest and frozen in fear, waiting for him to do something horrible. His hands capture my waist, holding me securely.

And he just watches me.

I stare back. At his short, neat beard. Those deep brown eyes of his. His chest is damp, and a droplet of water rolls from his collarbone down his muscles and gets lost among the black hairs on his chest.

He's watching me look at him, getting used to all his bare skin and muscles. Even though he's nearly twice my age, he's kind of sexy and he knows it, but not in an obnoxious way, like Vinicius. His lap is large and warm and his fingers ever so slightly massage my lower back.

"I thought you wanted to talk," I whisper, and my voice comes out huskier than I'd like it to be.

"Do you have everything you need here?"

His deep voice reverberates beneath my fingertips. I pull my hands away, but he reaches up and puts them back on his chest, not breaking eye contact.

Kind of sexy?

Dangerously sexy.

"No, I don't. I don't know what I'm doing here. What do you

want from me?"

"We're trying something."

"You and me?"

Cassius shifts me higher in his lap so my thighs are hugging his hips. "All four of us."

These guys have been dropping hints about *sharing* and *three is better than one* for the past year. I'm not so naïve that I don't know people have threesomes and group sex, but is that really what they're interested in?

"I don't understand."

"Some years ago, after an experience that caused some..." He hesitates, trying to find the right word, "Damage, we decided we wanted to try something. The four of us. One woman. But we never found the right someone."

My mouth falls open. "Please tell me you're just making conversation and this has nothing to do with me."

One of Cassius' perfectly groomed brows quirks.

"You all want a...wife?"

"Closer than a wife, and not so traditional."

My nose wrinkles in disgust. "A sex slave?"

"Nothing so unwilling. A woman the four of us could share. That we could all protect. All cherish. In this life, having too many things you care about is hazardous to your health. And hers."

"So that's me? I hate to break it to you, but I'm not feeling very cherished."

He muses on that for a moment. "We didn't mean for it to be you, but things in our lives don't always unfold in predictable ways."

"Here I am, so you may as well have sex with me? How flattering. I'm not interested, so let me go."

"You asked me for help, and I'm helping you. I let you go, and you'll end up dead. You know I'm right."

"What about Salvatore?" I ask desperately. He won't want me dead just because I've been kidnapped, will he?

"Why? Did you fall for him?" There's an edge to his voice and I sense we're on dangerous ground discussing his ex-friend.

"Of course not."

But pain blossoms in my chest as I remember Salvatore's face as his ex-friends stole me at the church. I didn't *fall* for him. I grew to like him a little, but he spoiled that the night of my eighteenth birthday.

You're beautiful like your mother, and you're going to end up like her, too. That mouth of yours is going to be the end of you.

If I feel nothing for Salvatore, why does that hurt so much? "What happened between the four of you? He wouldn't tell me anything except that you weren't friends anymore."

Cassius holds up a long forefinger. "Rule number one. No talking about that *pezzo di merda*." Piece of shit.

"I have rules?"

"Yes."

"That's ridiculous. I'm already your prisoner."

He grasps both my wrists behind my back and yanks my T-shirt up. I'm not wearing a bra because none of them fit properly, and Cassius slaps his hand across my nipple.

I yelp in pain. "Ow! What was that for?"

"Talking back. Which brings me to rule number two. No talking back. Rule number three. No trying to escape."

He slides his thumb over my nipple and I brace myself for him to tug it viciously, but he doesn't. He rubs my nipple firmly in a way that makes heat dart through me.

Cassius' voice grows husky. "Rule four. Do as you're told at all times, by all of us, or I'll punish you."

My breath hitches at his touch. "So, if I'm good you say *good girl*, and if I'm bad you'll punish me?"

"Sì, *bambina*." He squeezes my breasts in his hand and my head tips back. Asshole.

"Can I try to kill Lorenzo again?"

I expect him to smack his hand over my nipple again, but to my surprise, Cassius laughs, a deep, rich sound. The vibrations travel from my nipples down to my pussy that's pressed tightly against him.

"What's life without a little unpredictability? Just remember that he'll probably kill you first. I'd rather you didn't die yet."

"Yet?"

"You like playing with fire, *bambina*. You nearly died several times this year and it's only thanks to us and Salvatore that you're still breathing."

He means that Geak guy who nearly killed me. Probably my father too, come to think of it. "I wasn't in any danger until you all came into my life."

"We're here now. Let us worry about the danger. You just follow the rules."

"What if I don't?"

He raises his hand to slap my nipple again and I quickly say,

"Okay, okay! I get the message."

"What are your rules?"

"No talking about Salvatore. No talking back. No trying to escape. Do as I'm told."

"And are you going to follow them?"

"Yes."

No.

Of course I'm not.

As soon as I find a way out of here, I'm going to run.

Fuck Cassius' rules.

He wraps his arm around my waist, hauls me up against his chest, and pushes my joggers and underwear down my legs. Then he settles me back into place and grips my hands behind my back again, taking a good long look at my breasts and my…my everything.

Looking me dead in the eye, he licks his thumb and strokes it across my clit.

I gasp and squirm in his grip. "What—what are you doing?"

"What I always do with girls who do what I say. A little positive reinforcement." He circles his thumb over my clit, tortuously slow. "This is what you get if you're good."

The last thing I want to do is be *good* for my captors, but there's something about the way this big man talks to me and how his voice rumbles so soothingly in my ears. After Lorenzo's viciousness, Cassius' lap and his pet names, and even the pain he inflicts, is making me melt.

My pussy is melting as well, all over his fingers. I roll my hips back and forth across the bulge beneath his towel, working myself against his fingers and enjoying his hard breathing.

"Do you like it, too?" I whisper.

"*Sì, bambina*, I like it, too."

"Your plan won't work. I'm happy to say that Lorenzo would rather set himself on fire than touch me."

"You let me worry about that," he murmurs, pushing his fingers deeper to reach where I'm slippery, and then back to my clit. I moan louder, thinking how easy it is to pretend to follow his rules when he's about to make me burst apart in pleasure.

As I come, Cassius works his fingers faster on my clit and leans forward and clasps one of my nipples between his teeth. The pleasure and pain rocket through me and I cry out, my head falling back.

Boneless from my release, I fall against his bare chest, which is big and warm, and rest my cheek against his shoulder. My arms come around him automatically. I've never been held by a man before, and with the aftershocks of my orgasm racing through me I want to get even closer to him.

Cassius shoves me off him and stands up, leaving me shivering in the sudden cold on the sofa. When I look up at him, that indulgent expression has been replaced with cold indifference.

"Remember what I said, or I'll be the one to punish you. You won't fucking like it if I really punish you, so be good for me, and be good for Vinicius and Lorenzo."

I wrap my arms around myself to cover my nakedness and glare at him. "I can't be good for Lorenzo if I'm going to kill him."

He strides out of the room, the light shifting over the heavy muscles of his back. "I'd advise you not to try. I'd like to fuck you while you're still in one piece."

CHAPTER FIFTEEN

CHIARA

I open my eyes in the darkness, not knowing how I know, but certain there's someone in my room. No, in my *bed*. I keep as still as I can, straining for the sound of someone breathing, or the feel of the bed dipping under the weight of a heavy body.

Cassius? Panic floods through me—no, it must be Lorenzo, here to murder me because I had the audacity to be kidnapped by him.

As carefully as I can, I lift my head and peer around.

A voice speaks behind me, deep and familiar. "You're awake."

I roll over. It's Vinicius, his head propped on his hand. He's under the blankets in my bed, his shoulders are bare and he seems to be wearing nothing but a smile. "I heard Cassius left you hanging earlier. I thought you might need a cuddle."

"Are you *naked*?"

He glances down at himself, and then back up at me. "Why don't you find out?"

"Get out!" Predictably, he keeps smiling and doesn't move. "What are you doing here in the middle of the night?"

"I told you. I thought you might need a hug after what happened earlier. Cassius can be…distant."

Downright callous, more like. "How did you know about that?"

"We're in a group chat."

I stare at him, baffled by the image of these three bloodthirsty men chatting away via text. Do they share mafia memes? "Cassius just blurted out everything we did together? You guys are messed up."

"You don't need to feel embarrassed."

"A group of guys discussing getting me off? Sure, nothing to be embarrassed about."

"Cassius told you a little about the arrangement the four of us— the three of us, sorry—have considered. We're not a *group of guys*. We're three extremely close men who are trying something out for the first time to see if it will make sense for us, and for you. We talked about you in the most respectful terms."

"You were all *respectfully* discussing my pussy?"

He fights a grin. "Cassius had nothing but the best things to say about your pussy."

I reach out and shove his chest, my face flaming. "Oh, shut up."

Vinicius covers my hand with his and pulls me closer. "Come here. Everyone always says I give the best cuddles."

"You're *extremely* naked."

"It's just skin. I don't bite."

"It's not just—you don't—I've never been—"

"Chiara, I know. Come here." He pulls me into his arms, but the blanket is bunched between us so I'm not actually touching him.

"Those two men are closer to me than brothers, Chiara. No one understands me like they do." For once there's not a trace of teasing in his voice. I wonder if this is the first time that Vinicius has spoken the absolute truth to me.

He wraps his arms around me and speaks softly in the darkness. "We know that we're severely lacking in whatever makes a good partner. Kindness. Understanding—"

"Sanity?"

He laughs softly. "Each of us have a little piece of what a woman might grow to love. Between us, maybe we're one decent boyfriend."

Cassius and Vinicius? Possibly. Lorenzo? He's got nothing that I or any sane woman could want, and Cassius and Vinicius are in la-la land if they think this dynamic is ever going to work. It would be hard enough to get off the ground if they were the loveliest and most considerate men on the planet and not a bunch of murderous kidnappers.

"What about jealousy?"

"Among the three of us? There'd be nothing to be jealous about because you'd belong to all of us. Is that nice?" he whispers in my ear as he pulls me further into his arms.

He plants a kiss on my throat, and another on my jaw. Warmth washes over me. That does feel nice, actually. He turns my face up to his and presses his mouth to mine in a slow kiss, as sweet and delicious as chocolate. Then as burning hot as fiery peppers.

In the back of my mind, I remember that Vinicius is just as dangerous as the others even though he doesn't act like it. In fact, I seem to remember that he can be even more dangerous because he knows how to break down all your defenses with that silver tongue of his.

But it's been a rough week and I crave the comfort of his touch. And God, how comforting he is with his hands rubbing circles on my back and his tongue just flicking at my lips. When he draws me closer, I push my hands beneath the blanket so I can stroke his bare chest. Such warm, silky skin over hard muscles.

Vinicius eases me onto my back and our bare legs tangle together. I'm wearing an oversized T-shirt and underwear, making it easy for him to stroke my waist and squeeze my hips. My eyes open wide in the dark as his fingers loop into my underwear and start to drag them down.

Wait, wasn't this about cuddling? "You tricky bastard."

He wriggles down the bed a little and kisses my bare midriff. "Me, kitten? I just want to make you feel good. I'll stop if you want."

Want.

I've been learning a lot about *want* lately, but there's still so much that I don't understand. Why my pussy gets wet the instant these men touch me, for one thing. I can feel my own slipperiness now, just waiting to be discovered by Vinicius. He eases my underwear down my hips and legs until I'm naked from the waist down.

Then he slips between my thighs and plants a kiss on my clit.

"Have you got another one in there for me?" His voice is dripping with heat and desire. Another orgasm.

Laying there and panting is all the answer he needs. I'm going to escape. Meanwhile, I have to be what Cassius calls *good*. Letting Cassius and Vinicius make me come is a hardship I'll bear while I seek a route out of here.

I let my knees fall open, push my fingers into Vinicius' thick, golden hair and stare at what's happening. Vinicius, between my thighs, licking me. So this is what his devious mouth can do. His tongue homes in on my clit, and those mischievous eyes of his glance up to see what he's doing to me.

Wonderful things. Vinicius is all delicious heat and pleasure.

"Who are you?" I gasp, watching him lick me and feeling the hot sensations roll through me. I ride each wave higher and higher.

"Who do you think I am?" His words vibrate against my clit.

"A con man. Someone who steals by telling lies."

Vinicius sucks my clit. "Among other things. I don't like to box myself in."

"Why do you do what you do?"

He takes his time answering, massaging me with his tongue until I'm crying out. "For money. Power. Because I can."

My hips lift up from the bed involuntarily and I moan. He seems to know my clit better than I do. "But why trickery?"

"Baby," he murmurs. "Baby, baby, baby." He laps at me with every word. "Because it's so delicious to get what I want with just my..." another lick. "Tongue."

Oh, fuck me, what a tongue.

I'm breathing hard, my chest lifting and falling as everything down there begins to coalesce into something devastating and wonderful. "Vinicius, you—"

But he's too busy licking me to ask what I'm trying to say. He wraps his hands tighter around my thighs, pressing me open as my pelvis rocks back and forth. My head tosses side to side on the pillow. I need a little more. Just a little more.

"*Please*, Vinicius."

But he's not giving me more. His tongue is just lapping against me, the lightest of licks. He's deaf to my cries, holding back what I need in favor of drawing out my pleasure until it's almost agony.

Finally, Vinicius laughs softly and ups the pressure of his tongue. My orgasm slams into me and my back arches up off the bed, head thrown back, mouth open wide in a strangled scream.

I feel Vinicius move up the bed toward me, still between my thighs. Something hot and blunt bumps against my pussy. My body is limp and heavy but I drag my eyes open and look down. I've never properly seen a man's cock before. I barely got a look at Salvatore's before he was shoving it into my mouth.

I stare at the swollen head of his cock as he grasps the base in his fist and slides the tip through my wet folds. With his heavy, muscular body between my knees, I can't close my legs.

"What are you doing?"

"I'm not doing anything, kitten." But his sharp eyes are glinting. The head of him briefly presses into me and then the pressure is gone again. It's not enough for him to be inside me but a little more pressure and he'd start to penetrate me.

This doesn't feel like nothing. This feels very...vulnerable.

When I look up, Vinicius' beautiful eyes are foxlike. "Don't worry. I'm just imagining what it will be like."

"What it will be like?"

His mouth tilts in a heated smile.

Fucking me.

"Okay, but you should probably imagine it with your mind, not with your dick."

He pulses his hips forward and his cocks slides up through my pussy and against my clit. "People do this all the time when they're not going to have sex."

My eyes narrow. "That seems unlikely."

"It's true. Am I hurting you, my pretty little virgin?"

"Well, no…"

"You can take the whole tip of my cock and it won't change anything about you and it won't hurt. Watch."

He pulls back until he's right there at my entrance and with a small amount of pressure I feel myself give and stretch around him.

"Vinicius—!" I press my palms against his chest and pant with desire and alarm. The tingling, slippery heat between my legs makes me want to grasp his hips and beg him to slam into me.

His eyes are gleaming and he leans down to lick my lip with his tongue. "See, that doesn't hurt at all, does it?"

"You're tricking me into something. I know you are."

"Your hymen is actually quite far in. I can go even farther."

I inhale sharply as he slips deeper into me and I stretch wider. The stretch starts to burn. "This *really* doesn't feel like we're not having sex anymore."

His deep voice is hypnotic. "If we were having sex, I'd be thrusting deep, over and over."

His hips begin to work against me in a slow rhythm. I watch, wide-eyed, as another quarter inch of his cock disappears inside me. "Yep, you've tricked me. Oh fuck, oh God—"

There's a sound from the doorway. Cassius has opened the door and is standing there, stark naked. His curls are rumpled like he was asleep and we've woken him up.

Vinicius bares his teeth in annoyance. "What do you want?"

"Get your cock out of her."

Vinicius smirks, not moving. "It's just the tip. It doesn't count."

My face burns at the sight of Cassius' thunderous expression. I'm practically having sex with Vinicius and Cassius has walked in. This isn't normal. These guys are so not normal.

Also, if Lorenzo is right and Vinicius and Cassius only want me here so they can have sex with me, why isn't Cassius letting him?

I'm so confused. I'm excruciatingly embarrassed as well, and I try to wriggle out from beneath Vinicius but succeed in only working him deeper. The burn in my pussy becomes an ache.

Cassius lifts a finger and points at him. "If you break her, Scava and I will kick your fucking teeth in."

"I'm not going to. We're just playing. Aren't we, kitten?" Vinicius still doesn't pull out. He seems like he's enjoying winding Cassius up. "Why don't you come join us? I bet our *bambina* is great at giving head."

Cassius' expression is stony, but as I watch, his cock is thickening. It's getting bigger, and bigger. My eyes widen. I thought Vinicius was big enough, but Cassius is a *beast*.

"Kitten, could you stop staring at another man's cock when mine is just about inside you?"

"Vinicius," Cassius growls in warning, taking a step toward us.

"You should feel her. She's so tight, Cassius. Just an inch more."

"Don't you fucking dare."

"Or what?"

"We agreed."

This is news to me. "What did you all agree?"

The two men glare at each other for several more seconds and then Vinicius pulls out and sits up. "Fine. No harm done."

I grab my underwear and pull it back on. So much for just having a cuddle. I should have guessed it wouldn't have been *just* anything with Vinicius.

Cassius steps forward and scoops me into his arms, saying, "You can stay in my room tonight. I don't trust him not to try this again the second I fall asleep."

"And we're supposed to trust you?" Vinicius calls after us as Cassius carries me to his room.

"Of course. Good night."

Trust Cassius not to have sex with me, he means? What the hell is going on?

I open my mouth to ask Cassius why I'm here if it's not for sex, but as he puts me down on the mattress his expression is thunderous. Also, his semi-hard dick is right there. There have been two dicks right in my face in the last minute. This is two hundred percent more dick than I'm used to. Suddenly, I'm tongue-tied again as Cassius tucks me beneath the bedclothes, gets in the other side, and lays down with his back to me.

The silence is deafening.

Excruciating.

"Cassius?"

"Go to sleep."

"What agreement do you all have?"

He's silent for a long time. "Let's not discuss this right now."

"But it's about me so I feel I should know. Is it about which of you has sex with me first? That's a pretty screwy thing to have an agreement about."

"*Bambina*, it's late."

He's not even denying it, or defending what they're doing. I don't suppose it is defensible, but I still want to know what their agreement entails. Apparently they can touch me, but they can't fuck me. Until when? Why?

I remember what Lorenzo snarled in my face the other day. *The other two've had a hard-on for you for the past year. I don't know why they're not getting the hell on with it.*

I gaze at Cassius' back, imagining what it would be like to be pinned beneath him like I just was with Vinicius, receiving soft kisses from him as he murmured *bambina* in that deep, sexy voice of his. Heat darts between my legs. Maybe it wouldn't be awful if Cassius…

Nope, not thinking about that. I tuck my hands beneath my pillow and go to sleep.

The dream seems to begin the second I close my eyes. A figure shimmers in the darkness, outlined in gold.

Mom, and she's eating soup dumplings and smiling. I run toward her, but my body feels heavy. When I look down at myself, I see I'm wearing a wedding dress that's been sewn all over with bullets. I struggle over to her, my legs burning and my lungs heaving, and throw my arms around her.

"Mom, I've missed you. Where have you been?"

But there's something in my hand. Lorenzo's knife, and as I've hugged Mom, I've slashed her throat. Her smiling face becomes fixed and her eyes grow glassy. Blood pours down both of us from the gaping wound in her neck.

"*Mom!*"

I'm jolted awake, sobbing hard and covered in clammy sweat.

Arms come around me in the darkness. Big, strong arms that fold me against a steadily beating heart. I burrow into that sound, my tears damp against his chest.

"*Non piangere. Sono qui e non permetterò che ti succeda niente di brutto. Shh.*"

Don't cry. I'm here, and I won't let anything bad happen to you. Shh.

I sob harder as the deep, rich timbre of those tender words twine through me. I don't think Cassius knows that I can speak Italian. He squeezes me tighter in his arms, murmuring words against the top of my head as he kisses me.

"*Mia dolce bambina.*"

My sweet little girl.

All I've wanted for the past year was for someone to hold me while I cry for Mom. "I miss her. I miss her so much," I sob.

"*Lo so,*" he murmurs. *I know.*

It's pitch dark and I can't see his face. We could almost be dreaming the same dream. I feel like he understands my grief. Beneath my fingers, deep in his heart, flows the same sadness. Maybe that's why he wouldn't let me touch him earlier, because his grief simmers so close to the surface.

Slowly, my sobs subside into shaky breaths and he rocks me gently. He murmurs sleepily and keeps me tight in his arms.

"Cassius…"

"It was just a dream. Go back to sleep."

Sleep in my kidnapper's arms. The man who I asked for help and who repaid me with captivity. His warmth surrounds me and lulls me back to drowsiness.

"Why are you doing this?" I whisper.

But his breathing has deepened, and he doesn't reply.

I wake up in an enormous bed and turn to find Cassius. His side of the bed is empty, and disappointment ripples through me. In here, naked and vulnerable, he might have answered my questions. Businesslike Cassius in his crisp white shirts is always so guarded and severe.

I sigh and roll onto my back. What a strange night that was. Vinicius is a troublemaker. And Cassius…

The plan the three of them have is crazy and will never work. Sharing a woman because they feel like they'll be able to protect her more easily, and so she can feel like she has one whole boyfriend from the broken pieces of the three of them? More like all of them keeping one woman captive and at arm's length at the same time. Lorenzo hates me. Vinicius is sneaky and mercurial. Cassius has too much baggage and a bad temper.

I gaze at the space in the bed beside me. But maybe he has a sensitive side as well, only it's withered away like an unused muscle.

I sit up and hear noises coming from the kitchen. I pad out in bare feet and my oversized T-shirt and see Cassius standing at the coffee machine. He glances at me, his eyes flickering over my face before falling to my bare legs.

He doesn't smile as I walk toward him. In fact, he looks tense and uncomfortable, and turns back to what he's doing. "Coffee?"

He's dressed for business in a white shirt and black pants. Everything about him is neat and fresh, from his manicured black beard to his leather shoes. This is the face he likes to present to the world, but I've seen him vicious with bloodlust as he dragged Griffin from his car.

I've seen him vulnerable, too. Or felt him be vulnerable, at least.

"Yes, please." I stand close to Cassius while he makes a latte in a mug, but he doesn't once look at me, even when he passes me my coffee.

"You, um, give nice cuddles," I whisper into my mug as I take a sip. "And what you said last night was so sweet."

Cassius slams a button on the machine like it insulted his mother's ziti. "What?"

"*I'm here and I won't let anything bad happen to you, my sweet little girl*," I repeat. "What you said when I woke up from a bad dream."

Cassius stares at me, shoulders bunched tight and anger sparking in his eyes. Maybe he was sleep-talking, but I don't think so. I think he remembers exactly what he said to me.

He just didn't realize that I could understand him.

"I speak Italian. I took classes all through high school."

"Congratulations," he growls.

My eyebrows creep up my forehead. "Do you hate showing me affection that much?"

"I'm busy and don't have time for your childish moods."

There's nothing childish about what I'm saying or how I'm acting. If anyone's being a child, it's him. "Is being affectionate to me so horrible to you? I don't think so. I think you liked it, and that's scary to you."

"Is that so?"

Yes, that's so. I think I'm figuring Cassius out, and he resents it. Too bad because I'm not going to stop.

"That guy from the Geaks, I attempted to have sex with him because he was safe. He didn't make me feel anything when I was close to him. I hated that I felt things when you touched me. I *feel* things when you touch me."

Of all of them, Cassius is the one who I crave most to wrap me in his arms and hold me tight. The morsels of affection he's given me are not enough, and I sense just how warm and loving he could be if he gave in to it.

Either I escape and flee Coldlake for good, or I find some way to exist here safely.

Maybe that way is with Cassius.

Do I want it to be with Cassius?

I put my hand on his chest. "Don't you? Feel things for me?"

Cassius bats my hand away and steps back. "I don't know what you're talking about. If you haven't got anything better to do, read a fucking book."

Before I can say another word, he turns away and strides out of the room.

CHAPTER SIXTEEN

CHIARA

Days pass and Cassius doesn't say a word to me. It's like living with an enormous, sulking bear. One who sneaks looks at me when he thinks my attention is elsewhere.

If Cassius doesn't want to have any sort of relationship with me and he's not trying to ransom me to Dad, why keep me here? Kick me out, send me back to Salvatore, *anything*. This limbo is making me crazy.

I carry my frustration with me everywhere I go, and I'm on edge whenever I'm with Cassius. When I'm alone, I'm stewing with anger and boredom.

One afternoon Cassius is out doing Cassius things and I'm

sitting on the couch with a magazine, when I hear the elevator ping and the doors slide open. Lorenzo strides out, dressed in black jeans and a black jacket, his blond hair messy and his dark brows drawn together. His T-shirt is cut low at the neck and there are tattoos on his chest.

I sit back when I realize it's not Cassius. "Oh, it's you."

"Hello to you, too," he sneers, heading past me. He and Vinicius show up occasionally at random times. I presume Cassius has a safe or a computer that they need to use for criminal purposes.

"Oh, like you give a damn whether I say hello. Go fuck yourself, Lorenzo." I'm asking for trouble giving shit to a man who's crazy, jacked up, armed, and hates my guts, but in this moment, it just feels so good to take out my Cassius-related frustrations on someone.

Lorenzo freezes, then swerves toward me. My belly swoops in alarm. "You mouthy little bitch. Why don't you get out of here? Just leave. Go on, fuck off."

I jump to my feet and yell at him, "I can't leave because you're all *keeping me here*."

"Then find some way to fucking escape! You're not even trying."

"Call that elevator for me and I'll leave right this second." I expect Lorenzo to tell me to go fuck myself, but he hesitates. Hope flares in my chest. "Lorenzo, please open that elevator. You'll never have to see me again."

He passes his hand over his mouth and looks between the elevator and me. "Just to be clear, you're asking for my help. Mine. Not the others?"

Cassius and Vinicius wouldn't help me because they don't want me gone. Lorenzo is the only one who would be happy never to see my face again. "I know, I can't believe it either. Get me out of this building, *please.*"

Lorenzo glares at me for a moment longer, and then strides over to a door and opens it.

"You can't use the elevator. There are cameras. Through here is the door to a stairwell. It opens with a passcode. Four-two-double-three-nine."

Holy shit, he really is helping me. "One second. I'll be right back."

I run to my room and pull on a sweater and shoes with my jeans and scoop my hair into a ponytail. There's nothing else I want or need from this apartment. I don't know where I'm going without any money, phone, or passport, but I'll figure that out later.

I hurry back to the lounge, reciting the passcode under my breath.

As I pass by Lorenzo, he grabs hold of my ponytail and seethes in my ear, "You don't know where you've been since the wedding. A group of men kept you in a dark room and you never saw their faces. If you go to the police or rat on us to your father and Salvatore, I'll slit your fucking throat."

It's on the tip of my tongue to remind him he showed everyone his face at my wedding, but now isn't the time to be pedantic. "I know you will. I'm not stupid."

"Could have fooled me." He lets me go and gives me a shove.

My fingers shake as I punch the numbers into the door. I more than half expect the code to be rejected and for Lorenzo to heap scorn on me for believing that he'd help me, but the little light goes green, the door unlocks and I pull it open with a cry of shock.

Turning around, I see Lorenzo giving me a sarcastic wave.

Then I run.

It's a long, long way down. I grow dizzy from the turns but I hold the stair rail and keep running. Several minutes later, I burst out of the stairwell and into an underground garage. A black Mercedes is parked in front of me, and Lorenzo is leaning against it with his arms folded.

I brace my hands against my knees and struggle for breath. "What are you doing here? I thought we already said our goodbyes."

"Every entrance to this building has a security camera. When Cassius finds out that you're gone and checks them, he'll see me arrive and leave around the same time as you disappeared. I don't want to get mixed up in your shit. You can't be seen."

He goes around to the back of the car and opens it. "Get in."

"In the trunk? No way."

Lorenzo bares his teeth at me in a snarl. "I'm not tying you up and kidnapping you. I'm driving you a few blocks down the street and then letting you out. Get in the fucking car or I'll drag you back upstairs right this second."

He'll do it, too. Motherfucker.

I straighten up and walk toward him. "Only as long as this really is the last time I see your face."

"Who would have imagined Little Miss Annoying would have asked for my help. One more thing. Pass me that cloth." He points to a folded chamois in the trunk, the sort used to polish a car.

"What? Why do you need that?"

"Do you have to argue every step of the way? I said fucking give it to me," he snarls.

"Fine!" I pick up the chamois and pass it to him. The second his hand closes around the fabric, his expression morphs from annoyed to menacing. As quick as a snake, he shoves the cloth into my mouth all the way to the back of my throat.

I'm gagging when he rips a piece of duct tape from a spool he's pulled out of nowhere and slaps it over my mouth. Then he grabs a zip tie from his pocket and tightens it viciously around my wrists. He's so fast I've barely struggled for one breath in the time it's taken him to completely disable me.

"Idiot. You practically kidnapped yourself." Lorenzo grins and shoves me into the back of his car, straps me down, and slams the door.

I lay on the floor of the Mercedes, making angry buzzing noises in the back of my throat and kicking the side of the car.

I was nearly free. I was so close. You *asshole*, Lorenzo.

Chiara, you fucking idiot.

The car door slams, the engine starts, and we're moving. These are probably my last few minutes on earth and I'm spending them being humiliated and murdered by Lorenzo Scava.

I *hate* him.

Sometime later, the car descends as if into a garage and he turns off the engine. The back door opens and Lorenzo unhooks the straps and hauls me over his shoulder. I can't see anything but his back and his heels as he walks along a concrete passage. A familiar concrete passage. Then we're going upstairs, and then up another flight of stairs. I thrash about, trying to dislodge myself from his shoulder, but he holds me tight.

I'm set on my feet in a carpeted room and Lorenzo rips the duct tape and the chamois from my mouth. I stare around, trying to see where I am at the same time as I try to get some moisture back in my bone-dry mouth.

"This is your compound, isn't it? What are we doing here?" My eyes land on the bed over his shoulder, and I realize we're in the master bedroom. *His* bedroom.

Lorenzo gives a smile that could make an angel scared and horny at the same time.

My stomach hollows out and I back away from him. "Oh, no. No, no, no. Not that. Not *you*."

"That pussy of yours is causing trouble. Or should I say—that virgin pussy. I'm going to do everyone a favor and make it mine."

I start to shake in fear. No one hates me more than Lorenzo Scava and he's going to make this as brutal as possible. Then, he'll throw my battered body down in front of Cassius and Vinicius and they'll turn away in disgust.

Ruined.

He's going to utterly destroy me so they don't want me anymore.

Lorenzo pulls his T-shirt up and over his head. He moves slowly, the muscles of his stomach and biceps rippling. There are tattoos across his torso and down his arms. His eyes are burning with the same twisted delight as they were the night of my seventeenth birthday.

He's going to make me suffer, and he can't wait.

I turn and run for the door, but Lorenzo merely steps forward and wraps an arm around my waist.

My back is pressed against his scorching naked chest and his lips are against my ear. "We can do this the easy way or the hard way."

"Fuck you. We both know you're going to make this horrible for me."

"Ah, sucks to be you, princess." Lorenzo scoops my hair away and goes for my throat.

He *bites* me.

I suck in a panicked breath, braced for pain.

Lorenzo nips my throat with his teeth, and then opens his mouth wider and bites me again. Not hard enough to hurt, but I feel every tooth in my delicate flesh and his breath heats my skin. Lorenzo buries his fingers in my hair, stroking up the nape of my neck over the spot where he cut me, as if the marks are fascinating to him.

I stare at our reflections in the nearby mirror. My chalk white face. Lorenzo's savage beauty. His huge arms are locked around me and his eyes are closed as he works his teeth against me.

"I guess there's a silver lining to this."

"What's that, princess?" he murmurs, almost sounding like a lover.

"Once this is over, none of you will want me again. I'll be free."

And yet my heart contracts painfully at the thought of Cassius gazing at me in disgust because I'm used goods. Turning away from me. Throwing me out so he never has to look at me again. It's ridiculous that my virginity should make any goddamn difference to my value and I refuse to believe it does.

But it clearly matters to Cassius.

Lorenzo smiles against my throat. "Is that so?"

My blood freezes. I'm assuming he's going to let me live. Once he's finished with me, maybe he'll just kill me. Take me out to the desert and hunt me down like game, like he so lovingly described.

Tears shimmer in my eyes. At least then I'll be with Mom.

"Ah, princess. Am I so hideous?"

Lorenzo turns me around to face him, his hands on my waist and a smile on his lips. His blond hair is tumbling around his face and the light from the window is striking his high cheekbones and the hard line of his jaw. He's beautiful, but he can't hide the malevolence that shines from within.

My wrists are still fastened together. I reach up and touch his face. "Not here."

My hand slides down his jaw, over his tattooed throat and comes to rest over his heart. "Here. This is what scares me."

The smile fades from Lorenzo's lips. He almost looks like he's in pain. He glances in confusion at my bound wrists, his clothes on the floor, and then at himself.

I beg him with my eyes. Please, please realize what you're doing and that you don't want to hurt me.

Please, Lorenzo. Show me that you're not a monster through and through.

He steps away to pick up his jacket and fishes around inside it. He brings out his knife, clutched in his fist, and when his eyes meet mine they're sparking with fury.

I swallow hard. Oh, shit. Now I've made him angry.

"The others have told me how lush you are. Let's see what these clothes of yours have been hiding."

Lorenzo grasps a fistful of my top and slices through it. He does it over and over, grasps and cuts, grasps and cuts, until every scrap of fabric has fallen to the floor at my feet.

He wriggles the point of his knife beneath the center of my bra. "Aren't you fucking perfect. I've been dreaming about this."

I swallow down the burn of disappointment and force my voice not to wobble. If he's going to strip me bare then I'll at least keep my dignity. "I thought you said you couldn't stand me."

"I was fucking with you so I could win. You're just my type, princess." He slices through my bra with a flick of his wrist and it falls open.

"Win what?"

But Lorenzo's too busy cutting through my bra straps and throwing the tattered garment to the ground. His hungry gaze devours my body as he works. I stare straight ahead at his chest.

If I can just get my hands on that knife. Even with my hands tied I might be able to stab him in the neck, just how he taught me. The idea of him bleeding out in seconds is the only thing keeping me going.

Lorenzo notices me glance at his knife and throws it aside, laughing. "I like my neck how it is."

I screw my eyes up. Stupid, stupid Chiara. I made it so obvious what I was planning.

He turns his attention to my jeans and pulls them down my legs. He tugs them meaningfully when they reach my ankles so that I have no choice but to step out of them, nearly losing my balance. Lorenzo catches me around the waist and steadies me, and his fingers just slip beneath my briefs at my lower back.

"How about we make things interesting? Vinicius told me you couldn't resist his wager. If I get these panties off you and they're not soaked through, I'll take you back to Cassius."

I frown at him, perplexed. Back to Cassius. Not Cassius and Vinicius?

"I see how you look at my friend. Like you're half a breath away from falling to your knees and begging for him to save you." There's an edge to his voice, almost like he's jealous.

He *is* jealous. Not of Cassius touching me. Of me feeling affection for the man.

He grips my hair and forces my face up to his. "I saved you, too, remember? We all did. We're all your knights in shining armor, not just Cassius."

I remember Lorenzo's cold and brutal expression as he advanced on me with that hypodermic. "You're one messed-up knight. All you care about is scaring the hell out of me. If you wanted me to like you, you shouldn't have gone out of your way to be so horrible to me."

He laughs without humor. "Yeah, I did, didn't I?"

Lorenzo draws his finger around the inside of my briefs, and I shiver despite the hatred burning in my heart. "It doesn't matter now. What do you say to this little wager?"

I've got nothing to say to such a messed-up bet.

"Princess." A delighted smile breaks over his face. "Are you wet for me already?"

"Screw you. I'm not wagering my body over anything." Not a second time. I did that once and I was totally humiliated.

He hoists me up against his chest with an arm beneath my knees and one around my waist and carries me over to the bed. "Refusing the bet is not an option."

I'm placed gently on the mattress, but there's nothing gentle about Lorenzo's expression. He slips between my legs and my inner thighs rub against his rough denim jeans. Looming over me, he takes my breasts in both hands and rubs my nipples between his thumb and forefingers.

I brace for an excruciating assault on my nerve endings. Instead, a delicious sensation expands through me and burrows deep inside me to blossom between my thighs. Every squeeze, every stroke of his fingers, makes the heat grow.

"No," I moan. Not again. I don't want to enjoy this. I want to give him the hatred he deserves, not the satisfaction of seeing me pant for him.

Lorenzo bends over me, the bulge at the front of his jeans tight against my pussy. He takes one of my nipples in his mouth and sucks at the same time as he grinds his hips against me.

I twist futilely at the zip tie binding my wrists. I can't believe this is happening. I'm filled with self-loathing.

When he sits up, his lower lip is reddened and wet with saliva. He hooks a finger into my underwear and drags them down my legs. He lifts them up and rubs his finger over the slippery wetness that has gathered in them, a triumphant smile on his lips. "Fuck, I love it when you do that."

He throws them aside, puts his hand between my thighs and spreads them open. "I win."

"No, wait—" But my protest is lost when he slides down the bed and his tongue swipes my clit.

My whole body jumps in response. *Fuck.*

"You taste like heaven," he murmurs between lashes of his tongue.

I screw my eyes up tight. He doesn't feel like heaven. He *doesn't*.

"Has anyone ever licked you before, princess? Wait, Vinicius got his lying mouth all over you, didn't he? And you came so hard for him." Between words, he laps at my clit, his lips vibrating against me. "How I fucking loved hearing about that. As soon as I read the text from him I was so hard. I pumped my cock up and down in my hand, thinking about your tight, dripping snatch. I was right here in this bed, imagining you moan for me as I slammed into your pussy."

I feel my back arch as my hips rock against his mouth. As he's spoken, my eyes have opened and so have my knees, and I'm watching him murmur filthy words into my pussy.

Lorenzo glances up at me. "You must have imagined what it was like to be licked by a man, but the real thing isn't what you thought it would be. My tongue's soft, isn't it?"

Softer than I expected, especially from Lorenzo. As hot and slippery as I am, my pussy and his tongue feel like they were made for each other. He spreads me wider with his fingers and laps at my clit, and I can't control the cry that tears from my lips.

Lorenzo's arms slide around my hips and hold me tight as his eyes close and he keeps licking. What the hell is happening to me? This feels so wrong, but the wrongness seems to be spicing my body's reactions.

I'm so close to coming when he sits up, and I'm frantically trying to get a grip on myself when I realize he's taken off his jeans. His cock is jutting out beneath his belly, thick and aggressively swollen.

Oh, Jesus. He's really going to do it. I whimper and struggle against the zip tie that's cutting viciously into my flesh.

"Hmm. This isn't right."

My head lifts in surprise, wondering if he's had a change of heart. He gets up for his knife, cuts my wrists free and then throws the weapon out of reach. Then he slides back between my legs, his cock nudging my entrance.

I press my palms against his burning chest. "Don't, please," I sob, but not with tears. With need and self-loathing. Being free is worse. I look at my hands splayed against his tattooed muscles and it feels like he's my lover.

Once this is done, it's all over. I'll have nowhere to go. No one who'll want to keep me safe. They'll all throw me aside. Lorenzo. Cassius. Vinicius. Salvatore. Dad. They all made it plain that I'm worthless without my virginity. I don't want to be anyone's prize, but the thought of being used and discarded is even worse.

Used and discarded by a man that I'm burning up for. After he's finished with me, Lorenzo will mock me for the ways he made me come, and then throw me out onto the street.

"Don't do this, please."

But Lorenzo doesn't listen. He grasps his cock and slides it through my wetness.

"I fucking hate you," I say, my chest heaving with every breath as I stare at the shiny head of his cock.

"So fight me if you're feeling so guilty for getting turned on.

It won't stop me, but at least you'll be able to tell yourself that you weren't asking for it."

My muscles are locked up with fear and desire. I don't want to fight. I just want to burn up in shame and humiliation. This is worse than if Lorenzo beat me first. This is so sick and twisted.

His eyes narrow and he doesn't move. I don't know what he's waiting for. He's getting exactly what he wants and there's nothing I can do to stop it even if I did fight him.

"You want to feel like I'm making you?" Lorenzo asks, reaching into the bedside table.

I hear an ominous click, and then something cold and hard is pressed under my chin. I look down and see he's holding a gun, the barrel pressed against my jaw. Lorenzo's fingers flex on the gun grip. "Aren't I good to you, princess? Hands down on the bed."

My palms hit the mattress.

"If you resist me before I'm through, I'll blow your brains out."

"If I resist you, you'll be screwing a corpse."

His eyes flash. "Don't mind one bit, princess. Your pussy will stay warm enough for me to finish even with your blood and brains all over the pillow."

The sight of the gun pressed against my jaw and my body prone beneath him seems to excite him. He's braced on one hand by my head. "Reach down and take hold of me."

"What? No!"

The barrel of the gun presses viciously against my jaw. "That's your last warning."

Lorenzo Scava is so messed up he's making me help him take my virginity against my will. I reach down between our legs and wrap my fingers around his length. He's burning hot and iron hard, but velvet soft to the touch.

He groans as I enclose his girth. "That's it, princess. Guide me in."

I squeeze my eyes shut for a second. Lorenzo is watching me, his eyes filled with delight and anticipation. I push the broad head of his cock down my inner lips and feel my body give against his. He surges forward with a heavy groan, sinking into me, so deep it's shocking.

I almost reach up and grab his shoulders before I remember his threat to shoot me in the head. I grip the sheets with both hands instead as pain burns through me.

"Fuck, your pussy," he groans, moving slowly. Then he hesitates. "You okay, princess?"

His cock is thick, a blunt weapon deep inside me. The pain is subsiding, but the humiliation is only getting worse. "You don't care."

"Well, fuck you then." His pale blue eyes flash and he looks down between us. "There's no way you can tell me that doesn't look insanely hot."

I grip the sheets harder. I'm not looking. I won't look.

The only other place to look is into Lorenzo's face, so I take one glance down between my thighs. He slides into me, and then out again, his length glistening wet and smeared with red. Is that my blood?

Oh, Jesus. That's weird and…and kind of hot.

Without thinking, I look up at him.

The same time as he looks up at me, his face just inches from mine.

I'm trapped in Lorenzo's eyes as he fucks me deep and slow. The pain has been replaced by a delicious stretching sensation every time he bottoms out inside me.

"Your little clit is so swollen. My hands are full here. Stroke her for me."

His voice is heavy with desire. Even with the gun to my head he sounds like he's coaxing me.

I don't have a choice, so I do as he tells me, lifting my hand from the bed and sliding it down over my hip and circling my clit with my middle finger. His tongue sensitized me so much that just a few strokes of my finger has my breath deepening. I watch my fingers move as he thrusts, fascinated by the strange sight.

"Look at me," he breathes.

I do, and I wish I hadn't. That expression on his face. I've never seen him look so...*normal*. Not a trace of viciousness or cruelty. I could swear he's wondering how the hell this is happening as much as I am.

I see it again.

A tiny glimpse of the humanity inside Lorenzo.

Everything's starting to slide out of my control and without thinking, I reach up with my other hand to grasp his shoulder.

Lorenzo doesn't seem to notice my mistake. His teeth sink into his lower lip and he groans. "Princess, I can feel your pussy squeezing me. You're going to come and it's going to make me blow."

Heat flashes through me. Blow. Come inside me. My finger keeps working on my clit as he continues to thrust. This is so wrong. This is so fucking wrong. I'm panting hard and moaning for a man who's holding a gun to my head. I'm squeezing his shoulder like a lover while he pounds my pussy that's so wet for him I'm practically gushing.

His eyes have me pinned to the bed even more than his body does. A surge of pure pleasure breaks through me, taking me prisoner. Wave after wave of heat slams through me in time with his cock.

"Jesus fucking *Christ*," he growls, animalistic and rough, like feeling me come has set something off in him. He starts pounding me faster. Now both my hands are up on his shoulders as his body moves. The aftershocks of my orgasm have moved deeper and are gathering right where his cock is thrusting.

"Lorenzo," I whimper, panting with need as he drives into me in the most heavenly way. Not saying his name because I have anything to say. Saying his name because it's the *only* thing I can say. "*Lorenzo.*"

The door flies open. In a flash, Lorenzo whips the gun out from beneath my chin and points it at the intruders. He sits up, still buried deep inside me, his chest and brow glowing with sweat.

Cassius and Vinicius.

Cassius looks thunderstruck as he stares at me. My hands have trailed down Lorenzo's chest to slip around his waist. My thighs are tight around his hips. I rip my hands away from his stomach as if they're suddenly burned, but my legs are locked and won't let go.

Vinicius merely raises one brow and casts his gaze down my naked body, interested and amused.

"Stay right there till I'm done with our princess," Lorenzo says with a smile. "But feel free to watch."

Cassius strides forward and swipes the gun out of Lorenzo's hand. He grasps the blond man under the armpit and hauls him off me. Then he scoops me up in his arms and pulls me tightly against his chest.

Cassius.

I wrap my arms around his neck and hide my face in his chest. Again, he's seen me with another man. Again, he's pulled me away from them and back to him. Why does he have to keep tormenting me like this, pulling me close only to push me away again?

"Take me out of here, please," I whisper, so soft that only he can hear. "Take me back to your penthouse. Anywhere but here."

I feel Cassius stroke my hair and hold me closer, and my heart leaps. For a second I think he's going to do as I ask.

Instead, he walks over to a sofa and sits down, with me in his lap.

"How did you do it, Scava?"

Lorenzo flexes his neck from side to side, smiling. "My good looks and charming personality."

Vinicius laughs and perches on the windowsill. "No, come on. How did you do it?"

"Instead of asking me how I won, ask yourselves why you lost. *You* were too busy trying to cheat. 'Just the tip.' Are you fucking thirteen?"

Vinicius grins. "I couldn't help myself. Look at her, she's perfect."

Lorenzo shoots me a heated smile and pushes his damp hair back from his face. "Yeah. She is. Best bet I've won in ages."

I look from one man to the next. "Bet?"

"We kept arguing about who got to sleep with you first, so we decided to make it interesting," Vinicius tells me with a grin. "The first one to gain your trust, he'd get the green light to take you to bed."

I turn and look at Cassius, expecting him to deny such a ridiculous story, but he says nothing.

"I thought Cassius would make you melt because he's such a softie. I'm fucking crushed I didn't win." Vinicius is grinning as he says this, though, as if the game was so fun it didn't matter that he lost.

I start to scream and struggle. "So it was a trick? Why do you all think it's so funny to mess with me?"

Cassius holds me against him. "No, *bambina*. We want you to learn. You need to think two, three, four steps ahead."

"Speak for yourself. I just wanted to fuck her," Lorenzo says, reaching for me. "Now, hand her over. I'm not done."

I shrink away from Lorenzo and closer to Cassius.

Lorenzo's eyes narrow. "He won't protect you from me, princess. We don't work like that, and don't pretend you hate me so much when a few minutes ago you were coming all over my dick."

Everyone's gaze is on me and I feel my whole face reddening. "I hate you."

"Yeah, you do. That's what makes the sex so hot."

"Everything you guys do is a trick. What's next, is Salvatore going to walk through that door?"

Cassius grabs my throat and squeezes. "Rule number one, *bambina*," he growls, his eyes growing dangerously dark. "In fact, rules number two, three, and four as well. What are they?"

"No talking about Salvatore," I gasp around his fingers. "No talking back. No trying to escape. Do as you're told. Screw your rules! You say the three of you want one woman to protect, but you don't act like it. You can't protect me by keeping me prisoner and forcing me to have sex with you. That's not protection."

Cassius lets go of my throat slowly. "Then we need to discuss how this is going to work between the four of us from now on."

My eyebrows shoot up. From now on? But Cassius was so intent on keeping me for himself. He won't want me now that Lorenzo has had sex with me. That's why they had their stupid bet, because my virginity is such a goddamn prize.

Why are men *like* that?

"What do you mean, from now on?"

"Nevertheless," Cassius says, speaking over me. "We had an arrangement and you broke it. You have to be punished before we move on."

I swallow and gaze at him in apprehension. "Lorenzo already punished me enough."

"I dispense the punishments. He was claiming his winnings."

"And I haven't even had them all yet. My balls are fucking aching," Lorenzo says, sitting down in an armchair. He leans back, knees spread, completely naked and still hard. "Go on and spank her. I want to watch."

"Screw you," I snarl, but he just smiles at me.

I start to fight my way out of Cassius' lap. He wouldn't dare punish me. Not after I've just been thoroughly humiliated and used.

Cassius grasps my wrists. "Are you going to let me, or do I have to make you?"

"Oh, please make her," Lorenzo says, his deep voice heavy with desire.

"No, I'm not going to *let* you. You made it clear enough that you don't care about me."

Cassius and I stare at each other for a long time. There's a tic in his jaw as if his teeth are clenching. I would have stayed with him if he'd opened his arms to me that morning, but he didn't. If he's mad that Lorenzo screwed me first, he only has himself to blame.

You know what? I'm mad at *him*. I didn't have to suffer through Lorenzo kidnapping me, cutting my clothes off with his knife and fucking me with a gun to my head. I wouldn't have suffered if Cassius had welcomed my affection. The first one to earn my trust gained the right to my body. That was their bet. But instead of accepting my trust, he pushed me away and I had no choice but to turn to Lorenzo.

"Fine," he bites out. "Then we'll do this the hard way."

He yanks savagely on my wrist until I'm face down over his lap. I struggle and swear at him, but he's too strong for me. I'm pinned over his thighs as he raises his hand.

"Don't you—"

Dare.

That's what I was going to say.

But he does dare.

He strikes my bare ass with his hand and I squeal in indignation. Pain and heat burn in my flesh. Cassius spanks me over and over while I struggle and scream at him. Every now and then, his hand dips between my legs and feels how wet I am, and then his fingers seek my clit and he torments me with his touch. Pleasure rockets through me as fierce as the burn from his spanking.

"Get your hands off me," I pant, thrashing around in his lap. Everyone's looking at me. All three of these hateful bastards are enjoying my humiliation.

Cassius captures my chin in his hands and purrs, "I thought you weren't going to like it, but you do, don't you, *bambina*?"

I yank my chin from his grip and sink my teeth into his fingers.

"Ow. Aren't you feisty," he scolds, but he doesn't pull his fingers away. I keep my teeth sunk into him as he spanks me again. He eases his finger from between my teeth and pushes it deeper into my mouth.

"Suck," he whispers, and I do. "Good girl."

Heat darts through me at the silky warmth in his voice. I suck harder on his finger, eyes closed. A moment later I hear Lorenzo groan and realize what I'm doing.

I pull my mouth away and glare at Cassius. "Are you finished?"

"I told you there would be consequences for your actions. How will you learn to trust me if I don't follow through?"

I look at each one of the three men in turn. Cassius' stern expression. Vinicius' wicked delight. Lorenzo's heated interest as he grips the base of his erect cock. "How are you three going to keep me captive forever? I will find a way to escape on my own."

"You'll learn in time what we're about, and then you won't want to leave," Cassius says. "Nothing worth dying for happens overnight. One day you'll understand."

I look at the other two and see that they have utter conviction in what their friend has said. Cassius releases me and I sit up slowly, but he keeps hold of my waist. I settle on the sofa next to him, my heels against my burning ass, and push my hair off my face. "You all trust each other that much? You would die for each other?"

"Completely," Vinicius says, the afternoon sunlight playing across his cheek and making his eyes glow golden. "After what we went through together we learned to trust each other implicitly."

"But what about—" I almost say Salvatore's name.

Vinicius narrows his eyes. Even he turns cold and threatening at the mention of his ex-friend.

"Nothing. Never mind."

Cassius strokes his fingers through my hair. "I know it's strange. We really do mean it, though. We'll look after you and protect you. We'll die for you if it comes to that. But you have to trust us first."

Die for me. My heart aches as it recognizes the pure, unadulterated love of someone who would die for you.

It's the only kind of love that's worth anything.

"This is a lot for one afternoon, *bambina*. We can talk about it more later. But for now, get over there and finish Scava off."

Lorenzo wraps his hand around his still erect cock and beckons me closer. "I've felt that pussy of yours, princess. What that mouth do?"

"Rip your dick off with my teeth."

Cassius slips his hand between my thighs and massages my clit with his fingers, glancing at the other two. "How about the three of us ask nicely from now on? What does that promise sound like, *bambina*?"

"Utter garbage," I reply, but I can't help the way my eyes close and I moan at his touch.

"I have to ask nicely? Define nice," Lorenzo growls.

My eyes open and I glare at him. "Not kidnapping me would be a start."

His eyes widen in amusement. "Fine. No kidnapping. Now, get over here."

I stay right where I am, leaning against Cassius' strong chest while he touches my pussy. Cassius is the one who deserves me. Lorenzo can sit there with his blue balls and watch.

Cassius puts his lips against my ear as he rubs my clit in slow, tormenting circles. "*Bambina*, your pussy is so wet. I can feel how much you want to come again. Do you want that?"

I look into his deep brown eyes and I caress his jaw. "You all make me want fucked-up things."

"We noticed," he says, and kisses behind my ear. "That's what we liked about you from that first night."

"Liar," I whisper. "You hated me."

"You think so?"

I recall the pain and disgust on his face as he'd prized my fingers from his arm.

I'm sorry, I can't help you tonight. You have to wait. I promise I'll be back.

Not disgust at me, I realize. At what my father had done.

"We'll go home," he whispers. "But first, go back over there and finish Scava off. I know you want to."

I wrap an arm around Cassius' neck and arch my back as he continues to rub my clit, and then turn to Lorenzo. "Maybe I'll just stay here."

Amusement quirks the corner of Lorenzo's mouth. "Are you trying to make me jealous, princess? It won't work. I am getting impatient, though."

I glance at Vinicius, who's settled himself back against the window to watch. His beautiful eyes are alight with interest.

"What about you?" I ask him.

"Am I jealous?" Vinicius asks with a smile. "My brothers look happy for once. That's the only thing I want in this world."

I don't know about *happy*, unless Vinicius sees something I don't, but Cassius and Lorenzo do seem more relaxed than usual.

I get down from Cassius' lap and slide over to where Lorenzo is sitting, and kneel between his legs with my hands on his thighs. I sit there for a long time while we gaze at each other. If he tries to force me, I *will* find a way to kill him, that's a promise.

Lorenzo doesn't move.

I turn and look at Cassius, and then at Vinicius. Their expressions haven't changed.

Curious.

I gaze up at the handsome devil before me. "What if I use my teeth? Aren't you afraid of that?"

Lorenzo smiles. "Maybe I'll like it."

I expect him to grasp my hair and shove his cock into my mouth, making this as horrible as Salvatore did for me. Instead, Lorenzo leans down like he's going to kiss me. I realize he never has kissed me. My eyes drop to his mouth as I anticipate what his kiss will feel like. Intoxicating, and as hungry as a wolf.

But Lorenzo stops short of my lips and swipes the pad of his thumb over my lips, just once. Like a kiss. And looks deep into my eyes.

Maybe that's his version of a kiss.

It sends a fizz of heat and affection through me, and my lips part, hoping he'll do it again.

"I'll like whatever you do to me," he whispers. "I'm all yours."

I stare up at him in surprise. This vicious, tattooed asshole just told me he's mine. His fingers rub the base of my skull, making my body feel heavy and languorous. The tip of his cock is right there, just inches from my mouth, which waters at the sight.

I glance over my shoulder at Cassius and Vinicius. "Are you both just going to watch?"

"Would you rather they join in?" Lorenzo asks.

A hot sensation flashes through me at the suggestion. No, but…

"Do you like that idea? Hey, boys, why don't you—"

I reach out with my tongue and flick the tip of Lorenzo's cock. That shuts him up. He closes his eyes and groans as I enclose three inches of him in my mouth.

"Fuck, that's incredible, princess," he breathes as I suck slowly up his length and then down again. He continues to stroke his fingers through my hair. That's the first time he's called me princess without it sounding sarcastic.

Lorenzo being gentle. Lorenzo using pet names. What alternate universe is this?

I feel something brush against the backs of my legs, and realize it's Vinicius. He's kneeled down behind me and grasped my hips.

"Kitten, I can't stand this. I need to fuck you."

"What did we just say about asking nicely?" Cassius says from the other side of the room. I turn and look at him, relaxed on the sofa with his arm along the back, content to watch like he's some sort of referee. His cheek is resting against his palm, and there's a smile just curving his lips.

He's happy.

He's watching me with his two friends, hard as a rock in his pants, and he couldn't be more pleased.

Vinicius strokes his hands along my back. My bare pussy is just brushing the front of his pants and the sensations make me moan. "Please can I fuck you, kitten?"

Every time Vinicius touches me the world turns golden. The orgasm Lorenzo gave me feels like eons ago, and the heat from Cassius' spanking is making my pussy throb.

Two men at once, on the day I lose my virginity, with another one watching. My father would be horrified. This should probably feel slutty, but I've never liked that word. Anyway, right now I don't want to think.

I just want to feel.

Slowly, with my mouth still full of Lorenzo, I nod.

I hear the clink of Vinicius' belt and the sound of his zipper, and then the tip of him presses into me. He's not going to stop at just the tip today, though, and a moment later he thrusts deep.

Vinicius groans, a long, luxurious, "*Fuuuuuck.*"

I moan at the brief flash of pain, and then the longer burn of pleasure, and walk my knees open.

"She likes that. She's sucking my dick harder," Lorenzo says.

"I fucking like it too," Vinicius growls. He reaches down between my legs to rub my swollen clit as he pounds into me. I close my eyes and work my mouth in loving strokes up and down Lorenzo's cock. The blow job is messy and without rhythm as Vinicius sends heat and pleasure rippling through my body, but Lorenzo doesn't seem to care. In fact, he's entranced.

"You look so good getting fucked, princess. You should see what

I see. That's it, get your pretty mouth around me and suck."

My hands press against his belly as I moan with my mouth full of him. A decadent feeling washes over me and I feel the attention and desire of all three of them.

Each time Vinicius bottoms out inside me, I feel myself being coaxed closer and closer to my peak, until my whole body goes rigid with my climax and I push Lorenzo to the back of my throat.

Vinicius pulls out suddenly, and something warm and wet shoots over me.

"He's painted your ass with his cum. Oh, God, princess. Fuck, that's…" But Lorenzo doesn't have the chance to tell me what it looks like because he comes himself, flooding my mouth with the taste of him.

Vinicius draws me back against his chest and holds me tight. "I've been waiting a year to do that. Worth every second, kitten."

I turn my head and look at him, and then at Lorenzo slumped back in his armchair. Both their faces are flushed and they're smiling. As I swallow, Vinicius wipes the corners of my mouth with his thumb.

"Good girl," Vinicius murmurs in my ear. "Very good fucking girl."

Cassius holds out his hand to me. "Come up here so I can talk to you."

Vinicius lets me go, but I hesitate, glancing down at myself. I can feel Lorenzo in my mouth. I can definitely feel Vinicius on my thighs.

Cassius raises a dark brow. "You think I'm squeamish about that? Don't be a baby."

I get up and go over to Cassius, and he pulls me onto his lap and against his chest. "That was intense. You did well."

Awkwardly, self-consciously, Cassius wraps both arms around me and holds me. Out of the corner of my eyes, I see Vinicius and Lorenzo exchange surprised glances.

"I didn't think you liked giving affection," I whisper, so only Cassius can hear me.

"I'm trying, for you," he says tightly. His grip is as tight as his voice. It's like being hugged by a metal cage.

"Relax your muscles. I want you to feel soft."

Cassius takes a deep breath and lets it out. Slowly, all the tension melts from his arms and chest. I sink into him and rest my cheek against his shoulder.

"Did you enjoy that, *bambina*?"

I glance up at him, sheepish and exhausted. "I...did, actually."

"Good girl."

They need to stop saying that. I'll get addicted. Cassius' warm words cascade through me and I close my eyes. What an afternoon. Despite the terrifying way it started, the past hour or so was delicious. My mind travels backward through the events. Swallowing down Lorenzo. Vinicius pounding into me and coming hard on his cock. Coming beneath Lorenzo as he had a gun to my head. Remembering the bet sends a spurt of irritation through me. I'll bring that up later and tell them that if they ever pull a stunt like that again then they can forget about touching me, but for now, I let it go, and drift in the warm cocoon that Cassius has made for me.

I can hear Vinicius and Lorenzo talking quietly. Lorenzo. What a strange, terrifying man he is, but I glimpsed something in the middle of all that, didn't I? Someone more vulnerable than the face he usually presents to the world. I saw that person even as he held a gun to my head or shoved that horrible knife in my face.

The knife.

My eyes pop open.

The knife.

He used it on me, to threaten me and cut off my clothes. My stomach rolls at the memory. The same knife that was used to kill my mother.

I should never have begged for Cassius' affection. Being in his arms has made me feel again, and the first emotion that rushes back burns through me like fire.

Shame.

I scrunch my fingers in Cassius' shirt and press my face into his chest. "Can you kill me, please? I don't want to live anymore."

"*Bambina?*"

Revulsion pounds through me and tears pour down my face. "I deserve to die. I'm disgusting. I can't believe I let him do that to me."

"Who?"

"Lorenzo," I whisper. "His knife."

"His knife?" Cassius repeats. Lorenzo's knife is on the carpet on the other side of the room. No blood on it. No marks on me. "I don't understand."

I wipe my cheeks and look over at Lorenzo, whose face is a tight, pale mask. He knows, even if the others don't.

Cassius strokes my hair. "Scava, what did you do to Chiara to win her trust?"

"Not much. I made her think I hated her guts and wanted to get rid of her. Worked a treat."

"I didn't *trust* him," I protest. "I believed him when he acted like he wanted nothing more than to see the back of me. I thought the hatred was mutual."

"But what did you say to her to make her hate you so much?"

He shrugs. "Everything I could think of."

Cassius cups my cheek and draws my face up to his. "What did he tell you, *bambina*?"

"It doesn't matter. I just want to die, please. You've broken me. You've won."

"Are a few of Scava's nasty words all it takes to make you give up, after everything you've been through?"

Cassius doesn't get it. If the only thing Lorenzo hurt me with was words then I could say a few of my own back. Words don't hurt me.

Sick, twisted, and depraved behavior, that's what hurts me. *My* behavior. I had sex with that monster, and I liked it. That makes me an even bigger monster than him, and I should be put down like an animal.

"He handed Dad that knife so he could kill my mother, the only person I've ever loved. He used that knife on me, and then I…then…"

I can't even say the words.

Cassius' jaw clenches. He glares at Lorenzo, and then awkwardly pats my shoulder, his body rigid again. I can feel how much he detests comforting me like this. "*Bambina*, he was lying."

"No, he wasn't. I saw for myself the knife Dad used to kill Mom. When Lorenzo cut that chip out of my neck, he used his knife on me just to be cruel. He used it again today to cut my clothes off."

Vinicius shoots Lorenzo a furious look. "You let her think that?"

Lorenzo forces a laugh. "What? I was trying to win a bet. You would have done the same."

The room remains silent.

"Tell her the truth," Cassius finally growls.

"Fine," Lorenzo mutters, and looks at me. "I was flipping the knife over my knuckles and your father walked past me and grabbed it. Happy?"

"No, I'm not!" I cry. "Why didn't you stop him?"

"Because it's not my business if a man wants to kill his wife. And I didn't use the knife to get the chip out of your neck. I used a scalpel, you just couldn't see what I was doing."

Anger burns through as I look at him. Maybe he didn't hand Dad the knife, but he let me believe that he did and then he *fucked me*.

"She hates you. I can feel it," Cassius says.

Lorenzo sighs impatiently. "I don't give a damn."

Vinicius is eyeing Cassius and me speculatively. "They'll all hate Lorenzo no matter who we choose. There's nothing we can do about that. At least Chiara's attracted to him."

"No, I'm *not*. I'm never letting him touch me again. This afternoon was a disgusting, horrible mistake. You guys aren't normal, making bets with each other about who gets someone's virginity."

"No kidding we're not normal," Vinicius shoots back. "And you're lying to yourself if you think you can be normal after what you've been through."

That's not true, I think desperately. I've always been Chiara Romano, the mayor's daughter, good in school and comfortable with everyone's attention. *Well-adjusted and conscientious,* that's what all my school report cards said. I clung desperately to this idea the whole year I was promised to Salvatore, and it was easy because most of the time, he just wasn't there.

These three men remind me of my pain whenever I look at them.

Cassius brushes his thumb against my cheek, and I realize tears have slipped down my face.

"The four of us have been through things together," Cassius says. "Painful, brutal things that bond you like nothing else. We need someone for us all to bond with. Someone at the heart of us."

"What could you have possibly been through that would mean you'd want that?"

Lorenzo slowly draws his thumbnail across his throat. For a second, I think he's threatening to kill me.

Then I realize he's telling me what happened to them.

"Was it someone you all loved?"

He folds his arms and glares at me. "Not in the way you're thinking, princess."

I turn to Cassius. "I'm sorry about that, and I mean it because I know what it's like, but I don't want three insane boyfriends."

"No one ever seemed right," Cassius says. "You didn't seem right, at first, but…"

"But I watched Mom die, and that's something you can all relate to?" I finish.

Cassius gives a tight nod.

United through destruction. A blood bond. That's what he thinks the four of us will have.

"I won't do it. *He's* crazy," I say, nodding at Lorenzo. Then I look at Vinicius. "All he does is lie. And you," I finish, gazing at Cassius, "showing me even one drop of affection is taking decades off your life. You don't want something *closer than a wife*, you want a toy, and I'm not playing. Find some other girl, preferably someone as crazy and damaged as all of you are, because it's not going to be me."

CHAPTER SEVENTEEN

CASSIUS

If you love something, let it go. If it comes back to you, it's yours forever. If it doesn't...

Then you need to go and *get* it.

Three days after Scava stole Chiara away from my apartment, I finish my meetings early and head home. Chiara's reading on the sofa when I stride out of the elevator, her hair in a messy bun on the top of her head and a crop top baring her midriff.

Fuck, she's cute. Whenever I look at her, I feel pain and pleasure in equal amounts. I swore I'd never let myself get attached to another person after Evelina was killed, and Chiara being younger and just so fucking adorable makes me think of her more than I have in years.

I hate it. I crave it. My moods swing unpredictably and I know that's not fair on her. I don't know if I can get past the impulse to shove Chiara away.

But I'm trying.

I lean over the back of the sofa and gaze at her. "I missed you today, *bambina*."

She blinks, seeming surprised that I've spoken from the heart. "Where's everyone been? I haven't seen the others in days. I've barely seen you."

"We thought you might like some space." Actually, I told the other two to back off for a little while, for Chiara's sake, but maybe for selfish reasons, too. I want to share her, I want to see her with the others, but right now I feel like I'm lagging far behind. Scava was the first one to get her into his bed.

Scava. For fuck's sake.

Between him snarling at Chiara and Vinicius trying to sneak his way into her panties, *mio Dio*, I thought I had more time to get over my…problems. I shouldn't have underestimated Scava's need to win at any cost, and just how much he's attracted to our sweet little blonde.

She rubs her hands over her face. "I've done nothing but think. I'm exhausted."

I come around the sofa and sit down beside her. "Can I ask what you've been thinking about?"

Chiara sighs and plucks at a cushion. "Mom. I think about her all the time and the fact that Dad murdered her and suffered no consequences whatsoever." She clenches her head in her hands and moans. "I'm so angry all the time. I don't know what to do."

I wish I could give her advice, but when it comes to the pain and anger of loss, I'm as stuck as she is.

"You know, I asked…you-know-who to kill Dad. He wouldn't do it, though."

Salvatore. He wouldn't kill the mayor. That doesn't surprise me. "You want your father dead?"

She thinks about this for a long time. "I was brought up Catholic. Mom took her faith seriously. Love thy neighbor. Forgive those who trespass against you." Chiara stares straight ahead, her eyes burning. "If the choice is between Dad facing no consequences for what he's done or some vigilante justice, then he should be murdered in a back alley."

I sense a question on the tip of her tongue.

But she doesn't ask it, and so I scoop her up in my arms.

Her blue eyes open wide and she wraps her arms around my neck. "Where are we going?"

"My bed. I haven't been able to stop thinking about you."

A pink flush blooms across Chiara's cheeks as I set her on her feet at the end of my bed. "Three men in about as many days," she whispers. "I've imagined explaining to my old friend Nicole what's been happening since I came here. We haven't been friends in a long time but I still talk to her in my head sometimes. You know those friends you're just not ready to give up on?"

"Yes. I know."

Chiara strokes the collar of my shirt. "She's the most levelheaded and traditional person, and no matter how I go about pretend-telling her that three men are touching me and undressing me and making me come, she disapproves utterly."

"Do you want me to stop?"

In answer, Chiara comes up on her tiptoes and presses her lips against mine. I freeze, and my hands lock on her wrists.

"Sorry. Do you not like that?" When I don't reply, she presses her lips to mine again, soft, fluttering kisses like the brush of butterfly wings. Each one burns through me like an ache.

"You're killing me, *bambina*."

"Do you want me to stop?" she echoes.

I take her face in my hands. "Never."

I slant my mouth over hers and kiss her hard. I take the kiss that I've been thinking about for a year. Her lips are plush and yield to mine, and she opens her mouth for my tongue. While she undoes the buttons of my shirt, I pull the clothes from her body and take greedy handfuls of her. Her plump little ass. Her breasts. All mine, I think selfishly. I'm happy to share, I love to watch, but just sometimes, I want her to be all mine.

I pull her up onto the bed and her naked thighs slip around my hips as I nudge at her entrance with the tip of my cock. She gets wet so fast, and my resolution to take this slow flies out the window as she gazes up at me with needy eyes.

I grasp the base of my cock and sink into her.

Chiara breathes in sharply. "Cassius, oh my fucking God."

"You want me to stop?"

"Stop and I'll kill you. But do you have to be so much?"

I look at her small hands pressed against the dark hair on my chest. Her slender thighs wrapped around my hips as I thrust into her. "This is as much as I am. Relax, *bambina*, and let me fuck you like I need to."

I ease up a little, not pushing quite so deep for a few strokes so she can take deep breaths and let her body go supple.

"That's it," I murmur coaxingly. "Good girl. Aren't you pretty stuffed full of my cock?"

Chiara moans and rolls her hips. "You have the cutest dirty talk."

I laugh softly. "It's just what you inspire, *bambina*. I've been aching to touch you like this for a year. I've watched you with the others and it's been making me crazy."

"Jealous crazy?" she asks.

Jealousy is when someone is stealing what you believe should belong to you, but never did. Chiara belongs to all of us, and we could never take her away from each other. Even when she's in here with me, in my bed, she's still ours, not mine.

"I felt impatient. And envious as hell when I saw Scava balls deep in you. You were both insanely hot for each other. That moment looked perfect."

"He had a gun to my head," she points out with a moan, as I thrust deeper, her head tipping back.

"Maybe you like that, too. You like me pushing your limits, don't you, *bambina*? Look." I cradle her head and lift it so she can see how much of me is buried inside her.

All of me. Every inch.

"Wow," she whispers. "That's so much cock. Where did you go?"

I feel myself smile again. And I'm the one who's supposed to have the cute dirty talk.

I roll over onto my back until she's straddling me, hungry to watch her ride me. Slowly, tentatively, she rocks her hips against me, gaining speed and confidence with every stroke. Soon she's biting her lip and her head's falling back, and then she comes with a cry, her inner muscles ripping along my length.

Before she can finish coming, I grasp her hips and pound up hard into her, selfish hard thrusts that have my orgasm rushing up. At the last second, I pull out and hold Chiara tight against my chest as I finish in my fist.

I slump back against the pillows and groan with my girl laying on me. Better. Much fucking better.

She sits up and rolls onto the sheets beside me. "You're all careful about not coming inside me. It should have occurred to me earlier."

"We will keep being careful, and we're all clean. Scava made sure of that before we brought you here."

"Oh yeah, the *doctor*," Chiara mutters with a wrinkle of her nose.

I reach out and stroke her cheek. "I know he terrorized you, and he can be frightening, but he'd be the first one to protect you if you were threatened."

Chiara doesn't agree, or even nod. Scava is going to have to work hard to prove himself to her.

"You could have won," she whispers, tracing her fingers through my chest hair.

The bet between Vinicius, Scava, and me. The morning after she slept in my bed, Chiara would have walked into my arms if I'd held them open for her.

"Let me tell you a secret, *bambina*. I barely thought about the bet. I was too busy obsessing about you."

Her face breaks into a smile and she wraps her arms around my neck. "That's why I like you, Cassius."

I sit up in bed and scoop Chiara into my lap, holding her against my heart. *I like you, Cassius.* Fuck, that's too much, and at the same time, just perfect.

"I taught my baby sister to read like this," I say, trailing my fingers through her hair. "Sitting on my lap with her favorite books. She was such a little angel."

"What's she doing now?"

"She's dead."

Chiara winces. "I'm sorry. Is this who you meant when you said you lost someone?"

I nod, focusing on Chiara's hair slipping through my fingers.

"Ginevra Fiore told me that her sister was killed, too. You all lost family members?"

"The four of us lost little sisters. We knew they were in danger and we tried to protect them by ourselves. We failed, one after the other, until they were all dead."

Chiara reaches up and touches my face. "That's terrible. I'm so sorry. And you never found out who did it?"

"*Bambina*, we barely even know why." The ache in my chest is as fierce as it was the day I discovered Evelina was dead, and how brutal the end had been for her. I gather Chiara closer to me and whisper into her sweet-smelling hair. "It's never felt right to hold a woman like this because I wouldn't know if I could promise to keep her safe.

We all promise. Vinicius and Scava will lay down their lives for you, as will I."

"It can never be just you and me?"

"No, *bambina*. It can never be like that. Not for me." Their pain is my pain. Their happiness means as much to me as Chiara's does.

"But the three of you can't be that bonded if Sal…" She bites her lip. "I want to be able to talk about him without you going to crazy town on my ass."

I know what she's going to ask. How can the three of us be so sure that we want to do this when recently we were just as certain it would work with four?

I am sure. One day, Chiara will understand.

"We'll talk about Salvatore. But not now. For your sake, not his."

"My sake? But—"

I brush my lips over hers. "Trust me. Not now."

"I wish you'd just tell me. I can't take any more shocks."

I run my fingers through her hair, remembering the jolt I felt when she reached out to me for help in the minutes after her mother was killed. Looking over at the traffic lights and seeing her sitting in a car with a Geak. Listening to her berate the four of us for the way we treated her on her seventeenth birthday.

The envy and triumph at seeing her hands lovingly caressing Scava as he fucked her with a gun to her head.

The press of her lips against mine for the first time, so pure and sweet. A litany of surprises as devastating as nuclear bombs. "I sometimes think the same, *bambina*. But don't ever stop, will you?"

"Silly," she mutters with a smile, and puts her head down on my chest.

I hold Chiara in my arms until she falls asleep, and then I tuck her beneath the bedclothes and send a text to Vinicius and Scava.

Then I go to the kitchen and grab three glasses and a bottle of vodka. We're going to need it.

When they step out of the elevator, Scava looks around right away. "Where's our princess?"

"Asleep in my bed."

Vinicius raises one eyebrow and smiles. "Did you…?"

I nod. "She's…" Words fail me, but it doesn't matter. I've seen her with Vinicius and Scava. They already know. "It's not going to work like this."

"It's not going to work at all," Scava growls.

Vinicius takes a sip of vodka and shakes his head. "Great attitude, Lorenzo."

"I'm right. There's no point in trying to make her ours when she hates our fucking guts."

"*Your* guts," Vinicius counters. "Maybe this would have worked if you hadn't taken things too far just so you could fuck her first."

Scava's lips press into a white, angry line. He knows when his brothers are right.

"She doesn't hate us," I say. The other two turn to look at me. My lips are still tingling from Chiara's soft kisses. "Not even you, Scava. She's told me she's been having arguments with an old friend inside her head about us and what we're doing with her. She's conflicted and, most of all, she's still stuck on the night of her seventeenth birthday, watching her mother die."

"Yeah, that'll fuck you up," Scava mutters.

Vinicius nods. "She's as damaged as the rest of us. That's actually the reason I don't want to give her up."

Which is exactly what I've been thinking.

Scava rubs his eyes with his thumb and fingers, muttering to himself.

"What was that?" I ask.

"Neither. Do. I," he says through gritted teeth.

"Good. We're agreed. So, what are we going to do about it?"

CHAPTER EIGHTEEN

CHIARA

The morning light is glimmering behind my eyes when I feel the bed sink beside me. I smile, remembering that I'm in Cassius' bed. I reach out without opening my eyes and feel a large warm hand slip my fingers into his.

I squeeze, and after a moment, he squeezes me back. I take a long, luxurious stretch, extending my legs and pointing my toes, dragging the sheet from my naked body.

"Damn, you've got great tits."

My eyes pop open. It's not Cassius gazing down at me. It's Lorenzo. I rip my hand from his and yank the sheets back over me.

Lorenzo folds his arms and glares at me. My heart races as I anticipate a wave of venom and hatred from him.

Before I remember that he was faking it. "You've really messed with my head, you know that?"

A muscle flexes in his jaw like he's just clenched his teeth, but he doesn't say anything.

"I truly believed you hated my guts, and now I don't know if I'll ever stop thinking of you as a cruel and vicious person."

"Probably for the best."

Is it? When we were alone in his bed together he felt…different. Softer. More vulnerable. I wonder if I'll ever get to see him like that again, or if it was a one-time thing. I liked Lorenzo in that moment even though he had a gun to my head, which is another argument I've had with Nicole. I've started thinking of her as the good fairy sitting on my shoulder, and I'm the bad fairy sitting on my own shoulder pointing out that Lorenzo Scava is as hot as sin and a complicated man as well as being dangerous, vicious, and crazy.

"What's with that look on your face?" he snaps.

"What look on my face?"

"I don't fucking know. Like your dog's just been run over."

I sit up slowly, keeping the sheet wrapped around me. I was remembering how he sounded when he called me princess. When I had him in my mouth and he was stroking his fingers through my hair like I was precious to him.

God, listen to me, romanticizing Lorenzo rather than coming to terms with the fact that I enjoyed having sex with a ruthless killer. "What are you doing here? Where's Cassius?"

"You like Cassius, don't you?" Lorenzo asks, a sly glint in his eyes.

"Please get out. I want to get dressed."

Lorenzo gets to his feet and gives me an ironic bow. "Of course, princess."

When I'm alone, I get dressed, the sound of that mocking *princess* reverberating through my skull.

Out in the lounge, Cassius passes me a coffee, and our fingers brush. His lips are just touched with a smile, and I feel myself melt inside.

"We want to talk to you," he tells me.

I glance at the others. "I want to talk to all of you, too."

"Ladies first," Vinicius says with a smile.

"Fuck that. Us first," Lorenzo interrupts, and turns to me. "You in or out, princess? Either what Cassius explained to you the other day appeals to you and you're staying, or it doesn't and you can fuck off."

I take a sip of my coffee and give him a sarcastic smile. "Oh, Lorenzo. You do care."

His jaw tightens. "I want shit to get back to normal. Babysitting someone who doesn't want to be here is wasting all of our time."

"Things won't be normal or easy with Chiara around," Vinicius points out. "She's not just someone you can screw. We need to keep her safe from our enemies, which includes the Mayor of Coldlake and everyone he controls."

"You think I won't kill anyone who touches her?" Lorenzo says, a dangerous edge to his voice.

Cassius is following the conversation but doesn't say anything.

"Anything to add?" I ask.

He shakes his head. "I want to hear what you want to talk about first."

"I want to talk about my father."

Lorenzo pulls his knife out. "Say no more. He's dead."

"Stop it. No." I take a deep breath. "*I* want to kill him."

I think I do, anyway. Look at what it's done to these four men to have their sisters' deaths go unavenged. I lie awake at night burning with anger that she died because of a selfish and cruel man. Mom deserves justice and I'm the only one who can get it for her. Even pretend-Nicole doesn't argue back when I point out that a man as powerful as my father is untouchable by the law.

Their expressions are stunned. Then a smile slides over Lorenzo's lips as he puts his knife away. Vinicius' brows rise, and then he nods slowly, like he's impressed.

Cassius is the only one who's frowning. "No. It's too dangerous, and you don't know how."

"Would you let someone else avenge your sister?" I ask him.

Cassius puts his coffee down. "Think of what you're saying. Imagine you're going to shoot him. You need to get close to your father, look him in the eye and then pull the trigger."

I hear the gunshot in my head. I see the expression of shock on my father's face as he collapses to his knees. It's just one moment, and then it will be over. "I can do it."

"No, you can't."

"Cassius, I like it when you baby me and call me *bambina*, but not about things that are important. This matters to me, and I'll never forgive you if you stand in my way."

"She has this chance. We probably never will." Lorenzo's eyes are wild with bitterness and hatred. He notices me staring at him. "What?"

"I'm just surprised you're on my side."

"Vengeance. It's the one thing we have in common, princess. You want to kill the bastard? I'll hold him down for you."

"Thank you. But I want to do this myself."

Vinicius folds his arms and regards me seriously. "Have you really thought this through? Killing someone changes you forever."

Lorenzo makes a dismissive gesture. "I fucked her with a gun to her head and she came on my dick. She's not so innocent anymore."

"She is innocent, but she won't be after we put a gun in her hand!" Cassius shouts.

"Ever held a gun?" Vinicius asks.

I shake my head.

"Then first things first. I'll teach you to shoot." He glances at Lorenzo. "Can I use the compound?"

Lorenzo gets to his feet. "Be my guest, but I want to watch. Are you coming?" he asks, turning to Cassius, who's glowering from one of us to the next. "Stop babying her. If our girl wants to indulge in a little murder, who are we to stand in her way?"

In the end, all four of us go. I ride with Cassius, sensing that there's more he wants to say and that it will be easier for him to get it off his chest if we're alone.

We get onto the freeway and his hands tighten on the steering wheel. "I don't like this."

"I know. But it's all I can think about. I'll go crazy if I don't do something to avenge Mom."

"You're innocent, and it's our job to keep you that way. You begged for my help, remember?"

"I begged Salvatore to kill Dad. I tried to use that Geak to take my virginity. I wanted Lorenzo to help me escape. Every time I've asked someone else for help it's blown up in my face. This is something I'm going to do myself. Besides, who said it was your job to keep me innocent?"

"I said so," he growls.

"You guys are a bunch of criminals and I'm the daughter of a corrupt, murderous mayor. That's not a recipe for a virtuous future together."

He glances at me. "You're thinking about our offer to stay with us?"

Be theirs. Belong to all three of them. I look out the window at the passing city. "I don't know. I can't see past tomorrow, let alone that far ahead."

At Lorenzo's compound, I ask Cassius to stop before he drives down into the garage so I can take a look at the house and yard. There's not much to see apart from a dark gray house that looks secure as hell and a neat lawn with nowhere to hide.

Lorenzo pulls up next to us and rolls down his window. "Reminiscing about our time together, princess? Me, too."

His smile is devilish. I wasn't thinking about being in bed with him, but now I am.

"I didn't get a good look at the place the two times I was brought here against my will. This is where you live?"

"It's my home and my headquarters. There are armed guards, dogs, security cameras, fourteen-foot walls, and motion sensors. No one gets in or out without me knowing."

"You live in a prison," I point out.

"And I sleep like a baby. This whole city will be baying for your blood if you murder your father. Think about that." He speeds into the underground garage and disappears.

Good point.

I get back into Cassius' car and we follow him down, Vinicius in his Ferrari right behind us. The place is a lot bigger underground than the ground level would have you believe. The concrete walls and warren of corridors aren't lovely, but they feel as secure as a nuclear bunker.

Lorenzo has disappeared somewhere and Vinicius leads us down a corridor.

"What does Lorenzo do here?" I ask.

Oh God, what if it really is organ harvesting?

Vinicius laughs. "That's a long story. Maybe Lorenzo will tell you himself one day."

He turns into a long, narrow room with two booths and man-shaped targets at the far end. Cassius stands near the door, his arms folded, disapproval radiating from him in waves.

Lorenzo appears a few minutes later with two handguns and a box of ammo, and lays them on the table inside one of the booths. "Here you go. Baby's first guns."

The weapons look heavy and too large for my hands, but Vinicius picks each one up and nods in approval. He starts to load them and runs through some safety rules. The main takeaway seems to be don't point it at anything you don't intend to shoot.

My neck prickles and my hands feel clammy. Even looking at a gun is making my heart pump with a sick feeling.

Vinicius is a good teacher, speaking slowly and calmly as he explains how a gun works. "You ready to try firing?"

I wipe my sweaty hands on the seat of my jeans and take the gun he holds out to me. "It's too big. I don't think I can handle it."

"Bet that's what she said to you the first time, huh, Cassius?" Lorenzo says behind me.

I purse my lips but keep looking straight ahead. "Can you guys go do something else? I can't concentrate while you're staring at me."

"*Bambina*, if you can't pull the trigger with us looking at you, then you won't be able to when you're looking down the barrel at the mayor. And, Scava? Shut the fuck up."

Vinicius adjusts my grip on the gun. "You want the gun to be a good size in your hand to help you absorb the recoil. This is a 9mm but it's still going to kick."

I gaze up at him and smile. "If you were a teacher at my school, we'd all be fighting to get into your classes."

Vinicius grins. "Two hundred Catholic girls calling me Mr. Angeli? Sounds like fun."

His voice and instructions have calmed me down, and I take a deep breath and aim at the target.

"Squeeze, don't pull," Vinicius says when my finger is on the trigger.

I squeeze, and there's an enormous bang and the gun kicks in my hand. I realize my eyes were closed and I have no idea where the bullet went.

"Did I hit the target?"

"Ah, no, but that was a good start." Vinicius puts his arms around mine and adjusts my aim. "Take your time. You're doing great."

I turn my head slightly to look at him. "I'm not, but thank you."

He plants a kiss on my lips, slow and encouraging. Vinicius' kisses always catch me by surprise with how delicious they are. "All it takes is practice."

"You really want me to do this," I realize.

"Amalia never got to take revenge on the men who hurt her, and neither did I. When you face your father and pull that trigger, I'll be cheering you on."

Amalia. That must be his sister's name. I've never seen one flicker of grief or pain in his handsome face. He must hide it deep down where no one can ever touch it.

"Thank you," I whisper.

An hour and a dozen reloads later, I've managed to shoot the target in the chest at various distances.

When I've unloaded the guns and put them down, Lorenzo comes up beside me and picks them up, and the box of bullets.

"Nice work. That was hot as fuck."

To my surprise, he plants a kiss on the side of my neck. Actually, it's more like a nip with his teeth, and I glare at him. Just because he took my side over committing murder, doesn't mean I forgive him for everything he's done.

You are cordially invited to the wedding of Salvatore Fiore and Chiara Romano.

"Is this going to work? I feel like they're going to guess it's a ruse," I say, examining the invitation card printed with formal calligraphy.

"Your father's greedy," Vinicius says, taking the card from me. It's an extra, and the real thing was sent to Dad and Salvatore two days ago. "He'll hope that it's true, and even if he suspects it's not, all we have to do is get you in the same room as him." He makes a gun with his thumb and forefinger. "And pow."

He has a point.

Cassius comes out of the elevator into the lounge holding a wedding dress in a clear plastic sleeve. He had it made in less than a week while I was practicing shooting with Vinicius. The idea of me killing my father still doesn't sit right with him, but he's doing everything he can to make sure that I'm prepared.

I take the dress from him and hold it to the light. An embroidered, strapless bodice and a long tulle skirt. "Cassius, it's beautiful."

Heavy, too. Even heavier than my first wedding dress.

"I'll help you get dressed," he says, and follows me to my room. I've already done my hair and makeup, and I strip down to my underwear and let Cassius help me into the dress.

He laces the back up tight and then pulls me into his arms, my back against his chest. "I wish I was going in there with you."

We debated it, but if the three of them step foot in that house, Dad won't show his face because he'll know it's a trap.

He thinks I'm weak. That's my advantage.

"Come back to me. Don't let them keep you. Don't let them *hurt* you." Our eyes meet in the mirror and he strokes his knuckles over my cheeks. "*Sei bella.*"

You're beautiful.

"*Grazie. Per tutto.*" *Thank you. For everything.*

Lorenzo comes into the room holding a bouquet of pale pink roses. I weigh it in my hand as he passes it to me. "Heavy."

"Yeah. It's fully loaded. Ready to go?"

Vinicius appears in the doorway. I stare at each of their reflections, three beautiful men who would gladly ambush Dad on some dark road and end his life for me. They would kill for me, but would they let me go? I can feel Lorenzo itching to take me prisoner in his compound after I kill Dad. This isn't over between the four of us as far as they're concerned, and I'm replacing one tyrant with three more.

But that's a problem for tomorrow. I haven't ever stood up to Dad, even before he murdered Mom. He treated us like his accessories, and I'm not going to be anyone's decoration or pawn ever again.

"I'm ready."

The four of us get into Lorenzo's Mercedes and drive until the roads are as familiar as my own hands. They let me out at the far end of the street, out of sight of the house.

Lorenzo turns around and gives me a nod. "Three in the chest, and when he's down, shoot him in the head."

In the front passenger seat, Cassius passes an agitated hand through his black curls.

Vinicius grips his shoulder. "She'll be all right. You know she will."

A meaningful moment passes between them, and I sense words

that have been spoken out of my hearing. Whatever they've said, it doesn't matter right now. My heart's beating wildly and I need to focus.

"Go get him, kitten. We've got your back."

I take a deep breath, get out of the car, and start walking. My heavy dress rustles on the sidewalk and I keep my chin lifted and my pace slow, as if I really am walking down the aisle of a church. The walk I never got to take the day of my wedding.

My home appears before me, huge in its splendor with its grand columned entrance and sweeping front lawn. After today, I'll have no mother, and no father. There'll just be me, and the men who want to claim me as theirs. I walk up the steps and push the doorbell.

I'm home.

CHAPTER NINETEEN

CHIARA

Sunlight dances on the surface of the water. The swimming pool is vivid blue and casts refracted light on my wedding dress. I stare at it, remembering ribbons of blood blooming through the water. Mom's been near me all year, but now I can feel her hovering closer than ever.

I look up at Dad and Salvatore, dressed for the occasion in suits and suspicious expressions.

"Sorry I'm late," I tell them.

Salvatore's eyes narrow at my attempt at levity. Now I'm the unpredictable one, and he's the one warily watching me and wondering what I might do.

His eyes scour my wedding dress and snags on the engagement ring that he gave me, and I gave away. He flinches, almost like he's hurt.

"Where have you been?"

My heart squeezes painfully. I was half in love with Salvatore when Cassius carried me out of that church. Our marriage would have been a disaster, but one filled with passion. Heat. *Need*.

And blood.

The others are raw and bleeding with Salvatore's loss. There'll be a power vacuum in this city once Dad is dead, and the most powerful men in Coldlake will be at war.

"With your friends."

"Why did they let you go?"

I think about that carefully. "I guess they thought it was the right thing to do."

"Since when did those three ever care about what's right?" Salvatore sneers.

But I'm not here to discuss Cassius, Vinicius, and Lorenzo with Salvatore. The four of them have got nothing to do with why I'm here.

My problem is standing before me in a black suit, eyes narrowed with mistrust, silent at Salvatore's side. I try to imagine him as a man-shaped target at the other end of Lorenzo's shooting range, but the adrenalin coursing through my blood tells me he's not.

He's Dad.

He's a living, breathing human being, and the man who brought me into this world. I watch him closely, wondering what he felt in the moments before he murdered Mom. Did he hesitate, and ask himself what the hell he was doing? Or did he plan what he would do in cold blood if she stood in his way?

Did Mom recognize the footsteps behind her or the scent of the man wielding the knife? On the one hand, I hope that Mom didn't know it was Dad, but that would mean her last thoughts on this earth were that Lorenzo was killing her.

No, baby, I hear her murmur in my ear, calm and sweet. *My last thoughts on this earth were of you. Only of you.*

I breathe in sharply and blink to clear my eyes. *I was loved*, I think fiercely.

If I never feel that deep and pure kind of love ever again, at least I had it once in my life.

Even if I die today.

"When you first became Mayor of Coldlake, did you set out with good intentions, or did you let yourself become corrupted along the way?"

Boredom and impatience flash across Dad's face, and he starts to turn away. Just like that, he knows I'm not here to marry Salvatore, and so I have no purpose to him.

No *value*.

His own daughter.

I pull the gun out of the bouquet and hold it up. Lorenzo's gun, feeling heavy but secure in my hand. My finger over the trigger just how Vinicius taught me.

Squeeze don't pull. Three times in the chest and once in the head. Do it quickly. That's what Cassius would want, so I can safely return to him.

To all three of them.

But it can't end like this, when Dad hasn't even bothered to say a word to me.

My hand starts to tremble. "Stay right there. I want to talk, and you're going to answer my questions."

He's going to talk, even if it kills me.

Women who don't do as they're told by men like you end up dead.

Dad turns back to me. "You can't always get what you want, Chiara, and I've got better things to do." He turns to Salvatore. "Well? I won't blame you if you don't want her anymore."

Salvatore casts his eyes over me. "Did any of them fuck you?"

Any of them. If he only knew what I'd done with his ex-friends.

"Did *all* of them fuck you?"

I still have the gun pointed at Dad's chest but my gaze flickers to Salvatore for just a second.

Yes, all of them.

And I liked it.

His lip curls. I'm ruined. I've lived past my usefulness. Dad shakes his head and starts to turn away again.

I step forward, the gun shaking in my hand. "No! You're going to talk to me. You owe me this."

Salvatore gazes between me and Dad, and silence stretches. Water laps at the edge of the pool.

Just do it.

Do it.

But he was supposed to beg for my forgiveness.

That's what I wanted, I realize. Not to kill him.

To force him to see me.

To make him show me his pain over killing Mom. He has to feel sorry for killing Mom. He can't be human otherwise.

I beg him with my eyes to give me something. *Anything.*

I don't want to do this.

I won't do this if you just give me that.

Please.

But Dad's lips stay closed, and his face is blank and cold.

With a growl of frustration, Salvatore produces a gun from inside his jacket, lifts his arm and takes aim at my stomach. "She's probably already pregnant. Useless."

The sky breaks open with an enormous *crack.*

A force hits me so hard I'm knocked backward. I look down, and blood is running down the front of my dress and staining the white tulle. The gun slips from my fingers and clatters on the tiles.

Dad stands there with his hands in his pockets, no expression on his face.

Nothing.

I stagger backward, and my foot slides off the rim of the pool. Dad's cold face is the last thing I see before the water swallows me up.

I'm going to die just like Mom did.

The water wraps around me, feeling like my mother's arms. *It's over, baby. It's all over.*

I can feel her already. I can hear her.

Don't cry. I'm here, don't cry.

All the pain, all the heartache, spreads out through the water. I slip into the darkness, and let it take me.

EPILOGUE

CHIARA

I'm blinded by chlorine and my midsection feels like I'm being crushed to death by an iron weight. I fumble for my belly and hold my hand up in front of my blurry eyes.

Wet and red.

Blood and pool water, that acrid, familiar scent. Someone has pulled me out and I can feel their hands on me.

Just push me back in. Let me die and be with my mother.

I'm shaken vigorously. "No, you don't. Open your fucking eyes."

I feel someone's mouth against mine. My lungs forcefully expanding. Then the world goes black.

Cold.

Alone.

Then shocking white. Light pierces my eyes. Water erupts up my throat and I can't breathe—*can't breathe—can't breathe*. Spots dance in my vision as I cough. Desperate, hacking coughs that feel like they will rip my lungs right out of my chest.

"Chiara? Chiara!"

I take rasping breaths, my eyes streaming. I can't see. I don't know where I am. My hands are gripping muscular shoulders as I fight to stay conscious.

Lips against my lips. A mouth that's kissed mine so many times, always stealing my breath and my heart. Lips that demand I answer him.

"Chiara? Kiss me so I know you're still breathing."

Second Comes War *(Promised in Blood, 2)* is available now

AUTHOR'S NOTE

Phew, what a cliffhanger! Sorry to leave you hanging like that, but I swear all the answers you crave are in *Second Comes War*. There are also a few clues scattered through this book about what's really going on.

I have to thank my lovely editor Heather Fox for all her help on my reverse harem journey. I couldn't have asked for better support!

If you're curious, two things inspired this book. The first was season one of the podcast *Crimetown*, which examined how organized crime shaped Providence, Rhode Island, and the connection between the Patriarca crime family and the corrupt mayor Vincent "Buddy" Cianci. Cianci was beloved by the residents of Providence but his jovial, smiling public persona hid a scheming and violent nature. Cianci is, of course, the inspiration behind Mayor Romano.

The second inspiration was a snippet of Roman history that lodged itself in my brain years ago and has nagged at me ever since. Honoria, sister to Roman Emperor Valentinian III, was promised in marriage to a (probably very boring) senator. Honoria had a reputation for being ambitious and promiscuous (no judgement here, girl) and instead of doing what she was told, she hatched a plan.

No one in Rome was going to help her, so she looked farther afield to Attila, King of the Huns, sworn enemy of Rome and probable stone cold fox. Just listen to how he's described in one source:

He was a man born into the world to shake the nations, the scourge of all lands, who in some way terrified all mankind by the dreadful rumors noised abroad concerning him. He was haughty in his walk, rolling his eyes hither and thither, so that the power of his proud spirit appeared in the movement of his body.

I mean, I would.

Honoria sent a letter to Attila pleading for his help and enclosed her engagement ring as payment. It's not clear what sort of help she was hoping for. Possibly she expected him to invade Rome and cause such a mess that the wedding would be called off. What is clear is that Attila took one look at the ring and decided that Honoria had proposed to him, and he demanded his bride and half of the western empire as dowry.

Can you imagine how red-faced and infuriated Honoria must have been when her brother the emperor stomped into her bedroom and asked her what the *hell* she's playing at, proposing to his enemy?

Attila never managed to carry off his bride, but someone else did. Bad-tempered, overbearing Cassius has the heart and soul of a barbarian in an expensive Italian suit.

With one important difference: he just *loves* to share.

Finally, a big thank you to you for reading *First Comes Blood*. That was pretty sexy of you, I have to say. If you enjoyed this book, please consider leaving a review.

ALSO BY LILITH VINCENT

Steamy Reverse Harem

THE PROMISED IN BLOOD SERIES (complete)
First Comes Blood
Second Comes War
Third Comes Vengeance

THE PAGEANT DUET (complete)
Pageant
Crowned

FAIRYTALES WITH A TWIST (group series)
Beauty So Golden

M/F Romance

Brutal Intentions

Printed in Great Britain
by Amazon